TECHNICALLY
Yours
IN
VEGAS

TECHNICALLY Yours IN VEGAS

Sabrina Wagner

Stay Connected!

**Want to be the first to learn book news, updates and more?
Sign up for my Newsletter.**

https://www.subscribepage.com/sabrinawagnernewsletter

**Want to know about my new releases and upcoming sales?
Stay connected on:**

Facebook~Instagram~Twitter~TikTok
Goodreads~BookBub~Amazon

**I'd love to hear from you.
Visit my website to connect with me.**

www.SabrinaWagnerAuthor.com

Books by Sabrina Wagner

Hearts Trilogy
Hearts on Fire
Shattered Hearts
Reviving My Heart

Wild Hearts Trilogy
Wild Hearts
Secrets of the Heart
Eternal Hearts

Forever Inked Novels
Tattooed Hearts: Tattooed Duet #1
Tattooed Souls: Tattooed Duet #2
Smoke and Mirrors
Regret and Redemption
Sin and Salvation

Vegas Love Series
What Happens in Vegas
Billionaire Bachelor in Vegas
Behaving Badly in Vegas
Technically Yours in Vegas

Spotify Playlist

Circus~ Britney Spears
Shivers~ Ed Sheeran
Constellations~ Jade LeMac
Love on the Brain~ Rihanna
Champagne Kisses~ Jessie Ware
Vegas High~ Kylie Minogue
Lose Control~ Teddy Swims
Beautiful Things~ Benson Boone
Truly Madly Deeply~ One Direction
Unwritten~ Natasha Bedingfield

Listen and Enjoy!

Prologue
Aurora

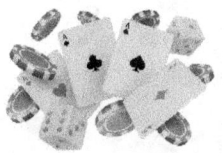

When Tom asked me to be his date for his sister's wedding, I was ecstatic. I thought he might finally see me as more than his quirky neighbor from across the hall. I dreamed about us spinning around the dance floor, laughing and having a good time. But as the night dragged on, it was clear I was stuck in the friend zone.

Everyone was dancing but us. Instead, we sat at a table on the edge of the action while Tom babbled incessantly about the secret project he'd been working on. It was finally finished, and he was ready to meet with investors. "I'm telling you, Aurora, this has the potential to change the casino and gaming industry."

"Uh-huh." I appreciated his enthusiasm, but the last thing I wanted to talk about was work. The star-studded night and Colorado mountains were the perfect backdrop for a romance-filled evening, and he was ruining it. The one time we danced, there was enough room to drive a Mack truck between us, and no matter how much I wished otherwise, his hand stayed firmly planted on my hip. It was middle school all over again.

"If Brett invests in my idea, I'll finally be able to quit my job at Mystique. This is what I've been working toward."

Having heard enough, I nudged his leg with my foot. "Tell me why you don't like Charli's new husband?"

"Hunter?" His face scrunched up. "Let's say he's an acquired taste I've spat out a dozen times. I still can't believe out of all the men in Vegas, she chose Hunter Dorsey. It gives me heart palpitations."

I chuckled. "He can't be that bad."

Tom sighed. "You have no idea. Even worse, he's my boss's brother, so I have to play nice."

"Well, Charli looks happy, and if she's happy, you should be happy for her."

"I'm trying."

I pinched his cheek. "Try harder. Now, get up and go dance with your sister."

He eyed the dance floor skeptically. "Don't you think it would be rude to interrupt?"

"I think she'd like to dance with her brother. Tell her how happy you are for her."

"Alright." Tom stood from the table and ran his hands down his slacks, then straightened his bow tie. Walking onto the small dance floor, he tapped Hunter on the shoulder. After some back and forth, he took Charli's hand in his.

I watched them longingly. It was silly to be jealous of Tom's sister, but I wished he would have danced with me the way he danced with her... without ten feet of space between them.

Penny, whom I'd met when we arrived yesterday, waddled over to me and plopped herself in a chair, rubbing her big belly. "Uh-oh. I know that look."

"What?" I asked innocently, hoping my feelings weren't written all over my face.

She motioned in Tom's direction with her head. "You like him."

"Of course, I like him. He's a great guy."

"That's not what I meant, and you know it." Penny laughed. "That's the same look I used to get when I fell in love with Brett. Admit it. You've got a crush on our little tech genius."

I pinched my fingers together and held them up. "Little bit. Doesn't matter though, because he only sees me as a friend. The nerdy neighbor girl."

Penny eyed me up and down, taking in my shimmery blue dress and stiletto heels. "You don't look so nerdy to me. Besides, Tom is the nerdiest guy I know."

"Yeah, but he's like a Clark Kent nerd." I sighed. "I keep wondering what he'd look like without his glasses and shirt on."

She laughed, then winced and held her side. "This little dude keeps kicking me in the kidneys. I can't wait until he comes out." Penny readjusted herself in the chair. "Anyway, never say never. Who would have thought Brett, the *Billionaire Bachelor of Vegas*,"—she finger quoted—"would fall for me? Now we're married with a baby on the way. You never know what could happen."

I'd read all about her Cinderella story in the *Las Vegas Not So Confidential*. The notorious gossip rag documented their entire relationship with intrusive photos and less-than-flattering commentary. I knew how it felt to constantly be under scrutiny, but it didn't seem to faze her.

Looking away, I caught Tom walking toward us and so did Penny. "Don't be afraid to take a chance," she whispered to me.

I wished I had her optimism. I feared this date was doomed before it even started. But it wasn't a real date, was it? More of a favor, so he didn't have to come to the wedding alone.

"How are you feeling?" he asked, putting a hand on Penny's shoulder.

"I feel like a balloon that's ready to burst. I don't think my skin can stretch much further. I look like the Pillsbury Doughboy; even my feet are fat. Two weeks left to go, and he'd better be on time." She stabbed her belly with a finger. "You hear me, little one? This is not your home."

Tom chuckled. "You look beautiful, and it'll all be worth it in the end."

"He's right. You're glowing," I assured her. "Make your hubby rub your feet when you get back to your room."

"I'm going to do that sooner than later. That man owes me big-time." Penny pushed out of the chair and gave both of us hugs. "It was nice talking with you, Aurora. Enjoy your night." She winked at me and waddled away in search of her husband.

"I really like her," I said, wondering if I'd ever see her again after tonight.

"Yeah, Penny's hard not to like. I've worked with her for a couple years. She's a bubbly little ball of sunshine. Doesn't let much get her down." Tom tapped the leg of the table with the toe of his dress shoe. "You want to get a drink?"

I shook the ice in my empty glass, tired of sitting at the table. "You bet."

We headed to the patio bar and sat at the end of it. Holding up a finger, Tom flagged down the bartender. "Two glasses of your best bourbon."

"Fancy," I said with a smirk.

"Hunter's paying for this shindig, might as well take advantage of it. Tonight, we drink like we're rich!" he exclaimed with a slap on the bar top.

The bartender arrived with two glasses of amber liquor. I took a tentative sip and shuddered as the fiery liquid flowed down my throat. I was more of a Cosmo girl than a bourbon girl. Tom, on the other hand, tossed his back like it was water and motioned to the bartender for another.

I'd never seen him drink more than a beer, so I wondered how this was going to play out. The more he drank, the more his eyes sparkled behind his glasses. He finally relaxed, telling me about the small town he grew up in, not far from the Denver resort we were staying at. Tom laughed while he recounted a story about hacking into the high school's computer system and changing Charli's grades to keep her from getting grounded. "No one ever said a damn thing. You'd think schools would have better firewalls, yet cracking them is child's play."

"You're lucky you didn't get caught."

He looked indignant. "I've never gotten caught, Aurora." Tom tapped the side of his head. "There're a lot of brains up here."

The bartender came back and refilled Tom's glass. I'd barely drunk half of mine, so when he held the bottle over my glass, I put my hand on top of it. I was already feeling tipsy and didn't want to get drunk. Who knew what would come out of my mouth? I was liable to declare my love for Tom in front of the whole resort.

Shivers shot down my spine when he put his hand on my bare knee. "You want to hear a joke?"

I liked this version of Tom. "Oh, you've got jokes now?"

"Bah! Lots of 'em. How does a computer get drunk?"

"I don't know."

"It takes screenshots."

I shook my head and laughed. "That's terrible."

He held up a hand, trying to contain his laughter. "Wait, wait, wait. Here's another one. What do you call an iPhone that sleeps too much? ...Dead Siri-ous."

My body vibrated with giggles. "These are getting worse by the minute."

Tom threw back the last of his drink. "What does a printer have in common with a rock star?" I shrugged my shoulders. "They both keep jammin' all the time. Ba-dum-dum." He air-drummed the rhythm, accentuating the punch line.

Although the jokes were corny, I couldn't keep from laughing. This was the most animated I'd ever seen him. He was way past drunk. "Alright, funny guy, I think it's time to call it a night." I took him by the arm and hauled his heavy body from the barstool.

"But I have more jokes."

"And I'll look forward to hearing them in the morning."

His legs wobbled as he leaned into me, a silly grin plastered on his face. "Thank you for coming to my sister's wedding with me. You don't know how much I appreciate it."

I supported his weight as we walked through the lavish resort. "Are you kidding? Thank you for bringing me. I've never eaten or drunk so well in my life. Everything was exquisite." It wasn't a total lie. I just wish I'd gotten more of this version of Tom than the grumpy one who frowned throughout most of dinner.

"You know what was exquisite?" We stopped in front of our rooms. "You."

"Don't be ridiculous. You're just not used to seeing me in something other than jeans and a T-shirt."

He stared into my eyes and pushed a loose strand of hair behind my ear. "I'm serious. When did you get soooo pretty?"

It was everything I wanted to hear, but not right now. "You're drunk, Tom," I whispered.

"I'm not that drunk." He gently removed my black-framed glasses. "Your eyes are soooo bluuuuue. Like itty-bitty puddles I could splash around in."

Stunned, I stared back at him, the words I wanted to say stuck in my throat. My foolish heart screamed, *"Yes, yes, yes!"* But my rational brain warned me not to believe the words of a drunk man.

His gaze slid from my face to my ample cleavage. It'd been exposed all night, yet he hadn't paid a bit of attention to it until now. He leaned in, his mouth dangerously close to mine. My heart raced with anticipation as his thumb brushed over my bottom lip. "So soft."

Please kiss me.

Kiss me.

Kiss me.

But instead of kissing me, he mumbled, "I think I'm in love with you." With his eyes at half-mast, he nuzzled into my neck. "You smell so good. Like coconut and pineapples. I could eat you up."

I basked in those words even as my heart sank. He was far from sober and as much as the thought of us together thrilled me, it wasn't real. It was alcohol-fueled lust. From experience, I knew better than to believe the words of a man who'd been drinking.

With a firm hand on his chest, I created the space between us he'd been so fond of all night. "You don't know what you're saying."

He twirled my hair around his finger. "I know exactly what I'm saying."

"Doubtful." The look of rejection on his face killed me and I almost gave in, but it was better this way. No awkward regrets for either of us. I took back my glasses and held out a hand. "Give me your key card. It's bedtime for you."

"That's highly disappointing." He patted his pockets and came up empty. "I dunno where it is."

I reached into his coat and pulled out the card. With one swipe, his door opened, and I shoved him inside. "Good night, Tom."

"Night, Rora," he mumbled as the door clicked shut.

Inside my own room, I leaned against the door. Disappointment swelled. When we drove back to Vegas tomorrow, he wouldn't remember a damn thing, but I doubted I'd forget a single moment.

Chapter 1
Tom

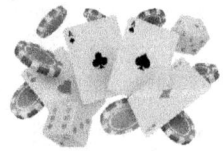

The red laser dot jumped all over the diagram on the screen as I practiced my presentation. "As you can see, once this program is implemented, it will improve operational efficiency, financial security, and the guest experience, all while identifying potential threats in real time." I pointed the laser at Aurora, who sat on my couch, accidentally hitting her in the eye with the red dot. "What do you think?"

Aurora held a hand in front of her face to block the light. "I think that if you blind your investor, you're going to end up owing *him* money."

"Sorry." I fumbled with the switch and turned off the gadget.

"Seriously, Tom, how many cups of coffee have you had?"

I looked at the empty mug sitting on the table. "A few. I've been busting my ass on this presentation for the last week. What did you think?"

My neighbor slapped a piece of red licorice against her lips as she thought.

When she still hadn't said anything, my shoulders slumped. "It was that bad?"

"It wasn't bad per se. It was very… techy."

I rolled my eyes. "What did you expect? It's a tech presentation." I'd been working on this project for months, years if you counted the time it took me to build the framework.

"I get that," she said, taking a bite of the licorice. "I understood exactly what you were saying, and I'll admit, it's genius."

My chest puffed up with pride. "I knew you'd get it." Aurora worked as a computer programmer, and she was sharp as a whip. It was rare to find a fellow nerd who understood programming and coding. The first time I met her, she was wearing a shirt that said *Talk Data to Me*. I knew right then we'd be friends.

"But will your investor understand it? I'm afraid your message will get lost with all the technical terms. You need to simplify it."

I flopped down on my couch next to her and groaned. "I've already dumbed it down. A lot."

Her face scrunched up in displeasure. "Don't say *dumbed it down*."

"Why not? It's the truth."

"It may be the truth, but it makes you sound arrogant. Not everyone's brains work like ours. Technology can be overwhelming for people. You need to explain it like you would to a five-year-old. It doesn't matter if they understand the terminology. It's the concept that's important."

Aurora was right. My entire future hinged on this project. I'd developed a few apps over the years and sold them for decent money, but nothing that could sustain me long term. This project had the potential to provide financial stability for the rest of my life.

Not only for me, but my parents and sister. Even with Hunter doting on Charli, showering her with the kind of security his million-dollar bank account could buy, I wasn't ready to trust him. Being around Hunter was like standing on a glass floor—although assured the glass was secure and stable, I proceeded with caution in case it cracked, and the bottom fell away. Charli, on the other hand, tap danced across it without a worry in the world. She'd always been the more courageous of the two of us.

This was the riskiest thing I'd ever done.

Every dollar I had was invested in this project. The software I bought to build the framework and user interface, not to mention the testing hardware, cost me more than I made in a year. I knew the risks when I decided to go this alone instead of taking it to an investor up front. They would have wanted to bring in their own tech team and I wasn't one for group projects… too many cooks in the kitchen and all that. This was my idea, and I wanted complete control.

But autonomy came at a price.

As a result, I was flat broke. I had enough money left to buy a year' supply of Ramen noodles. If I didn't get financial backing soon, I'd have to ask Hunter for a loan and I'd rather stick my head into a vat of acid than do that.

In two days, I'd be sitting across from Brett Kingston, hoping he'd buy into my security software and beta testing plan. Although my connection with Penny got me an appointment, I hadn't mentioned the proposal to her. This wasn't about pulling strings or leaning on favors. I wanted to earn Brett's support on the merit of my work alone.

Resting my head on Aurora's shoulder, I looked up at her with puppy-dog eyes. "My brain is fried. Help me?"

She patted my cheek. "How can I say no when you look so damn pathetic?"

I knew I could count on Aurora. She was a good sport about being my date for Charli's wedding. We were buddies who watched sitcoms and played *Scrabble*, so asking her to spend the weekend in Colorado with me was a bit out of the box. Asking her to help edit my slide presentation was more in our wheelhouse.

I ordered pizza, and we sat in front of my computer as she pointed out what could be simplified. With a beanie on her head and minimal makeup, she looked more like the Aurora I knew than the woman who accompanied me to the wedding. That woman sucked the air right out of my lungs. I'd never seen her in a dress. With her caramel hair flowing down her back and curves on full display, she was a complete smokeshow. It took everything I had that night not to stare at her lush lips, voluptuous breasts, and long legs. We didn't have that kind of relationship, and I didn't want her to think

I was some kind of creep. Unfortunately, my dick didn't get the memo, so I kept him at bay by filling our time with the most mundane conversation I could muster.

The memory of us sitting at the bar drinking bourbon was fuzzy. I rarely got drunk, but the hangover I'd woken with the next morning told me I'd done exactly that.

Aurora popped her last bite of pizza in her mouth. "Alright," she said with finality. "I think we're good now. Your presentation is sufficiently *dumbed down*."

All I could focus on was the way her lips moved and the tiny drop of sauce below them. "You've got a little something on your chin."

She swiped the back of her hand over the area, completely missing the spot. "Better?"

As if under a spell, I couldn't look away. "Nope, still there."

Her tongue poked out and danced over her lips, searching for the rogue sauce. Inappropriate thoughts flitted through my head of all the other things she could do with that tongue. "Now did I get it?"

"Let me help." As I leaned in and brushed my thumb across her full bottom lip, a sense of déjà vu washed over me. Something at the edge of my memory that I couldn't quite grab. It frustrated me. Unnerved me. Had me second-guessing if I'd crossed some invisible boundary last weekend. "Did anything weird happen at the wedding?" I blurted.

Aurora's eyes widened and she chuckled at my outburst. "You were there. Do you remember anything weird happening?"

I pulled on my hair, then patted down the strands. "That's just it. I don't remember anything after we went to sit at the bar."

"Well, you did have a good buzz going," she said with a smile.

"We were both drinking," I defended.

She held up a finger. "Correction. I was sipping. You were tossing them back. It was nice to see you loosen up a bit."

That information didn't make me feel any better. "Fuck. Was I an asshole?"

Aurora tapped my cheek. "You were a perfect gentleman."

I let out a sigh of relief. "Thank God. I was afraid I did something stupid."

"Nope. We walked back to our room, said good night, and that was it." She gathered up her things and headed for the door. "I have an appointment in an hour. If I don't see you beforehand, good luck with your meeting with Brett."

"Thanks to you, I'm going to kill it."

"I know you will." She gave me a wink and left with a wave of her fingers.

With my presentation finished, I could lay off the caffeine and breathe a little easier, yet something still niggled at the back of my brain, and I couldn't figure out what it was.

Chapter 2
Aurora

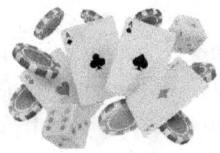

Squinting, I rubbed my temples, but it wasn't solely the blaring sun from the Vegas Strip that had me narrowing my eyes. It was Tom.

Spending time with that man was emotional torture. He didn't remember a damn thing from the night of the wedding, and I couldn't bring myself to tell him. Instead, I sat there on his couch like an idiot, chewing on a piece of licorice and waiting for his shirt to fall off.

It was ridiculous.

If the cocktail dress I wore to the wedding didn't get his attention, a pair of jeans and a T-shirt weren't going to do it. For a smart guy, he missed all the signals I threw at him last weekend. The short hemline, plunging neckline, and meticulous hair and makeup were wasted on a man who would never see me as more than a friend.

Yet, I couldn't forget that one little drunken slip.

I think I'm in love with you.

I should have let it go, but instead I clung to it like a lifeline.

It was pathetic.

Ugh! Where was the backbone I'd grown over the years? My mother raised me to be a strong, independent woman, but when it came to him, I turned into a spineless jellyfish.

I tried to put Tom out of my mind as I pulled up to Helping Hands. There were several homeless shelters in Las Vegas, but this was the most comprehensive. It offered hot meals, housing, transportation, as well as basic medical and employment services. A one-stop shop for those who needed assistance.

Dinner was served at five o'clock every day like clockwork. It was barely four and the line wrapped around the building with hungry people waiting for what might be their only meal of the day. It broke my heart that in a city where money flowed like water, many depended on others to fulfill their basic needs.

I walked past the winding line, saying hello to familiar faces, all the while searching for the one I craved to see. It'd become my obsession. A year had passed without a word, but I kept hoping that one day it would happen.

Going through the back entrance of the shelter, I tossed a few bills in the donation box before Kendra tackled me in a hug. "Thank God you're here. Two volunteers called in, and we're super short on manpower." She'd been running Helping Hands for a decade. It was subsidized by the city, but without donations and volunteers, there was no way it could provide the services it did.

"Where do you need me?"

"Can you restock the coolers and fruit bins?"

"Absolutely." I grabbed an apron from the hooks by the door and tied it around my waist.

"You're an angel." Kendra ran off with her clipboard into the hustle and bustle of the kitchen.

I wound my way through the busy workers. "Hi, Carl. That spaghetti smells heavenly."

Carl was one of the few paid employees at the shelter. Rumor was he'd fallen on hard times when he was younger and worked at Helping Hands to pay it forward. He was a big man, but nothing more than a teddy bear. And one hell of a cook. "Thank you, Rora. I can fix you a plate if you're hungry."

I patted my full belly. "Ate some pizza before I came."

"Bah! My spaghetti is better than greasy ole pizza."

"Maybe at the end of the night." It felt wrong eating when so many waited outside for his cooking. I grabbed a dolly and loaded crates of milk, water, and other assorted beverages, then rolled it to the end of the cafeteria-style counter and emptied them into the waiting coolers. After several trips back and forth, I moved on to the fruit bins. We tried to keep a variety of fresh fruit that people could take with them, such as bananas, oranges, apples, and pears. The selection of the day depended on donations from local vendors and whatever we could get for a good price.

Kendra dropped several boxes of snack bars next to me. "Can you empty these into the grab-and-go baskets?"

"Sure thing." I put more apples into the bin. "Hey, Kendra?"

She looked up from her clipboard. "What's up, honey?"

Although I'd been volunteering at Helping Hands for months, I'd never had the courage to ask the question burning inside me. "Do you keep records of the people who come here? You know, for food or shelter or anything?"

"Some. Why do you ask?"

My face fell. I was hoping there was a centralized database I could look at. "Curious is all," I said with a shrug, continuing to stack the fruit.

She put down her clipboard and placed a hand on my shoulder. "Oh, honey, are you looking for someone?"

I nodded. "It's a long shot. Everyone else has given up hope, but I keep thinking one day they'll turn up."

"There's nothing wrong with keeping hope. It might be a long shot, but that doesn't mean it won't happen. After the dinner rush, I'd be happy to show you where the records are."

"That'd be great. I appreciate it."

She looked at her clipboard again. "We're going to open the doors in about ten minutes. Are you good with serving tonight? Carl's spaghetti always brings a crowd."

I gave her a thumbs-up. "You bet." I never minded serving. It gave me a chance to see everyone who came through the line.

The bustling sounds of clanging pots and the hum of conversation filled the kitchen as I scooped noodles and sauce onto plates, keeping the line moving for the steady stream of people. We never turned anyone away, but there was no guarantee that there would be enough hot food for everyone. Sometimes we had to switch to sandwiches, which was why the line formed well before dinnertime.

Every face that came through had a story to tell. I scanned each one, my heart tightening as the night went on. With every minute that passed, I prayed this would be the day I found the person I'd been searching for.

My memories were a tangled mix of happiness and sorrow. My best friend had once been a source of comfort whose presence made the world feel steady for me. The thought of someone I cared so deeply about wandering the streets alone kept me awake at night.

When the last person was served, I helped wipe tables and collect trash, readying the dining room for the next influx of people arriving for breakfast in less than ten hours. It was an endless cycle of clean, prep, and serve. The time I spent volunteering never seemed enough.

After throwing the last bag of trash into the dumpster, I found Kendra organizing the intake of those seeking shelter for the night. Two large rooms full of cots separated the men and the women. There were also a few private quarters for people with children. Every night, it was a scramble to see who would fill the beds.

I tapped her on the shoulder. "Do you mind if I check out the records room?"

"Not at all, honey. Down the long hallway to the last door on the right. I hope you find what you're looking for."

Grateful for the opportunity, I set out with a renewed bounce in my step, only to find my worst nightmare. The room did indeed hold the records, but they were organized into paper boxes stacked nearly to the ceiling. Each box was labeled *medical*, *employment*, or *housing* and contained dozens of file folders with handwritten names on them. The chaos made my data-loving brain itch. It would take weeks to go through

16

all the boxes, if not months, with no promise that what I was looking for was actually there.

Resigned to the fact that this was going to be time consuming, I pulled a box from the piles and sat cross-legged in the middle of the floor. One by one, I opened each folder and scanned it. By the end of the fifth box, despair set in.

There had to be a better way. It was no wonder so many people got lost in the system and virtually disappeared. No one kept good records, which made it nearly impossible to track who came and went. The homeless were a tiny blip on the radar of humanity.

Helping Hands needed to do better.

Society needed to do better.

Just because someone ended up on the street didn't mean they weren't worth caring about.

Frustrated with how the night ended, I hauled my sorry ass home. For a split second, I considered knocking on Tom's door, but bothering him with my personal problems would pile more onto his already full plate.

After a quick shower, I crawled into bed thinking about how I could help the shelter beyond volunteering. There had to be more I could do.

As I reached over to turn off the bedside lamp, I kissed my fingertips and repeated the same thing I did every night. "I'm not giving up on you. One day I'm going to find you and bring you home." Then I touched my fingers to the framed picture sitting on the nightstand. "Good night. I love you."

Chapter 3
Tom

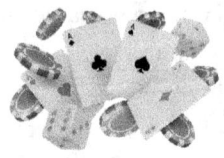

Have you ever felt like the universe was aligning in your favor?

That everything you'd ever dreamed of was dangling just out of reach, waiting for you to grab it?

That's exactly how I felt as I waited in the sleek lobby outside Brett Kingston's office.

I also feared my lunch was about to make a sudden reappearance and splatter all over his shiny marble floor.

I'd made a list and checked it not twice, but a dozen times.

My sales pitch was flawless, rehearsed so much I was sick of it.

The proposal in my hand rattled as my knee bounced uncontrollably. I wondered if this was how people felt when they went on *Shark Tank*, waiting for one of the entrepreneurs to tell them their idea was crap.

But my idea wasn't crap. It was brilliant.

Brett wasn't only a venture capitalist and the CEO of Kingston Enterprises; he was Vegas royalty. If Elvis was the king, Brett was the prince, ruling a kingdom of luxury and billion-dollar deals.

He was Penny's husband and my boss's best friend. But even with those connections, I felt like a crack he stepped over on the sidewalk.

We got even more entwined when Charli married Hunter. Family gatherings and work events had thrown me into a glittering circle of elites where Brett barely spared me a second glance. And now, here I was, hoping to win over the man who treated hundred-thousand-dollar decisions like buying lunch.

Working as a personal assistant for Trent was not my goal in life. I did it to support my sister when she moved to Vegas to be an aerial performer. Her living in the city alone wasn't an option for me. She needed a safety net, and I was more than happy to fill that role so she could chase her dreams.

It was a placeholder.

A way to bide my time, make some easy cash, and work on my real passion after hours. Now that she was settled, it was time to chase my own dreams.

The clickety-clack of approaching heels pulled me from my spiraling thoughts. A woman with graying hair and kind eyes that crinkled at the corners appeared in the lobby. "Mr. Kingston will see you now."

"Thank you." The proposal crumpled under the weight of my clenched fist. Rising to my feet, I smoothed my suit jacket and followed her down a hallway that seemed to stretch forever. The muted sound of my footsteps on the plush carpet did little to steady my racing heart.

Finally, she stopped at a set of tall double doors and knocked lightly before pushing one open. "Mr. Bently is here."

"Thank you, Maryanne. Please show him in."

Maryanne opened the door farther, and I stepped into the fanciest office I'd ever seen. It put the ones at Mystique to shame. Floor-to-ceiling windows lined two walls, offering an uninterrupted view of the Vegas skyline and the mountains beyond, jutting toward the clouds like majestic beasts keeping watch. The sunlight streaming through the glass gave the room an almost celestial glow, casting warm light on the rich mahogany desk and the sleek leather furniture. I stood frozen, struck by the contrast between the city's frenetic energy and the calm, commanding space Brett had built for himself.

But this wasn't the time to dwell on the view. The man who could make or break my future with a single word looked up from his desk with an expectant expression. "I have to say I was surprised when I saw you on my schedule today. What can I do for you, Tom?" He motioned for me to take a seat across from his desk.

This was my moment, my chance to prove that I was more than a personal assistant. "I have an investment opportunity for you that I believe could prove very profitable for both of us."

He leaned forward on his desk and folded his hands. "You have my attention."

"Remember last year when Mystique fell victim to employee theft and lost millions?"

"Of course. Trent was tied up in knots about it for months. Even worse, it wasn't the only casino on the Strip that got hit."

I smack the rolled-up papers into the palm of my other hand, making them look more like a high school term paper than a business proposal. "Exactly. What if there was a foolproof system, totally unhackable, to prevent employee theft and cyber threats, while increasing guest security?"

Brett leaned back in his leather chair, tapping his fingers together. "I'd say it sounds more like a pipedream than reality. Nothing is unhackable."

"Ten years ago, I'd have agreed with you. But since blockchain technology has emerged, it's become a reality. It's already being used successfully in cryptocurrencies. The technology was inspired by the need for a more transparent and secure system to manage records. Every transaction is verified and recorded in a decentralized ledger, making it nearly impossible to alter or hack. With this technology, any effort to skim funds off the top or steal customer information would set off major alarms and be blocked immediately."

Brett's lips twisted to the side. "It sounds complicated. You lost me at *decentralized ledger*. I've heard of blockchain technology, but I'm not going to pretend to understand how it works. Simplify it for me."

If Aurora were here right now, I would have kissed her. This was exactly what she warned me about. "I have a presentation." I pointed to the screen on the wall. "May I?"

"By all means," he said with a swipe of his arm. "Go for it. Fair warning though, I have another meeting in"—he looked at his Patek Philippe watch—"twenty minutes."

Twenty minutes? That was all the time I had to convince him to invest. I quickly set up my laptop and opened my presentation. I showed him how each input of information created a new block that connected to the previous one. Once a new block was created, the one before it was locked in place. It couldn't be changed, erased, or manipulated.

Brett stopped me. "This is all very interesting, but why can't it be changed? I'm not seeing how this makes it unhackable."

I tried not to let the interruption fluster me. "Now we're getting to the good stuff." I forwarded to the next slide. "Think about when you're staying at a hotel. You simply scan your key card to get into your room. Right?"

"Obviously. Get to the point, Tom." I was losing him, and my time was ticking down.

I forwarded to the next slide. "The point is, what you don't see is the hotel's backend system, where all that data is stored. Right now, that data can be compromised. A hacker could breach the hotel's system, duplicate your key card, or steal your information from a centralized database. That's the weak link most systems rely on."

"Well, shit. That's a scary thought. You're talking about addresses, phone numbers, emails... that type of stuff?"

"And credit card numbers. Not to mention getting into your room and robbing you blind."

Bret scrunched up his face as if the idea offended him. "And you can fix this?"

"Yes," I continued excitedly. "Now, imagine your hotel's data is locked in a vault that has a hundred locks, and each key is held by someone different. Even if a hacker gets through one, they'd have ninety-nine more to go." I showed him how, in this new model, the information was spread across several points of data, creating a decentralized system. "There's no

21

central place to hack. Once information is recorded on the blockchain, it's permanent."

"Totally secure?" he asked, with a raise of an eyebrow.

"As someone who's done some hacking in their lifetime, I can say with complete confidence that this system is impenetrable."

His other eyebrow shot up.

It was time to bring out the big guns and let him know I wasn't playing around. Leaning on his desk, I looked Brett in the eyes. "You didn't think that Trent and Hunter discovered where the money from Mystique was going on their own, did you?"

"I assumed they hired someone."

"They did. Me. It would have taken months, if not years, to cut through the red tape and subpoenas required to get information from the banks about the shell corporations that were set up. I did it in a matter of days. It might not have been legal, but they got definite proof against the thief in their company and prosecuted him. And I uncovered the scam Leonard and his son had been running for years. Thanks to me, the hotels affected recovered millions of dollars."

Brett leaned back in his chair and let out a breath. "Why did I not know about this? I'm flabbergasted that Trent didn't tell me."

"Hunter called it the triangle of trust. All three of us were sworn to secrecy. What I did doesn't come without risks." Maybe I shouldn't have told Brett about it, but I knew he wouldn't betray Trent. Their friendship was rock solid. Besides, since I had the most to lose, it was my secret to tell. Plus, it laid the foundation for my tech credibility, something I desperately needed right now.

Brett reached over and picked up his phone. "Maryanne, cancel my next appointment. I'm going to need some more time with Mr. Bently." Then he looked at me. "I assume there's more."

"So much more." Inside my head, I did a victory dance while I calmly explained how easily employee bonuses, vendor payments, and inventory purchases could be tracked. How my program could be used for auditing purposes of all transactions, and most importantly, how guest information would be protected.

"In addition to an added sense of security, guests could earn loyalty points based on all their expenditures and receive customized digital rewards to be used within the hotel, creating a top-tier experience. As you can see, once this program is implemented, it will improve operational efficiency, financial security, and the guest experience, while identifying potential threats in real time."

"And there's nothing on the market like this?" Brett asked.

"For now. Like I said, it's emerging technology. Once word gets out about our system, other tech companies will be scurrying to replicate it. The goal is to be the first and sell it to as many hotels as possible before that happens. This will revolutionize the hotel and casino industry," I said with confidence.

"I can't simply take your word on this. It has to be tested," he pointed out.

"Yes, beta testing is crucial and what better place than Mystique? It's a win-win for everyone. I'm already familiar with their current system, so implementation would be a smooth transition. Mystique gets a one-of-a-kind, cutting-edge security system and we get the endorsement of one of the top luxury hotels and casinos in Vegas."

Brett rubbed his fingers over his chin. "It's an intriguing proposal. I'm sufficiently impressed with your thoroughness and attention to detail. I bought a small tech company a couple of years ago. This would be an excellent asset to its portfolio. How much?"

I pushed my glasses up and asked him to clarify the question I already knew he was asking. "How much what?"

"How much are you selling it for, Tom? What's your price?"

A cold sweat broke out on the back of my neck. This is where I worried the train would fall off the tracks. "I'm not selling it."

He threw his hands in the air. "Then what the hell are you doing here?"

"Selling it would mean I get an up-front payout but miss out on the long-term benefits. Instead, I want an investor to build my own company. You fund the rollout, and in exchange, you get a twenty-percent stake in the company." I smoothed out my once pristine—but now raggedy—business proposal and set it on his desk. "I've laid out all the details. It's a good deal for you."

"I'm not so sure about that," Brett said, looking at the tattered papers skeptically.

"I've done the market research. With casinos having the highest security needs, this software will easily sell for millions of dollars per casino, with an added yearly fee for maintenance and upgrades. Once established as the premier technology, other casinos across the country will be clamoring to have it. And it's not only for casinos. Large hotel chains and resorts will want it too. It has the potential to go global."

Brett stood from his desk and walked to the windows overlooking the multitude of casinos on the Strip. "That seems a little optimistic. What justifies the price tag? They're doing fine without it."

I went and stood next to him, in awe of the unique view of Sin City. "But are they really? In one year alone, they'll recoup their initial investment cost. In the long run, this software will actually save them money through reduced fraud, efficiency in operations, and guest retention. They have the money to spend, and we're providing a solution to their number one problem—security. Selling it won't be an issue."

"I'm going to read through your proposal," Brett said, picking it up off his desk. "You've given me a lot to consider and now I need to do *my* research."

"As you should. I wouldn't expect anything less." I packed up my laptop and held out my hand. "Thank you for meeting with me today."

He grasped it in his. "It was an unexpected pleasure. You surprised me, Tom, and that doesn't happen very often. This is a huge leap from personal assistant to business owner."

His words gave me hope, but I pushed down my excitement. The deal wasn't done yet. "Steve Jobs launched Apple from his garage. Big ideas have to start somewhere."

He chuckled. "Very true."

As I walked to the door, Brett called out. "Hey, Tom. What makes you so sure I won't take your idea to my own tech team and capitalize on it?"

Then it was my turn to chuckle. "You could try, but *fair warning*, it will take your guys years to build this type of system. By then, I will have found another investor and you'll be eating my dust trying to play catch-up. Think about that when you're reading my proposal."

This time, he belly-laughed. "Penny always said there was more to you than meets the eye and I'm starting to believe her. I'll be in touch, Tom."

"I look forward to it." Once out of his office, I did a fist pump. It didn't go quite as planned; we didn't get to all my slides, but he was interested. I could feel it deep in my bones. Once he read through the proposal, not only would he see my software was a winner, but also how much money it would actually save casinos. The possibilities were endless and so were the profits.

On the other hand, if he decided the deal wasn't for him, it was back to square one. My threat of taking it to other investors wasn't a lie, but hunting down those investors would take months, and I didn't have that kind of time. Not when the bills were piling up.

I decided to focus on the positive—Brett's intrigue and interest. The deal wasn't signed, but he hadn't said no and that was something.

I could barely wait to get home to tell Aurora how it went.

Opening my text messages, I reread the ones she sent me this morning.

Aurora: You've got this! Keep it simple and don't let him intimidate you. If worse comes to worst, imagine him in his tighty-whities with a hairy chest and a beer gut. That should do the trick. Go, Tom! She added a string of emojis with pompoms, confetti, and hearts.

Aurora: In all seriousness, the software is awesome. If he doesn't invest, he's a fool. And remember, Brett's not the only investor out there. If he doesn't bite, someone else will.

Aurora: But he will bite. I know he will. Good luck today! More hearts and a kissy face followed.

They made me smile and eased the tension in my chest; however, they also caused a serious strain in my suit pants.

An image of her in that blue dress flitted through my mind. My god… that dress! I'd always thought she was cute, but at the wedding, I realized she was a stunner, as beautiful as she was smart and sweet. Since then, I'd mentally crossed the invisible line between us a multitude of times. I imagined what it would be like to kiss her soft lips, to hold her close, to feel every one of her curves in my hands. I'd woken with a hard-on for the past week.

She deserved a man who could take care of her right, who could provide her with everything she deserved, and that started with closing this deal. My meeting with Brett brought me one step closer.

On the way home, I bought a bottle of her favorite wine, ready to surprise the woman who had crept her way into my heart.

Chapter 4
Aurora

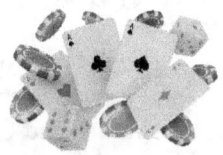

As I stepped out of the shower, three knocks sounded on my door. Water dripped down my body as I reached for a towel and rushed to put on my pink robe. It always worked this way. You could be sitting around for hours doing nothing and the moment you went into the bathroom, someone showed up out of the blue.

I wrapped the towel around my drenched hair and shouted, "Hold on! I'm coming!" My feet slipped on the wet floor, nearly sending me crashing into the shower doors. Catching myself on the counter, I straightened my robe and looked in the mirror. Black mascara rimmed my eyes like a raccoon. *Crap!* I wiped away the mess with a tissue. It would have to be good enough.

Another round of knocks came, and I rushed to the door. Standing on my tiptoes, I looked out the peephole. Tom's distorted face came into view, those blue eyes shining behind his glasses. My heart leaped. I wanted to talk to him, I really did, but my current state of undress wouldn't do.

Cracking the door open, I peeked out into the hallway and smiled. "Hey."

Dapper as ever in a gray suit with his signature bow tie, Tom held up a bottle of wine in one hand and two long-stem glasses in the other. "I wanted to tell you about my meeting." His eyes scanned my body from the towel on my head to the tips of my painted toenails. "Is this a bad time? I don't want to bother you if you're busy."

I shook my head. "It's not a bad time. I want to hear all about it. Give me five minutes?"

"Of course. I'll wait out here."

I held up a finger. "Don't go anywhere. I'll be right back."

He chuckled. "I'm not going anywhere."

Shutting the door, I sprinted to my bedroom, making the curtain of beads jangle, and pulled on a pair of panties and a bra, then slipped into a clean T-shirt that read *Nerdy by Nature* and cotton shorts. My legs were freshly shaved, so might as well show them off. I pressed a bit of powder to my face and applied a fresh coat of mascara.

I couldn't believe that, out of everyone, he wanted to share his news with me first. It meant something, right? He was still in his suit, so he must have come right here. The thought made me giddy.

The towel tumbled from my head to the floor in a damp pile. I ran a brush through the strands and used the hairdryer to get them mostly dry and not so stringy-looking. It would have to be good enough.

Grabbing my glasses from the bathroom counter, I hopped over a little black fur ball before she scurried into my room and under the bed. When I moved into this apartment months ago, I needed some company. I went down to the animal shelter and fell in love with the tiny kitten pressed into the back corner of her cage. She looked at me with soulful eyes, and I knew in that instant that she needed me as much as I needed her. "Be a good girl. We're having company," I called over my shoulder on my way to the door.

Opening it, I found Tom sitting on the floor beside his door, tie untied and the top few buttons of his shirt undone. "You could have changed." I motioned to his apartment.

"I didn't want to miss you." He ran a hand through his hair, mussing it up in the sexiest way. "Are you ready for me?"

In more ways than one. "Absolutely. Welcome to my humble abode," I said with a wave of my arm toward the open door.

Tom stood and sauntered into my apartment, his gaze sweeping the space with undisguised curiosity as he took in the Boho style and bright colors. "Wow! I did not expect this. It's the exact same layout as mine, but a completely different vibe. I like it." He wandered into the kitchen, setting the bottle and glasses on the counter. "How is it that I've never been in your apartment before?"

I followed him and bumped his hip with mine. "Just the way it worked out, I guess."

His lips pressed together in a thin line. "I've made it all about me, haven't I? Too much tech talk, and not enough real talk." He picked up a can of cat food from the counter. "You have a cat?"

"Yep. A little black one named Ailuros. She's shy around strangers, so she's hiding under my bed."

"You named your cat *Cat*."

I loved that he got it. "You know Greek?"

"Greek mythology, not the language. I went through a phase where I was fascinated with ancient cultures. It's all stored away up here in a file box," he said, tapping his temple.

I knew Tom was smart, but that was crazy. "Do you have a photographic memory?"

He laughed. "No, but I do know a lot of useless shit. Anything that interests me tends to stick."

"In this case, it wasn't useless; it was impressive."

"Never know when I might need to pull something out of that file box," he said with a shrug. "I can't believe I didn't know you had a cat. Usually, my observation skills are better than that." Glancing around my apartment, his eyes locked on my bedroom "door," which was nothing more than strands of colorful beads that nearly touched the floor. "I'm beginning to think I don't know anything about you."

"Sure you do." I rooted around in a drawer full of miscellaneous kitchen gadgets and pulled out a corkscrew. "You know what kind of wine I like." He turned the bottle around to show me the Moscato label. "You did good."

"That makes me feel a little better." He took the corkscrew from my hand and opened the wine, then poured each of us a glass. "At the risk of making it all about me again, I wanted to tell you how my meeting went. I got excited and now realize I should have texted first."

"It's fine. The wine tells me it went well." I took my glass to the couch and sat.

Tom followed and pushed aside a few tasseled pillows as he joined me. "To be clear, Brett didn't say yes." He held up a finger. "However, he didn't say no. He's interested. Highly interested and that's all thanks to you."

My hand flew to my chest. "To me? It was your concept and hard work that brought it to life."

"That's true, but…" He tipped his glass toward me. "Without you, my presentation would have flopped like a soggy french fry drowning in ketchup. Instead, it was solid and crisp, garnering Brett's attention."

The security software was one hundred percent all him. "I didn't do anything but make a few tweaks to the presentation." I took a sip of the sweetness in my glass. "Regardless, I appreciate the wine."

He put his hand on my bare knee, and a shiver ran through me. "You did more than you know. I think the slide of the vault with a hundred locks on it really drove the point home. It got him thinking deeper about security risks."

I tossed my hair over my shoulder. "Well, I will take credit for that."

He clinked his glass with mine. "As you should."

"Do you know when you'll hear back?"

His lips twisted to the side. "All he said was he was going to do some research, but I have a feeling I'll know sooner than later. He's not a guy who hems and haws."

"So, what's plan *B* if he says no?"

Tom dropped his head on the back of the couch and blew out a breath. "Honestly, I don't know. Look for a good cardboard box to live in? Every nickel I have is invested in this project."

The hair on the back of my neck bristled. It was a joke, just not a good one. And in all fairness, Tom didn't know I volunteered at the homeless shelter. "It won't come to that. I have a good feeling about this. Plus, you could always stay with your sister. I bet they have plenty of room."

He rolled his eyes. "You're kidding, right? I can't imagine sitting across from Hunter drinking my coffee. That's a living nightmare."

"I'm sure their bougie apartment isn't worse than living on the street. I volunteer at Helping Hands, and those people would switch places with you in a heartbeat." I didn't mean for it to come out so harsh, but there was a distinct sharpness to my words.

"Shit," he mumbled. "I'm sorry, Aurora. I didn't know. I feel like a total ass."

"It's fine," I said, finishing my wine. "Most people don't give the homeless a second thought. They think they're bums and alcoholics and drug addicts, but that's rarely the case. I've seen people in desperate situations they never thought they'd be in. All it takes is one unforeseen life crisis, like illness or job loss, to change everything. Not to mention that this country does a crap job with mental health. If you can't afford food, how are you supposed to see a therapist? It can quickly become a downward spiral into a dark hole with no ladder to get out."

Tom took my glass to the kitchen and refilled it. "You're right. It's nothing to joke about and I apologize for my insensitivity. What made you start volunteering there?"

The gears in my head whirred, deciding how much I wanted to reveal. *His* story was not mine to tell. "I knew someone who fell on hard times. They took to the streets and disappeared."

"This was a friend of yours?"

"My best friend," I answered, even though he was so much more than that. "Did you know that there's really no tracking system at the shelters? The records are practically nonexistent."

"I never gave it much thought, but I can't say I'm surprised," he said, coming back with my glass and setting it on the table. "I'm sorry about your friend."

"Thank you. Volunteering makes me feel like I'm doing something. Making a difference in someone's life."

"You are," he said with a soft smile. "They're lucky to have you."

"I don't know about that. It never seems like enough."

"It's enough to the people you help. You're a good person, Aurora."

I dipped my head. "Meh. I'm alright. Trust me, I have my faults." A feeling of guilt sat in my stomach. If I was a good person, I wouldn't have told him a half-truth. I don't even know why I lied, except out of loyalty and a sense of protectiveness.

"I haven't found any yet." He smirked.

His smile chased away my negative thoughts and got me back on track with the purpose of Tom's unexpected visit. "So, assuming Brett does say yes to your proposal, what's next?"

"Then we meet with Trent, Hunter, and *the* Mr. Dorsey—their dad. He's retiring soon, but I imagine he'll still get the final say. I'm hoping with Brett's endorsement and my experience at Mystique, they'll agree to let me use the hotel and casino as a testing ground. The only reason I could see Trent being against it is that he'd lose me as a PA."

"He can get another personal assistant," I said, waving off his concern.

Tom pulled on his lapels. "But not one as good as me."

I laughed. "True. Does he even know how overqualified you are for that job?"

"He knows *and* he sucks up all the benefits. There was talk about me moving to the tech department, but there was no bump in salary. It didn't make sense for me to change departments when I was working on something even better."

"I get that." One thing about Tom, he always had a plan. Everything he did was calculated. I loved how his brain worked. It was rare to find someone who could keep up with me intellectually, yet Tom had no issue. That was what drew me to him in the first place.

It didn't hurt that he was good-looking and didn't even know it. My heart pitter-pattered as I stared at the bit of skin revealed by the open buttons on his shirt. Why did he have to be so delicious? And clueless? The devil on my shoulder begged me to do something to urge him on. I may have been a good person, but I wasn't a good girl.

I didn't know if he was a leg man, boob man, or ass man, but I was willing to try anything. Stretching my bare legs out, I put my freshly pedicured feet on the table and wiggled my toes. Tom's eyes traveled from my thighs down the length of my legs to my pink toenails. His gaze lingered and his jaw tensed before he averted his eyes like a gentleman.

Dammit! Like Superman, he was bulletproof.

He stood and straightened his jacket awkwardly. "I should get going. You probably have things to do. I didn't mean to interrupt your... shower." A blush crept into his cheeks like a virgin schoolgirl.

My little stunt backfired. Instead of pulling him closer, it pushed him away. I removed my legs from the table and folded them underneath me. "You don't have to go."

"Yeah, I really do. I have some things to put together in case Brett does say yes. Presenting this idea to the Dorseys will require a slightly different approach."

I pouted as my heart sank. "Well, okay. I don't want to keep you from your work. Thank you for the wine." I held up my glass. "Do you want to take the rest of the bottle?"

He gave me a gentle smile. "Keep it. It's the least I can do."

"Hey." I jumped off the couch and tackled him in a hug. "Congratulations! No matter what happens, you should be proud." The smell of his cologne permeated my senses as I rested my head on his hard chest. It brought back memories of the Tom who nuzzled into my neck at the wedding, declaring his love for me. That man was completely uninhibited. And also—drunk as a skunk.

Sober Tom had no such inclinations. His arms loosely wrapped around me. "Thank you. That means a lot." He patted my back like you would do to an old pal from high school. "You're a good friend." Then he walked out the door, leaving me flustered and frustrated.

How in the hell did I trap myself in the friend zone and, more importantly, how was I going to get out of it?

Chapter 5
Tom

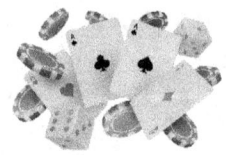

Penny slammed her hands on my desk and leaned forward. "Something you want to tell me?"

I quirked an eyebrow at the woman who had once captured my heart but gave hers to a billionaire. I couldn't blame her, but it taught me you had to have something more than kind words or a witty joke to offer a woman. Once I saw how much Brett loved her, I graciously bowed out and settled for friendship. "Shouldn't you be at home?" I answered back, trying to divert her away from the barrage of questions she was undoubtedly going to ask.

She rubbed her round belly. "I'm not due for three days. What do you want me to do? Sit around and watch television while eating bonbons?"

I chuckled. "Uh, yeah. That's exactly what you should be doing."

"I'd be bored out of my skull," she said emphatically. "Besides, Gia is training me to take over her job as director of events and entertainment, so when I come back from maternity leave, I'll be ready to go."

"You've been the PA for that position for years. You probably know the job better than her."

She held a finger to her lips. "Shhh! That's true, but don't tell her that. She's my bestie and I don't want to ruin it."

I mimed taking a key and locking my lips. "You'll do great."

"Honestly, not much is going to change. With Gia moving to head of public relations and marketing we'll still be working together. I'll simply have more responsibility."

"And a bigger paycheck."

"I'm not doing it for the paycheck. I'm doing it for personal satisfaction. I wanted that job before they ever hired Gia."

"You don't want to stay home with your baby?"

"I shouldn't have to choose between motherhood and a career. Men don't. Besides, they've agreed to a flexible schedule." She tapped her fingers on my desk. "Very sneaky. I see what you did there."

"What?" I asked innocently.

"You tried to distract me, and it almost worked. Why didn't you tell me about your meeting with Brett?" she whispered. "He was up all night researching blockchain and hotel security. Is this the secret project you've been working on for years?"

I looked around to make sure no one was listening. "Yeah. Please don't say anything. It's not a sure thing."

"This is the last time I'll speak of it." Then *she* mimed locking her lips. "Too many snoopy snoopertons around here. All I'll say is you got him thinking. He put extra security alerts on all our credit cards."

"That's good," I said with a smirk.

Trent poked his head out from his office behind me. "Tom, I need to see you."

"Right away, sir."

Trent rolled his eyes and shut the door.

Penny held up both her thumbs and squealed as she backed away to her desk.

I grabbed a notepad and pen, then entered Trent's office. He motioned to the chair across from his desk. "First of all, quit calling me sir," he said as he paced in front of the window overlooking the casino. "I've been telling you that for over two years and, frankly, it's getting old. We're way past the formalities."

I pushed my glasses up with one finger. "Noted."

"Second, are you sick? You don't look sick."

My brows furrowed. "I'm not sick. Why?"

"Because you haven't taken a day off since you started and yesterday you were gone. It felt like someone cut off my right arm."

I knew being absent would be suspicious. "I had some personal business to attend to. Is that a problem? I cleared it with HR."

He shook his head. "Not at all. I'm not saying you're not entitled to personal days. It was weird is all. You're always here. Do me a favor and give me a heads-up next time."

"Will do."

Trent ran a hand through his hair. "I'm anxious about moving up to CEO when my father retires. It's all I've ever wanted, but it comes with a shit ton of extra responsibility. I'm glad you'll be moving up with me."

I felt bad not telling him I might not be his personal assistant, but that would be getting ahead of myself. "I'm sure everything will work out. And with Gia taking your position, you know public relations and marketing are in good hands."

"Yeah. My wife is a ballbuster. It's the fiery redhead in her."

Hunter strolled into Trent's office uninvited and plopped into the chair next to me. He knew it made Trent crazy and there was nothing Hunter loved more than to get his half brother's goat. "What's up, buttercups?"

Trent ground his teeth. "What do you want, Hunter?"

"Seeing what my brothers are up to is all."

I glared at him. "We're not brothers."

He pointed to the ring on his finger. "This says otherwise. We're brothers from different mothers. Oh, wait! So are Trent and I. We should hang out together more."

"Hard pass," I growled.

"Hmmm. And I thought you were starting to like me. I did make you part of the triangle of trust." He gave me a big, dopey grin.

It was more like a square now, but Hunter didn't need to know that. "You make my sister happy, God knows why, so I tolerate you."

"So no kumbaya?"

"Again, hard pass." I should have been nicer to Hunter, knowing that he could piss on my security software parade, but it was better to keep things normal between us and that included animosity.

"Is there a reason you're sitting in my office?" Trent asked him.

"Actually, there is. I talked to Dad, and when he retires and you move into his office, I'm moving into yours. Gia can take mine. And before you get your panties in a twist, I deserve this office, and you know it." Hunter had been salivating over Trent's office for years. It was one of many bones of contention between the two of them since Hunter's office overlooked the dumpsters.

"Fine," Trent huffed. "But let me be the one to tell her."

"No worries. I saw your wife in the break room. I already broke the news to her."

"Fuck. How'd she take it?"

"More testy than usual. Must be the pregnancy hormones." Hunter's smirk told me he enjoyed breaking the news to Gia a little too much.

Trent ran his hands over his face and groaned. "The first trimester has been brutal."

"I got to skip that with Carina, seeing she was six months old before I even knew she existed." Hunter's daughter had been dropped on his doorstep with a note. Not something I would wish on anyone, not even him.

"It'll be soon enough before you find out," Trent assured him.

"Not too soon. Charli wants to focus on her career, not have babies, but we're doing plenty of practicing in the meantime," Hunter said with a smirk.

Although the back and forth was entertaining, this conversation was not something I needed to be involved in. The idea of Hunter and my sister *practicing* made me want to puke. "If there's nothing else, I'm gonna head back to my desk."

Hunter grabbed my arm. "Not so fast, Boy Genius. What's up with you and the woman you brought to the wedding? Aurora, right?"

The last thing I wanted was Hunter all up in my business. "She's a friend. End of story."

His lips tilted up. "A hot friend. Not that I noticed, being a married man and all. Did you tap that?"

Trent threw his hands in the air. "Jesus Christ! Could you be any more inappropriate?"

"It's a valid question."

This was why I didn't want to *hang out* with Hunter. "No, I didn't *tap that*." I finger quoted.

"Why the hell not? She's single. You're single. What's the problem?"

I looked at the ceiling and prayed for patience. "She doesn't see me that way. Besides, what do I have to offer a woman?"

Hunter scratched his chin. "You're a good-looking dude, objectively speaking, and you have a dick, so I'm not sure I'm seeing the issue."

"She could do better," I said with exasperation.

Trent frowned. "What's that supposed to mean? Besides, you know... what Hunter said, you're ambitious and smart."

"Money! I'm talking about money. You two don't get it because you both have plenty. I need to make something more of myself. She deserves that."

"Showing her your bank account is not a prerequisite for a booty call. Newsflash... poor people bang all the time," Hunter pointed out.

"Maybe I don't want to just bang."

Hunter rolled his eyes at me. "When did you get spayed? There's nothing wrong with hooking up. Or is it a plumbing problem? They have pills for that. Little blue ones. Take one of those babies and BOING! Took one back in college, and let me tell you, that shit works like magic."

I didn't miss his double burn. "I don't have a plumbing problem."

"Oh, shut up, Hunter. Tom really likes this girl. The last person he should be taking relationship advice from is you."

Hunter pointed at his ring again. "Successfully married. Take it from me, when you find the one, you've got to tie that shit down. If you don't, someone else will. A woman like her won't stay on the market forever."

The fact he was referring to my sister was entirely too much information. "Okay, I think this has been enough bonding for right now." I pushed out of the chair and headed for the door, practically running to make my escape.

"If you need any pointers, let me know!" Hunter shouted. "You know what Charli really likes?"

I slammed the door behind me, cutting him off before my ears bled. *Gross.*

Although I didn't appreciate Hunter's unsolicited advice, he was right about one thing. A woman like Aurora wouldn't stay on the market forever. Once this deal came through, if it came through, I'd be able to show her I was worthy.

Chapter 6
Aurora

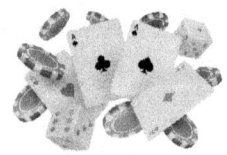

I was in the seventh circle of hell. I installed an update for one of our customers, causing their site to crash. After an extremely angry phone call, I rolled back the update, used the backup to get it running again, and spent the next six hours going through line after line of code. It was mind-numbing work, and by the end of the day, I was spent.

When I got Tom's texts, I couldn't help but laugh. It was the type of medicine you couldn't buy in any store, and I was in desperate need of it.

Tom: Sorry I flaked out the other day. I was a jerk for leaving so quickly.

Tom: I was thinking about what I said about not really knowing you and I want to remedy the situation. So, at the risk of making it all about me AGAIN, I'll go first. Below are five fun facts about me.

Tom: 1) I had a pet cat named Bartholomew when I was a kid. We called him Mew.
2) I didn't start talking until I was three, but when I did, it was in full sentences. My parents took me to lots of doctors, but nothing was wrong with me. I was always more of a thinker and a listener, I guess.
3) The first girl I said "I love you" to was my kindergarten teacher. She was sixty.
4) I've never eaten peanut butter.
5) My favorite color is blue, like your eyes.

Tom: Your turn. Tell me five fun facts about Aurora.

There was a lot to unpack in those few short sentences, number five being the most significant. *His favorite color was blue? Like my eyes?* Maybe everything he said at the wedding wasn't alcohol-fueled. Maybe there was more truth to his words that night than I initially thought. And if that was true… I covered my mouth with my hand and shrieked with giddiness.

He didn't remember, but there were still possibilities. He'd been acting as skittish as a cat in a dog pound, so I'd take it slow with him, nurture our friendship, until he realized we were meant to be. I was a patient girl. That didn't mean no action on my part, but it did mean subtlety.

Wanting to think of five good things and not seem overanxious, I tucked my phone away. I'd text him when I got home from Helping Hands.

Coming in the back door, the aroma of beef stew filled the air. "Smells good, Carl," I said, taking a big whiff.

He smiled and shoved a small dish at me. "I know if I asked, you'd say no, so I made you a bowl. It's already out of the pot. If you don't eat it, then I'll have to dump it in the trash."

I shook my finger at him. "Very clever. I would never waste your food, Carl."

"Go on, then. Take a bite." He nodded at me.

Lifting the spoon to my mouth, the flavors exploded on my tongue. By far, way better than my cooking. Or even my mother's, though I'd never tell her that. "It tastes like a cold night, wrapped in a blanket in front of a

41

fireplace. Comfort and a taste of home. You're going to make a lot of people very happy."

Carl beamed, the gap between his two front teeth on full display. "I hope so. That's the best compliment I've ever gotten. It's my Grandma Bessie's secret recipe, passed down from one generation to the next."

"I'm going to savor every bite," I said with a wink, carrying my stew to the assignment board. Looked like we had a full crew tonight, which was a blessing. Next to my name were the words *See Kendra*.

Huh? That was strange. I walked back to Carl. "Have you seen Kendra around?"

"She's been holed up in her office all day," he said, pointing a spoon at the hallway where I found the records. "Got some bees in her bonnet for sure."

"Thanks." I didn't really know what he meant but I finished my stew and headed that way. I found Kendra sitting at her desk surrounded by piles of paper. She chewed on a pencil, her brows furrowed in concentration. I tentatively rapped on the door and stepped inside. "You wanted to see—"

Her head snapped up. "Oh, thank god. I need your help." She motioned to the green plastic chair next to her.

"Sure. What's going on?" At first, I thought she wanted to see me because I'd done something wrong, but that clearly wasn't the case.

"The shelter is in trouble. Donations are down and the number of people needing help is up. I've exhausted all the city and state resources. If I don't do something, we'll be closed in six months."

I frowned. "Where will they go?"

Kendra sighed. "Other shelters, I suppose, but the prospect of them being able to handle the overflow is dim. It'll put more stress on their already strained budgets."

That news was depressing. "What about a fundraiser?"

She shook her head. "It won't be enough. What do you know about grants?"

"Very little."

She handed me a stack of papers. "There's a federal grant we might be eligible for."

I sifted through the papers, noting all the information required. "Okaaaay. You want me to write the grant proposal?"

She shook her head. "Nobody knows this place better than me. I can write the proposal." She took the papers from me and flipped to the last page, tapping it with the end of her pencil. "This is the problem."

I read the section she pointed to. *What specific metrics will you use to track the success of the project (e.g., number of individuals served, bed capacity, counseling, employment rates)? What methods will you use to collect and analyze data to demonstrate program impact?* My mind went back to the records room full of dusty boxes and my face fell as I looked back at Kendra.

"Exactly," she said. "Excuse me for saying this, but we're fucked. Helping Hands has an excellent reputation in the community and is a model for other shelters, but we've never had to prove our success before. Anyone who visits can see the good we're doing, but federal grants are an entirely different beast. They want hard facts and metrics. They're not going to be impressed to see we've fallen short on the record keeping."

I straightened my spine. "How can I help?"

"I've done some research, and we need to create a management information system. We'll need to have our clients complete intake forms to gather basic information, then correlate that information with what services they're receiving and update individual progress. The goal of any shelter isn't only to provide meals and a safe place to stay, but to get people back on their feet and help them become productive members of society."

"So, can we purchase a management information system?" There had to be some software available.

Kendra laughed. "We absolutely can, but here's the kicker... with the size of our facility, we can't afford it. There are licensing fees, implementation fees, training fees, support fees... the list goes on and on. And honestly, I'd rather that money go to the people than some big, money-hungry software company."

"I agree, but what will you do? If you don't get the data, then you won't get the grant." *And my chances of finding my best friend would sink even lower.*

She shuffled through some papers on her desk until she found the one she wanted. "You wrote on your volunteer application that you were a computer programmer."

I nodded. "I am. I mostly design interactive websites."

Kendra put the paper back on her desk and sighed. "It's a huge ask, and if you say no, I'll totally understand, but do you think you could create an information management system for us?"

My body filled with excitement as the gears in my brain whirred with possibilities. "That day in the records room, I wondered why you didn't already have one. It won't be that different than building a website, but with more backend data entry and analysis capabilities."

Kendra chewed on the eraser of the pencil, looking unsure. "I won't be able to pay you. It would be completely pro bono work."

I leaned forward and hugged Kendra. "It would be a privilege. This is the perfect opportunity to make a real difference."

She hugged me so tightly I could barely breathe. "Thank you. You have no idea how much this will help the shelter."

Grabbing a pencil from her desk, I scribbled notes on a pad of paper. "There will be some up-front costs, but not for the work itself. We'll need to pay for a domain and a hosting site, but those are relatively cheap. Also, I'm thinking tablets will be the best route for data entry. They're portable and affordable."

Kendra smiled. "You're already talking over my head, but I think we can manage that. You tell me what we need, and I'll set aside the funding."

"We'll also need to discuss the specifics of what data you want collected and the type of reports."

She rubbed her hands together eagerly. "Let's get to work."

I was jotting down initial ideas for the database structure when my phone buzzed in my pocket. My heart skipped a beat as I glanced at it.

Tom: Hello????

Tom: I'm patiently waiting for your five facts (fingers tapping). I want to know everything about you and commit it to memory. You interest me and my inquiring mind won't be satisfied until I do.

He followed with an exploding-head emoji and a smiley face.

Warmth spread through my chest. *I interested him?* Tom's texts, combined with the new shelter project, made me giddy. For someone who felt burned out a short while ago, my life was suddenly catching fire in all the right ways.

I tucked my phone away with a promise to respond later. Right now, I had a shelter to save—but tonight, I had five fun facts to carefully craft. Because if Tom was interested, I wasn't going to miss the opportunity to ensure it stayed that way.

"Aurora?" Kendra's voice snapped me back to the project at hand. "You're grinning like a Cheshire cat."

"I'm really excited about creating the database so Helping Hands can get that grant," I said, trying to redirect her curiosity.

"Uh-huh, I'm sure you are, but I have a feeling that smile has more to do with whoever texted you than the database."

I shrugged. "Maybe it's both."

It wasn't a lie. The prospects of finding Aidan and moving out of the friend zone with Tom were equally exciting. The future was full of possibilities and that was something to smile about.

Chapter 7
Tom

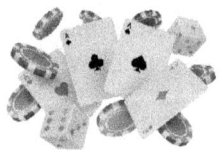

When I got the call from Brett, I didn't hesitate to meet him. He asked me to come to his penthouse since he didn't want to leave Penny alone. Couldn't blame him. She looked ready to pop.

The high-rise building was swanky as hell with its marble floors, crystal chandeliers, and elaborate floral arrangements. Even the concierge was fancy in his crisp maroon uniform and cap. Over the years, I had given up worrying about the opinions of others, but money was my Achilles heel. It was hard not to feel insecure when I was surrounded by wealth on a daily basis.

Stepping into the gold elevator, I opened my text messages and frowned. Aurora must have found my five fun facts cheesy. She'd read them but didn't respond.

I knocked my phone against my head. *Dumb, dumb, dumb.* Why did I send something so childish? How would she ever take me seriously if I couldn't get my shit together? My game needed work. I'd always been shy around women and my words never came out right. I thought it would be different with Aurora, but so far it wasn't.

I couldn't worry about it now, so I put my phone away as the elevator dinged and the doors slid open to a vestibule with two *apartments*. It surprised me Brett didn't have the whole top level to himself. Lord knew he could afford it.

When I knocked on his door, Penny answered quickly. "I'm so excited for you," she squealed, practically knocking me over in a hug.

"Then you must know something I don't," I said, hugging her back. She held her thumb and forefinger up. "A little something."

Brett rushed to the door behind Penny with a worried look on his face. "Dammit, Penny, I told you I would get it," he said, putting an arm around his wife and ushering her to the leather sectional.

"I'm not an invalid. I can answer the door. And just so you know," she said, wagging a finger at him, "I plan on going to work tomorrow."

"She's going to be the death of me," Brett said as he came back and shook my hand. "Thanks for coming."

I laughed. "You knew who you were marrying."

"That I did." He led me to the dining room table where the papers of my proposal were spread across its surface.

The penthouse was enormous with surprisingly modest furnishings. Bright portraits adorned the walls, and colorful pillows were strewn across the couch. Penny nestled into the corner of it and covered her legs with a blanket, then picked up a book from the end table as two orange cats jumped on her lap.

I sat at the table and folded my hands, trying to appear calm even though my stomach felt like I'd gotten off a Tilt-A-Whirl. "You've either called me here because you see the value in my software or to let me down easy."

"I've read and reread your proposal, as well as done my own research," Brett said, not giving anything away. "I have to be honest, I didn't understand the scope of the software until I really dug into it. What you've put together here is revolutionary."

It was encouraging, but he hadn't said the words I wanted to hear. "It is," I concurred.

"However, I have some amendments I'd like to make. If we can come to an agreement, I'm in. If not, I'll have to pass. You're asking for a large investment for only twenty percent of the company. That's not going to do it for me."

My fingers twitched and a bead of sweat trickled down my back, but I kept my face even. "I'm open to a counteroffer."

"I want a forty percent stake for an investment of one million dollars. I'm taking all the risk here."

My initial twenty percent was a lowball offer, but forty was more than I was willing to give up. I ventured a glance at Penny, who subtly shook her head. "It's generous, however, I think we both know you'll make your investment back within months. How many other investments have you made that can promise that type of return?"

He scoffed at my words. "Promise? I think you're overestimating the value of your product."

"And I think you're underestimating it. I'm willing to go to thirty percent. If that doesn't appeal to you, I'll take it to Rockford Industries. I already have an appointment with Wayne Rockford next week. He's always looking for the next big thing." It was a complete lie, but a little competition never hurt.

Brett visibly bristled. "Wayne Rockford is a dick. You don't want to do business with him."

"I'm not really concerned about his disposition. His money is the same color as yours. I came to you with the opportunity first out of respect for my friendship with Penny. I thought we could build something great together." If this strategy didn't work, I was screwed.

"You still have the option of selling it to me outright."

I shook my head. "This is my baby. No offense, but I'm not selling it to someone who doesn't even understand how it works."

"Then I'm out. It's forty percent or nothing," he said, calling my bluff and pushing the papers into the center of the table. "If Wayne doesn't bite, give me a call." Brett had the audacity to wink at me with a smug grin. His reputation of being a shrewd businessman wasn't unfounded. He would love me crawling to him with my tail between my legs.

"I'm sorry we couldn't make it work." Against my better judgment, I stood from the table and scooped up the papers, stacking them into a neat pile. "Thanks for meeting with me. I appreciate your time."

48

I headed to the door, sweat rolling down my spine faster with every step, hoping he was bluffing too and would call me back. Disappointment swelled when he didn't. I played with fire and got burned. How was I going to tell Aurora I blew the deal? That I let greed take over? I should have taken the forty percent, but it was too late to put the train in reverse. I'd look weak and foolish. "Good night, Penny. See you tomorrow."

She wiggled her fingers at me. "Good luck with Rockford. I met his wife, Charise, at a gala last year and we clicked right away. I'll call her and put in a good word for you."

I couldn't tell if she was lying or not, but her words put a smile on my face regardless. That was Penny... always positive even when everything went to shit. "Thanks. That would be great."

Brett stood with his hands on his hips. "Wait! What the hell is going on here?"

"I'm not sure what you're talking about," Penny answered innocently.

He swept his arm in her direction. "You would really call Charise? You're supposed to be on my team."

Penny pushed the blanket from her lap, the cats scampering down the hallway. She waddled over to Brett and poked her finger into his chest. "I've always been on your team—from the beginning. No questions asked. Tom brought this opportunity to you, and you passed. Why shouldn't I help him if I can?"

He furrowed his brows. "Because I hate Wayne Rockford."

"So what? Get over yourself. Just because you don't know a good thing when it's presented to you, doesn't mean Tom shouldn't take his offer elsewhere. Don't be greedy. If I can help him, I'm more than willing."

He ran his hands through his hair as he stared down at his wife. "I feel like I'm being tag-teamed."

"That's on you, not on me." She stood on her tiptoes and pressed a kiss to his cheek. "I'll always support you, but I'll also call you out when you're making a mistake."

Brett sagged. "Tom, come back. I think we can agree on something that'll make us both happy."

Penny patted him on the chest. "You're doing the right thing. You can thank me later." She grabbed her book from the couch and disappeared down the same hallway as the cats.

What just happened? I gained a whole new appreciation for Penny after watching that show. She was a genius. And a sneaky little manipulator, not that I was complaining.

"Listen, Brett, I don't want you to do anything you're uncomfortable with. If this deal isn't for you, then I'll walk out the door."

"My wife is right. She's always right. The last thing I want is Rockford getting his hands on your software. Let's sit."

I went back to the table and set the papers down. "What are you thinking? I'm open to negotiation, but I've put years into developing this security system, so I'm firm on the thirty."

"I'll take the thirty percent. However, I'm changing the investment structure: ten thousand up front, five hundred thousand after successful implementation at Mystique, and another five hundred after our first sale. If this software catches on like you say it will, that shouldn't be a problem."

Ten thousand would barely make a dent in digging me out of the hole I'd buried myself in, but what choice did I have? I'd already almost blown it once by being greedy. I couldn't walk away now. By my calculations, that would give me approximately a month to get the system up and running. If I paid my back rent and the minimum due on my credit card, it was doable. "I can agree to that," I said coolly, even as my heart raced. "However, if I need to buy any hardware for Mystique, it'll have to come out of the balance, not the initial ten thousand."

Brett tapped his chin and made a note on his paperwork. "I hadn't thought about that. That's completely reasonable. I'll open a separate line of credit for incidentals. Make sure you keep receipts for everything."

He made it sound like I would be purchasing cheeseburgers and toothbrushes, not thousands of dollars in technology upgrades. His demand to keep receipts was laughable and unnecessary. Not only would I have receipts, but a detailed spreadsheet of expenditures. Color coded. If nothing else, I knew how to keep records.

The thing that worried me about this deal was that everything hinged on the Dorseys. "What makes you so sure Mystique will consent to be the test subject?"

"Because it's that good. They'd be fools to pass up the opportunity. And if they do, I'll tell them we're going to offer it to Bellagio. That'll get their attention. I'm sure the Dorseys won't want this software to go to their biggest competitor first." Brett was all in now, despite his earlier hesitations.

"Trent's going to be pissed," I sighed, thinking about our recent conversation. "He's really counting on me to be his personal assistant when he moves to CEO. I'm not giving him any time to find a replacement."

"Trent's a big boy; he'll get over it. People quit all the time without notice, yet life carries on. If anything, he should be happy about what you're going to do for Mystique. He can find another personal assistant, but this opportunity will only come around once."

Well, when he put it like that... "You're right, but I don't like disappointing people."

Brett put his pen down and folded his hands. "Listen, you've been a dedicated PA to Trent for years. He's been lucky to have you, but you need to stop thinking like an employee. You're a business owner now, so start thinking like one. You do what's best for the business and leave your emotions out of it."

"I will," I said as I nodded. He made it seem so easy.

Making more notes on the original paperwork, he focused back on the plan. "This needs to happen fast. Penny could have our baby any day, and I want this deal in motion beforehand. How's tomorrow for a meeting with the Dorseys?"

I paled. He wasn't kidding when he said fast. "Tomorrow?"

"Yes, I'll have a contract detailing our agreement sent over for you to sign first thing in the morning. Have a lawyer review it if it makes you feel better, but be assured, I'm not trying to fuck you. Even if I wanted to, Penny would kill me, and I would never risk that." He made more rapid-fire notes. "I'll schedule the meeting for after lunch." Brett was in business-mogul mode as he kept talking about logistics.

And I was out of my league.

Yes, I had the product, but I also had zero practical business experience. I should have done more research. I dove right into the deep end without a plan, and I was drowning. There was no sense lying about it. "I'm overwhelmed. I don't know where to start as far as setting up the business end of this."

He lifted an eyebrow. "Lucky for you, you've partnered with the best. I'll have my people work with you. I've got the lawyers, the accountants, the marketing team. All you need to worry about is delivering on your promises. Welcome to the big leagues, kid." Brett stood and held out his hand for me to shake. "You've made the deal of a lifetime. Hold on because it's going to be a wild ride."

I shook his hand, both elated and nervous as hell. A wild ride indeed. "Thank you for believing in me. I'm glad we could come to an agreement."

"I'm looking forward to it." He let go of my hand and scratched his temple. "There's one thing bothering me."

"What's that?" The possibilities were endless, and I hoped whatever it was, I had an answer.

Brett narrowed his eyes and glared at me. "Were you really going to take this to Rockford?"

I barely kept the smirk off my face. "I did my research on you. I know Wayne Rockford is your nemesis. If it came down to it, I would have *tried* to get an appointment with him, but it was a long shot." Telling the truth was a gamble, but I hoped he would appreciate my strategy.

He shook his head and chuckled. "And my wife?"

"She didn't have a clue. That was just Penny being Penny. It wasn't planned."

With a slow clap, he said, "Well played, kid. You two got me good. Can't say I haven't bluffed a time or two in my life."

"Like taking the software to Bellagio?" I asked, referencing his plan for our meeting with the Dorseys.

"That's not a bluff, it's a promise."

Alrighty then.

I left Brett's penthouse with a skip in my step. I sealed the deal and had messages from Aurora.

Aurora: Sorry for the delayed response. I've been in a meeting and have big news. How about I tell you one fact now and the rest over drinks?

Aurora: When I was little, I wanted to be a ballerina. Turned out I was a terrible ballerina. At a recital, I got so into the spinning that I spun right off the stage and broke my arm. I never put on a tutu again.

Aurora: The Rabbit Hole. 8:30?

I laughed at the image she painted of a little girl with her hands raised high above her head, spinning out of control. She was probably an adorable kid. She was still adorable. And beautiful. And sexy. There was no denying I had it bad for her.

I messaged her back, confirming the place and time. I hadn't planned on a date with Aurora, but I should have. I should have made the first move.

Wait!

Was it a date or two friends meeting for drinks?

Well, shit!

Guess I'd find out when I got there.

Chapter 8
Aurora

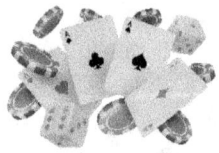

My leg bounced to the beat of the bass as I sat at a corner table drinking a Cosmo. Looking around, I couldn't decide if The Rabbit Hole was a good place for Tom and me to meet or not. I'd never been here, but it was highly recommended by a fellow volunteer. It was more of a club than a bar, full of twentysomethings, like us, drinking, laughing, and dancing. The air was electric with debauchery and pheromones. A sexual playground.

It might have been a bad choice... no, it was definitely a bad choice.

Tom was as tightly wound as his bow tie—but there was something kind of lovable about someone so committed to being himself. I should have picked a sports bar or a pub. Something more chill.

Second-guessing myself wasn't worth the effort because I spotted Tom by the bar, holding a beer and looking lost. I stood and waved my arms frantically to get his attention.

When he finally noticed me, he tugged his bow tie off and shoved it in his pocket, then headed my way.

Why did I find that little gesture so sensual? Hardly anyone wore bow ties anymore, but Tom always donned one for work. Religiously. It was quirky and unique, like him.

I stood and gave him a hug. "Hey, you made it."

"I wasn't going to miss out on hearing the rest of your fun facts. I bet you were a cute ballerina." He chuckled.

"Cute maybe, but I stunk at it." I groaned as I sank back into the chair.

"Well, you can't be good at everything," Tom said, taking a seat across from me. "I wanted to play football, but I was too scrawny."

That wasn't a word I would ever use to describe him. "You don't look scrawny to me."

"You didn't know me when I was fifteen. I had chicken legs, and it wasn't until college that I finally filled out." He took a sip of his beer. "There I go talking about me again. I'm gonna shut up now while you tell me your big news and dazzle me with your four remaining facts." He mimed locking his lips and throwing the key over his shoulder.

"I've been bursting to tell you this. Helping Hands is applying for a federal grant, and they asked me to design an information management system. Remember how I told you they didn't have a tracking system? I'm going to build one," I said.

"Wow! That's great. Is this a paid project?"

I shook my head. "It's pro bono. I don't care about the money, as long as it helps the shelter." *And helped me find Aidan.*

Tom nodded. "It would cost them big bucks to purchase one. Like I said before, you're a good person, Rora. If you need any help, let me know."

"I will." A bubble of guilt sat in my stomach. I might have been a good person if I hadn't had an ulterior motive. Instead, my actions were fueled by pure selfishness. "So, my facts…"

Tom drummed his fingers on the table. "Yes, I've been not so patiently waiting. Do tell."

I lifted my Cosmo and took a sip. You'd think it would be easy to come up with five things about yourself that were interesting, but it wasn't. My ideas were either boring or more information than I wanted to share. "I

55

grew up on the coast of California, spending my days on the beach. I tried surfing, but I was only marginally better at it than dancing. One time, the board came down on my head, resulting in a visit to the emergency room and ten stitches. Thankfully, my hair grows fast, so I only had to wear a hat for a few weeks before it wasn't so noticeable."

He chuckled. "I'm starting to see a pattern here. I'm guessing sports aren't really your thing?"

"I honestly think it's more of a balance issue than a lack of athletic aptitude. I'm really good at tennis. My backhand is to die for, thank you very much," I said, fanning myself proudly.

"Noted. Don't challenge Aurora to a game of tennis unless I want to embarrass myself by losing spectacularly." He pretended to write it on his hand. "What made you move to Las Vegas? If I lived on the beach, I'd never want to leave."

This question was bound to come up. Aidan disappeared almost a year ago. The last postcard I got from him came from Vegas, saying not to worry. How could I not? So, I left the West Coast and came here with one mission in mind: to find him.

The truth was too messy, so I went with a version of the truth. "I got offered a great job and it was hard to pass up."

His brows crinkled. "You work mostly remote. There must be a million programming jobs in California."

My story didn't make sense. People like me often worked from home, some from their parents' basement. There was no need to travel. I swallowed down the lump in my throat. "What can I say? They wanted me here, so I came." The lie tasted foul, especially knowing my answer would do little to quell Tom's curiosity. The story was fishy at best. "Anyway—" Suddenly, the lights flickered, dimmed, then went completely black. "What's going on?"

"You've never been here before?"

"First time."

"Then you're in for a treat. Sit back and enjoy the show." Tom moved his chair closer to mine as spotlights twirled around the room. "Ladies and gentlemen, I'd like to direct your attention to the main stage for the lovely Laney!"

A woman sat in a chair at the center of the stage wearing a tux with coattails and a top hat. Dread crawled up my arms, the hairs standing on end. "Did I ask you to meet me at a strip club?" Yes, I wanted to move things along with Tom, but this wasn't what I had in mind.

He wrapped his arm around my shoulders and squeezed. "Relax. It isn't a strip club. It's more of a striptease. All the naughty parts stay covered. I've been here before with the people from work. Laney is actually a friend of Charli's. She works at Oasis too."

"Thank goodness." It surprised me he'd been here before. Guess it wasn't such a bad choice after all. I breathed a sigh of relief and leaned back against his arm.

"Circus" by Britney Spears started and the woman snapped her head up, running her hand along the brim of the hat, her hair tucked underneath it. She seductively slid her legs apart and cracked a whip between them, commanding my attention, along with everyone else's in the room.

I was instantly drawn into her performance as she strutted to the front of the stage. Grabbing the lapels of her coat, Laney eased it down her shoulders, then pulled it back tight to her chest. After a few sexy denials, she slid the coat down her arms and flung it to the side. The room erupted in wolf whistles and catcalls as the dancer stepped on the chair and tipped it over while spinning the whip over her head.

Laney teased the crowd, cracking the whip in the air, then suggestively running it along her body before releasing her pants and letting them fall to her ankles. In a quick move, she stepped out of them and kicked the pants onto the lap of a guy sitting next to the stage. His friends cheered him on as he held them up like a trophy.

She gave him a wink, though her shirt was so long, the audience barely got a look at what was underneath. Laney strode toward the chair and picked it up, then did an elaborate routine of kicks and spins, extending her legs and arching her back in unnatural positions that showcased her perfect body. The dancer was a temptress in the art of seduction. It might have been the sexiest thing I'd ever seen.

Each wiggle of her hips, each kick, each piece of clothing she removed, made me more and more aroused. Had me clenching my thighs to stave off the dull ache between them. I put my hand on Tom's thigh and pressed closer, no space left between us as I melted into his warmth. His fingers traced lazy circles on my bare shoulder, and I wished he would move them lower. That in the semi-privacy of darkness, he would touch me. Kiss me. Anything.

My eyes closed and my body hummed as I imagined his hand sliding along the side of my breast, down my body, and between my legs. I could practically feel his fingers pressing into my wet center. Playing with me, rubbing against my clit.

"You like that, don't you, you dirty girl?" he whispered in my ear, his hot breath sending shivers down my spine.

"Yesss... so much."

His fingers slid inside me, and the world fell away. Nothing had ever felt so good. So forbidden. So erotic. He massaged me from the inside out, hitting that spot that made me go crazy, making me climb higher and higher. I clenched my thighs again, chasing the feeling.

A quiver racked my body as a release shook me, a quiet gasp falling from my lips. Endorphins flowed from my fingertips to my toes, a warm, dreamy sensation of floating on clouds. I snuggled into Tom's chest, inhaling his cologne... something comforting yet exhilarating I couldn't quite identify.

His fingers gripped my shoulder tightly and pulled me even closer, snapping me back to reality.

Oh my god! I came while fantasizing about Tom.

I opened my eyes to see Lacey strutting off the stage, her long hair swaying, in thigh-high black boots and a red-sequined bikini. I'd completely missed the end of her routine. Thank God it was dark, and he couldn't see the blush I was sure had crept into my cheeks. I blinked, praying for time to reverse itself. Instead, it stood still, punctuating the catastrophic collision between my dignity and humiliation.

As the lights came on, I pulled out of Tom's arms. "I need to use the ladies' room." Moving quickly through the maze of people, I didn't stop until safely locked inside a stall.

What the hell just happened?

Moisture beaded on my forehead, and my pits were wet along with my panties. I'd never spontaneously orgasmed before. Never. I didn't even know that was a thing.

Did I snuggle into his chest and sniff him? Was that reality or part of the fantasy my mind conjured?

I wanted to hide in the bathroom forever. How could I go back to the table and face Tom? I took deep breaths, trying to get my heart rate under control.

Inhale. Exhale.

Inhale. Exhale.

Inhale. Exhale.

Maybe he didn't notice. It was dark. The music was loud. His attention was on the stage, not me.

All I could do was hope I'd been quiet enough that he didn't hear me.

After cleaning myself up, I washed my hands with cold water and held them to my cheeks. They were still pink, but not as much as I had feared. Running my fingers through my hair, I tried to make myself look presentable and not like I'd orgasmed from a sexy fantasy. My eyes were glazed behind my glasses. I pressed my fingers into them, willing my pupils to shrink back to their normal size.

"You okay, honey?" another clubgoer asked.

"Yes, um… got overheated for a minute. I'm fine."

She shrugged and continued primping, painting her lips bright red.

After straightening my clothes, I left the bathroom and made my walk of shame back to the table. If I acted like everything was okay, maybe Tom would too.

Chapter 9
Tom

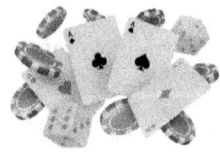

I was an asshole. When it came to Aurora, I kept fucking up.

She took off like her tail was on fire after the show, heels clicking and shiny hair swinging. When she'd shivered, I assumed she was cold. Pulling her closer to my chest was a mistake, an overreach, but she smelled so damn good, like coconuts and pineapple on a sunny day.

Dammit!

No matter how much I wanted our relationship to progress, I had to take it at her pace. Not make any more unsolicited advances. I thought meeting here was a date, but I'd read that wrong too.

And then there was my secondary problem.

Between Laney's show, Aurora's hand on my thigh, and the warmth of her against my chest... my pants were tented so much you could hide a small animal in there. I tried to think of the vilest things possible, but the sweet smell of Aurora had infiltrated my senses and all I could think about was holding her in my arms.

She'd been MIA for a while. *Did she ditch me?* I should have been focused on my meeting tomorrow, but instead I was sitting in a club, chasing a woman who saw me as nothing more than a friend.

When she finally returned, Aurora's cheeks were flushed and her shirt hung off one shoulder. For a brief moment, I wondered if she'd had a quickie in the bathroom. The club was full of guys who were more fit than I was, better looking, and had more to offer. I wasn't normally jealous or territorial, but with Aurora, the thought of some other guy with his hands all over her turned me into a green-eyed monster.

Then my rational brain kicked in and I dismissed the thought of her having crazy bathroom sex as irrational. It was possible, not probable. She wouldn't ask me here and then meet up with some other guy, but the mere possibility took care of the lingering problem in my pants. "Are you feeling okay?"

She put a hand on her stomach. "Yeah, I think that Cosmo hit me funny. I haven't had much to eat today." Aurora smiled, but it didn't quite meet her eyes. I could have been wrong, but I was sure she was lying. Her explanation was more likely an excuse to get away from me.

I stood and pulled out her chair. "Then let's get you fed. They have a great selection of shareable appetizers."

"Actually… would you be totally bummed if we called it a night?"

Yep, definitely trying to get away from me. This night hadn't turned out at all like I thought it would, but I tempered my disappointment. "Not at all. Are you okay to drive?"

She waved off my concern. "It's more my stomach than anything. My head is fine."

"Alright. I'll follow you home just in case." It was a quick ten-minute drive, but we were going to the same place anyway.

She lifted on her toes and pressed her lips to my cheek. "You're the best. Thank you for understanding."

I wanted to think the kiss meant something, but I'd been wrong too many times to count.

I didn't even get to tell her about my deal with Brett. It wasn't the right time or place, and she probably wouldn't care anyway.

The next morning, I swiped an overdue notice off my apartment door, hoping Aurora didn't see it. My financial problems weren't a secret, but it was demoralizing having them put on public display where anyone could see. Also, I might have downplayed the seriousness a bit. The crinkled note from my landlord sat at the bottom of my messenger bag as a reminder of what was on the line today.

As promised, an email from Brett came bright and early. Attached was the contract we'd agreed upon. I read it carefully and ran two copies, signing them both, before Trent showed up in the office. I prayed Brett brought a check with him to our meeting this afternoon, or I was fucked. The landlord wouldn't wait much longer before he taped a big red eviction notice on my door.

"Morning, Tom."

I flinched like a sixteen-year-old being caught with a hand down his girlfriend's pants. "Morning."

Trent narrowed his eyes. "You're jumpy."

"I've got a lot on my mind. As a matter of fact, there are some things I need to discuss with you." It was better to get this over with before our meeting. As much as Trent could be a pain in the ass at times, I liked him, and he'd been a decent boss.

He looked at his watch and frowned. "It'll have to wait. I have meetings all day. Could you pull up the notes on our last print campaign? The vendor is trying to fuck us, and I want to look at the fine print in the contract."

I pushed up my glasses. "Of course, I'll get right on it."

He gave me a rare smile. "Thanks, Tom. I don't know what I'd do without you."

My stomach sank. He didn't know it yet, but he was about to find out. I hated not giving him appropriate notice, but Brett's words rang in my ear... *leave your emotions out of it.*

I continued with my day, completing all the mundane tasks that made Trent's life easier, trying not to feel guilty. Shortly before one, Brett strolled up to my desk in a suit that cost more than a month of my paychecks and dropped an envelope. I pushed the two copies of the contract toward him, and he signed both, then folded one and put it in his suit pocket. "Are you ready?"

"As I'll ever be."

"He in there?" he asked, motioning toward Trent's door.

"Yeah, go on in. He's expecting you." Brett didn't need my permission to enter Trent's office. They'd been friends so long, they were essentially brothers.

Brett gave me a curt nod. "Get your shit together. I can practically smell your anxiety." Without knocking, he opened Trent's door and disappeared.

Making sure Brett's comment was figurative and not literal, I covertly sniffed my armpits. *Nope... fresh as a daisy.* I peeked inside the envelope, and there sat the biggest check I'd ever received. Ten grand. If nothing else, I could rest assured I wouldn't be evicted, but a whole other pile of bills loomed, and this wouldn't even come close to covering them.

Trent and Brett emerged from his office, laughing and patting each other on their backs. "Come on, Tom. I need you to take notes in this meeting. Brett's got something new he's trying to sell us."

I quickly grabbed my laptop and my presentation notes, along with the packets I'd made, and followed behind them to the conference room. Once inside, I sat next to Brett on one side of the table, while Trent, Hunter, and Edward, their father, sat on the other.

Trent narrowed his eyes and patted the spot next to him. "Tom?"

Brett put his hand on my arm. "Not today, Trent. Today, Tom is with me."

This wasn't exactly how I would have announced my partnership with Brett, but I let him lead the show.

"Excuse me?" Trent asked, rightfully confused.

Brett cocked his head to the side. "You'll see."

"What the fuck is going on?"

Hunter leaned back and crossed his fingers behind his head, "This oughta be good."

"Tom, would you like to explain?" Edward Dorsey said calmly, not fazed by his sons' outbursts.

I stood and cleared my throat. "Yes. I've recently partnered with Brett to develop a new security software."

"Don't be modest, Tom," Brett interjected. "He's the developer and mastermind. I'm merely the investor."

"What?" Trent looked between the two of us in confusion.

"About fucking time," Hunter said in an unexpected show of support. "You've been wasting your talents here."

"You're leaving Mystique?" Trent's face turned red.

"Relax, Trent. Let the man speak," Edward chastised his son.

"I'm not leaving Mystique yet, per se. I'd like to use this hotel and casino for the beta testing of my software."

Edward leaned forward and folded his hands on the table. "You have my attention. As you're well aware, we recently had a security breach."

"Fucking Leonard." Hunter shook his head in disgust.

Mr. Dorsey had no idea I was the one who traced the money and found the evidence that put Leonard Moroski behind bars. That information stayed in the triangle of trust. Now that Brett knew, Edward was the only one out of the loop.

"I'm aware," I said. "I began developing this software years ago and had it been in place, it would have saved Mystique millions. With this new software, such security concerns will be a thing of the past. May I?" I motioned to the screen on the wall.

Edward gave me a nod. "Please."

After going through the same presentation I did for Brett, with some minor modifications, I moved on to the efficiency and cost-saving aspects. "This blockchain system will give you top-tier, impenetrable security that will put you leaps and bounds ahead of other casinos on the Strip. It will also improve efficiency, reduce operational costs, and enhance the guest experience. We can integrate each customer's digital key with a loyalty program, allowing them to unlock personalized benefits based on their spending habits."

"That's all very impressive, but how much will it cost us?" Hunter asked. Being the CFO, it all came down to numbers for him.

"That's the beauty of the offer I'm… we're making," I said, glancing at Brett. "As a gift for allowing us to use Mystique for our first implementation, all of this will be completely free. That includes any maintenance or future subscription fees. All we ask in return is that you market the new upgrades for your hotel and help us create a buzz."

"Free?" Hunter raised an eyebrow. "How much would it cost to buy this new security software?"

"Based on the size of your casino and hotel, two million. That would include any hardware upgrades required. The annual subscription and maintenance cost is five hundred thousand. Those are our initial numbers, but depending on the success of the product, they may increase exponentially."

Trent tapped his fingers on the table. "Is this supposed to be a consolation prize for stealing Tom away from me? What's the catch?"

Brett leaned on the table. "First of all, I didn't steal Tom away from you. He came to me. Secondly, there's no catch. We're offering this to you because you've been my friend since we were kids. Your family is my family. Also, Tom is already familiar with your current system, so integration will be easy."

"And if we refuse?" Trent puffed up his chest.

"Then it will be your loss. Bellagio is next on our list. I'm sure they'll jump at the chance to get ahead of Mystique."

"Are you threatening us?" Trent stood, hands balled into fists.

Brett got to his feet and mirrored his stance. "I'm not threatening you. I'm telling you the way it is."

"You're supposed to be my best friend."

"I am, which is why I'm offering it to you first, but when it comes down to it, business is business."

Hunter winked at me. "Looks like the Bobbsey Twins are having a spat."

"Boys!" Edward interjected. "Take a seat. Tom has given us a lot to think about. This is a generous offer that we'll give deep consideration."

Both Trent and Brett reluctantly sat down, still staring daggers at each other. I never expected this offer to cause a rift. I was sure it was the Bellagio statement that threw Trent over the edge.

Gia, Trent's wife, stuck her red head into the conference room. "Sorry to interrupt, gentlemen, but Penny's in labor. Her water broke."

Brett grabbed his things from the table. "Holy shit!"

Trent jumped out of his chair. "I'll drive."

"I can drive my wife," Brett snapped.

Trent rolled his eyes. "The last thing we need is you getting in a car accident. I'll drive and you can sit in the back with Penny."

"Fine!" They both raced from the conference room in a flurry.

"Give Penny a hug for me!" I shouted to their backs. Without her, I wouldn't have this opportunity.

Hunter gave me a smug smile. "You've been keeping secrets. Does Charli know about this?"

"She knows I've been working on something, but I didn't want to give her the details until I made it a reality."

"Bravo." He clapped slowly and I couldn't tell if he was being an ass or was genuinely impressed.

"Trent is not on board," I stated the obvious.

"Don't worry about Trent," Edward said. "He's letting his emotions do the thinking. He feels blindsided."

"Yeah, he's more worried about losing his lapdog than the security of this hotel."

Wow! That stung. I didn't realize that's what they thought of me.

"Hunter!"

He looked at his dad. "What? It's totally true. Tom is the best PA Trent has ever had. He's butthurt that Tom is leaving to actually make a life for himself. Did he really think Boy Genius was going to stay here forever?" Hunter talked about me like I wasn't even there.

"Regardless, it's a decision we'll make together. Now, Tom, I have questions about how this would integrate with our current system."

"Absolutely." I gave them the packets I prepared, and we discussed the fine print, addressing all their concerns.

By the time the meeting ended, I'd won over two of the three Dorseys. Trent was a wildcard. If he bought in, I'd be able to put my financial worries behind me. If not, it was another less-certain pitch to Bellagio. More waiting. Time I couldn't afford to waste. Securing the next check was critical.

When I did, I'd be able to take Aurora out on a proper date and spoil her. I watched the way Brett and the Dorsey brothers treated their wives and wished I could do the same for the woman I cared about. However, I didn't even know where we stood after last night. She seemed more upset than unwell, and the deception didn't sit well with me.

I should have given up on the idea that we'd ever be more than friends, but I couldn't get the memory of her pressed against my chest out of my mind. There was something familiar about her perfume that tickled my brain and left me wanting more.

It was time to take two steps back. I had to face the truth: maybe the two of us weren't meant to be.

Chapter 10
Aurora

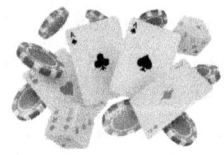

I'd successfully avoided Tom for the last three days, spending the weekend holed up in my apartment designing the information management system for Helping Hands. Throwing myself into the project kept my mind from rehashing my embarrassment.

It didn't take much to get me off, but spontaneously having an orgasm at The Rabbit Hole took it to a whole other level. Tom didn't say a word, but as much as I tried, I couldn't pretend that nothing happened. It was better to leave with the small shred of dignity I had left.

It was an utter disaster. When he walked me to my door that night, I could barely look him in the eye.

By Sunday evening, my refrigerator was empty, and I had no choice but to leave the safety of my apartment. Ailuros had gobbled down her last can of cat food while I'd stood over the sink munching on pretzel sticks and a single rice cake, so groceries were a must.

After a trip to the store, I hauled my bags to the elevator and stepped inside, hitting the button with my elbow.

"Hold the door!" Tom rushed into the lobby. I stuck my foot between the closing doors.

Sweat glistening on his chest, he hurried inside and tossed his shirt over his shoulder. "Thank you." He grabbed some of the bags from my arms. "Let me help."

"Uh… thanks." I'd never seen Tom without a shirt on before. He wasn't buff, yet his body was lean and his muscles well defined. I don't know what I was expecting, but I liked it. "I didn't know you were a runner."

"I don't do it as often as I should, but it's a good stress reliever. Helps me clear my head."

I tilted my chin and looked up at him, determined not to stare at his chest. "What are you stressed about?"

He ran a hand through his hair. "The better question would be, what am I not stressed about? It's hard to turn my brain off."

"Is it the security software?" He hadn't said whether Brett ever called him back, but I assumed he hadn't heard anything yet. Knowing Tom, he would have shown up on my doorstep with party hats and streamers.

"Among other things."

The elevator dinged and the doors slid open. He barely said a word as we walked down the hall toward our apartments. I set my groceries down, unlocked my door, and pushed it open.

Tom leaned in and set the bags on the floor, then backed away. "Have a good night, Rora."

His short answers and lack of conversation set off major red flags. I leaned on the wall next to my open door. "Are we okay?"

"Yeah. Why wouldn't we be?" He took the shirt from his shoulder and pulled it over his head, covering my fantastic view.

I shrugged. "I don't know. You seem a little distant. Are you mad at me?"

His eyebrows rose to his hairline. "That's the thing. I don't think I could ever be mad at you."

"Are you upset we left The Rabbit Hole early?"

Tom folded his arms across his chest. "Nope. I don't want you to do anything you don't want to do."

My hand instinctively went to my abdomen as if it could cover the lie I told. "I wanted to be there, it's just… I think I caught a stomach bug."

His eyes sharpened. "So you said."

I didn't know where the attitude was coming from, but this wasn't the same guy who brought over wine last week. This one was much colder and guarded. "Do you think I'm lying?"

"Honestly, I don't know. You appeared upset."

I was in too deep now to change my story. There was no way I'd admit I got aroused from a fantasy. "You didn't make me upset. I was having fun until my stupid stomach started acting up."

"Well, I hope you're feeling better. Take care." He turned his back on me and unlocked his door.

Desperate for him not to leave me standing in the hallway like a fool, I blurted out, "I'm sorry!"

He turned over his shoulder and stared at me, the tension in his shoulders dissipating.

"I'm sorry I flaked out on you. I did want to be there with you… that's why I suggested it. But then I got all hot and woozy, and my stomach flipped. I was embarrassed. That's why I wanted to leave." It was as much truth as I could bear without giving him all the sordid details. I wiped my damp palms on my jeans. "I'd like to make it up to you. Maybe we can go out later this week. There's a little Irish pub down the block. It'll be quieter and we can actually talk. I want to tell you about the progress I'm making on the project for Helping Hands and maybe get some input. Also, I want to hear about what's going on with you and Brett."

He leaned against the wall, his lips tipping up on one side, and rubbed the stubble on his chin. "Only if you *want* to. I mean… You do still owe me two facts. I feel like I got cheated the other night."

I nodded like a bobblehead, glad he didn't shut me down. "I want to."

"Then it's a date?" he asked, raising a brow.

"It's a date," I assured him. "How about Wednesday? We can meet right here at seven"—I pointed to the grungy carpet—"and walk over together."

"Alright. I'll put it on my calendar. Good night, Aurora." He opened his apartment door and went inside before I could respond.

I sagged and stared at the ceiling. I'd never asked a guy out on a date before. I never had to. This was a first and I gained an appreciation for the courage it took to risk rejection.

He didn't know about my orgasm, but he thought I was a liar, which was worse... and somewhat true. I was keeping things from him; not necessarily lies, but definitely omissions of the truth. Things that didn't matter now but might in the future. It was a sticky, yet necessary, web I was spinning.

Hopefully, when all was revealed, he wouldn't hate me.

Chapter 11
Tom

I officially put in my resignation last Friday, yet here I was at Mystique on Monday morning, ready to smooth things over with Trent. He'd locked himself inside his office before I arrived and hadn't peeked his head out or said good morning, a sure sign he was still pissed. I went to the break room and made a coffee to his exact specifications as a peace offering, then knocked on his door.

A gruff, "Come in," followed.

I cracked the door and stuck my head inside. "Can we talk?"

"Now you want to talk?" he grumped as he stared out the window that overlooked the casino.

"Yes." I pushed the door open and stepped inside, placing the steamy cup of java on his desk. "We need to."

"Seems like we needed to talk weeks ago. You should have come to me with this. It was highly unprofessional for you to drop a bomb like you did on Friday." He crossed his arms and scowled.

"Fair enough. I apologize for not giving you notice, but if you allow me to explain, I think you'll understand why I didn't."

"I can barely wait," he said dryly.

I stood next to him at the window, admiring the view Hunter was going to love when he moved into this office. "I've been working on this software for years, not weeks or months. It's always been a vision of mine to have something of my own. This job was nothing but a placeholder for me. I enjoyed working for you, but my tech skills far surpass what is required of me here. Surely, you know that."

Trent nodded. "I do. You proved it when you helped with the Leonard situation."

"What you don't know is that creating the security system wasn't cheap. I'm in debt up to my eyeballs. I approached Brett to invest in my idea, hoping he would help. Hoping. Never did I think that it would happen this fast. We signed the deal Thursday night, and he set up the meeting with you for Friday. Honestly, my finances can't afford to give you two weeks. I'm barely scraping by."

"I pay you a decent wage," he said defensively.

"I'm not saying you don't, but it's not enough. I'm treading water to keep afloat."

"You could have come to me. I would have given you a raise."

"Frankly, Trent, I didn't want to ask you for a raise. If you thought I deserved one, you would have given it without me asking."

His brows furrowed. "Well, you must be doing well now that you can afford to leave Mystique."

"I've gotten one check from Brett. It's enough to squeak by. I won't get the next installment until after the first successful implementation, whether it's here or somewhere else."

Trent let out a rough chuckle. "So Brett's running the show. It sounds like a shit deal."

"I agreed to the terms. Without him, I have nothing because, although I have the skills, I don't know jack about business. He's providing resources I couldn't obtain on my own. He's the best in the business, and you know it." Brett was throwing me headfirst into the world of entrepreneurship. I had meetings scheduled every day this week with his attorneys, marketing department, creative director, PR coordinator, and accountant. My head was already spinning.

"It still doesn't explain why you never said anything," he insisted.

"And tell you what? That I was working on security software? That I had no idea if it would ever become something? That I didn't know if I'd find an investor? That it could happen today or five years from now? Up until last week, there was nothing to tell. Be honest with yourself, it wouldn't have mattered if I gave you a day's notice or a month's; you still would have been pissed."

He stuck his hands in his pockets. "That's probably true, but with Penny gone, and now you, things are going to be rocky."

"I'll be around to answer questions and help if you need it. I just won't be fetching your coffee or answering your phone any longer."

Trent's lips twisted to the side. "Gia will make sure I hire another man. That cuts my options down significantly."

"True, but it's probably a wise choice. Happy wife, happy life and all that."

This time, he laughed for real. "I'm going to miss you. If I haven't told you, you're the best assistant I've ever had."

"Awww... I like you too. And you won't miss me too much because my sister is married to your brother. You couldn't get rid of me if you tried."

"Unless we get rid of Hunter. That would solve both our problems." He waggled his eyebrows.

"It would break Charli's heart, so that's not an option. He's growing on me. Kind of like a fungus, but yeah, it's happening." It was true. I never knew what would come out of his mouth, but it was always brutally honest, and I appreciated that. Whether Hunter was more excited about me starting my own business or leaving Trent high and dry, I wasn't sure. Either way, his vote of approval meant more to me than I anticipated.

Trent harrumphed his displeasure.

"Listen, I know you haven't made your final decision about the security software, but don't let your irritation with me be a factor. This is cutting-edge technology and we're offering it to you for free. I'll be here through the installation and implementation, and I won't leave until everything is running perfectly. It's a great deal for Mystique."

"I'll keep that in mind. We should have an answer before week's end."

I gave him a nod. "I'm going to finish cleaning out my desk and organizing files for you. I'm leaving at lunch, but if you need me, I'm only a phone call away."

"Thanks, Tom. By the way, how's it going with the girl from the wedding?"

Now that was the question, wasn't it? "I'm not sure, hopefully I'll have an answer to that by the end of the week."

He laughed. "Touché."

My relationship with Aurora was as up in the air as my security deal with Mystique. I thrived on control and order, but lately it felt like my life was a deck of cards that'd been thrown in the air and scattered by the wind. Every time I managed to grab one, two more blew away.

It was chaotic and messy. And I hated it.

The card that eluded me most was the queen of hearts. Aurora *was* apologetic last night. When she looked at me with those eyes, I couldn't hold my grudge about her wanting to leave the club early. Maybe she had been ill, but I still wondered if she was keeping something from me.

My own insecurities about women kept my head running in circles.

Girls like her didn't fall for guys like me.

Regardless, we had another date planned and hopefully this time I wouldn't end up being the joker.

Chapter 12
Aurora

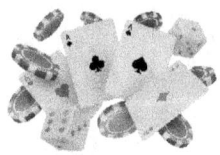

My phone rang, and I looked at the screen. I loved my mama, but dreaded her calls. It would be of no use to ignore it. If I didn't answer, she'd call again.

Resigned to a conversation that would probably make me want to throw my phone across the room, I answered, "Hi, Mama."

"Hello, my beautiful girl. I haven't talked to you in a while." It was so like her to butter me up, then come in with the sly accusations. What she really wanted to say was, *Why haven't you called?*

"I know. I've been really busy."

"Too busy to call your mom?"

Glad she couldn't see me, I rolled my eyes. "Don't be that way."

"Aurora, you know when I don't hear from you, I worry. I don't like you so far away, in Sin City no less, with no family. It's dangerous."

I sighed. "It's a really safe neighborhood and I've made friends. You don't need to worry."

She laughed. "I'm your mother. I'm going to worry. You'll understand when you have children of your own. I don't like my baby bird away from the nest."

It was always the same response from her. Never mind the fact that I was a grown-ass woman. At twenty-six, it would be worrisome if I were still in the nest. "I'll try to be better about checking in."

"That's all I ask. So... any luck?" I could practically see her sitting out on the back deck, tapping her fingers on the table, hair and makeup picture perfect. My father expected it.

"Not yet. I've been doing a lot of volunteering at the shelter, but I'm going to need to step it up. I guess I thought I'd walk in and there he'd be." In hindsight, that was foolish. There were a dozen shelters, but I thought I'd get lucky with this one.

"You and Aidan have been two peas in a pod ever since you were little. He's been knocking on our front door since he was five. Nothing shocked me more than when he left and joined the military."

It was true.

We'd been best friends since kindergarten. Aidan and I were inseparable. The older we got, the more our fathers liked the idea of us together. Not for us, but for them. To combine the forces of two powerful families. To further their own careers.

We tried the romance thing, but there was no spark. When we said as much, our fathers said a good marriage wasn't based on love; it was based on mutual respect and understanding. The understanding being that we'd both be cut off financially and removed from their trusts if we didn't agree.

Aidan's solution was joining the military to buy us time. "He had his reasons."

"That boy came home with demons, and I'm not sure if he's chasing them or they're chasing him," my mother said, sadness lacing her words. Aidan had always been like a son to her.

When he left for the Middle East, I wrote to him every week. I never knew exactly where he was, but the letters made it to him. At first, he responded diligently, telling me about the other guys in his unit and the pranks they pulled on each other. As time went on, there was a shift. His letters became less frequent. Darker. Haunted. Eventually, they stopped coming altogether.

The day he came home after being honorably discharged still plagued me. A warning I should have listened to.

I waited on the porch, watching the neighborhood kids play baseball. A ragtag setup with overturned buckets for bases took up the width of the street. The kids ran to move the buckets, waving the driver through when a black truck approached. I'd have known that pickup anywhere, it was Aidan's pride and joy, bought when he was seventeen with the money he saved from cutting lawns. We had a ton of memories in that truck, aimless drives up the coast and bonfire nights sitting on the tailgate.

My spirit thrashed when I saw him behind the wheel. This had been the longest we'd gone without seeing each other. Way too long.

Eager to see him, I ran down the driveway as he pulled up and threw myself into his arms, practically knocking him over before he was fully out of the truck. "I missed you so much."

Aidan squeezed me to his chest. "You're a sight for sore eyes."

"So are you." I held his face and looked up at him. He seemed to have aged ten years since I last saw him. There was a sternness in his expression and a blankness in his eyes I didn't recognize.

Kicking the door shut, he spun me around in circles. "Goddamn, I missed you." He brushed his lips against my temple, as he always did.

I pressed my hands against his chest, forcing some distance between us. "They're already talking about a wedding."

"Fuck. I've barely been home an hour." He leaned his forehead against mine. "Don't worry, we'll figure this out. I won't let them do this to us."

The truck shook as a sharp metallic clang echoed around us like a gunshot.

I screamed as Aidan threw me to the ground and wedged me against the front tire. "Get down!" He pulled a knife from the sheath attached to his belt and dropped to one knee, pointing it out at the street as he shielded me with his body, breath ragged and eyes scanning.

I peeked around him and saw... nothing. No threat. No danger.

Just a baseball on the driveway and the kids who were all staring at us, eyes wide. One took a cautious step forward, a mitt on his hand. "Sorry about your truck, mister."

"Aidan." I put my hand on his trembling arm. "It was a ball. That's all."

He lowered the knife and dropped his head to his chest. "I'm sorry. I thought..."

I picked up the ball and threw it back, then kneeled in front of Aidan. "It's okay. You're home. You're safe. I'm safe. Everything is fine."

But everything wasn't fine. I should have known then, things would never be the same. The months that followed were torture. No one knew how to help the man who came home, mostly because, in a lot of ways, he never did. There were so many things I should have done, yet I turned my back on him like everyone else. Not a day went by that the guilt didn't eat at me. It was my fault he joined the military in the first place. "I'm going to find him."

"I know you will, honey. Be prepared for the fact that he might not want your help. We tried."

Emotion clogged my throat, and a tear ran down my cheek. "We didn't try hard enough."

"Aurora..."

"No, Mom. He deserved more. He deserved for me not to give up on him."

She sighed. "You can't shoulder that blame, Aurora. He gave up on you long before you gave up on him."

There was some truth to that, but it didn't mean I would quit trying to find him. "I know."

"One more thing... I hate to ask, but you know your father. He's concerned. Are you being discreet?"

Concerned about his reputation. It pissed me off. Some things were more important than keeping the pristine family image my father liked to brag about. He wouldn't want anyone to know his daughter was *slumming it* at a homeless shelter. "Tell him I'm keeping a low profile. No one here has a clue who I am."

No one. Not even Tom. And that wasn't the biggest secret I was keeping from him. One more thing to feel guilty about.

Ready for our date, I stepped into the hallway at 6:59 p.m. to find Tom already waiting for me. In retaliation for his shirtless appearance the other day, I chose a low-cut sleeveless blouse that showed plenty of cleavage. His eyes went right to the girls, but quickly snapped to my face.

"You look pretty," he said, sporting a mile-wide smile.

I blushed as I not so slyly appraised him from head to toe. He wore dark blue jeans that fit him perfectly in all the right places, paired with a black button-down shirt with the collar undone and sleeves rolled up, showing the slightly raised veins on his forearms. I resisted the urge to run my fingers over the raised trails on his arms, knowing I wouldn't want to stop at his elbow. I'd never seen him dressed in that type of casual attire. Usually, it was dress pants with a sweater vest and bow tie or shorts and a T-shirt. This cool and confident man was a total turn-on. Now that I knew what was hiding under that shirt, I wanted to peel it off him. "You're looking spiffy too. Shall we go?"

"We shall."

I took the lead as we went down the hallway to the elevator and pushed the call button. The doors opened and we stepped inside the crowded car. The teenagers next to us were talking smack about who had the best jump shot. One pushed the other and he careened into my shoulder, knocking me off balance. Tom gave them a death glare and pulled me in front of him, my back to his chest and his hands on my hips. "You smell like summer," he whispered in my ear.

His warm breath on my neck ran shivers down my spine. Taking a chance, I leaned into him. I didn't want there to be any misunderstandings about my intentions tonight. He wrapped his arms around my waist, and I sagged into him.

The smell of his cologne enveloped me. Being in his arms felt like home. Like a place where I could live happily. Safe and comforting. A perfect little bubble.

The elevator jolted to a stop, but when the door opened, I couldn't make my feet move. Impatient neighbors pushed past us in their rush to exit, but I was in no hurry. I tilted my head back and stared at his handsome face. "Hey, you."

He smiled at me. "Hey yourself." The door was almost closed, and I thought he might kiss me, but then a man's sneaker appeared between the sliding panels. The doors opened and a big, burly guy stepped around us, frowning. "We should get off."

"Yeah." My voice came out breathy, a wisp on the wind.

When I still didn't move, he put his hands on my hips and gave me a gentle nudge forward. Tom chuckled and led us out of the building into the balmy evening air. The sky was splashed in pinks and purples as the sun started its gradual descent, making it a romantic evening for a walk.

Tom took my hand in his and wove our fingers together. "Is this okay?" he asked, holding up our joined hands.

"Yes, it's more than okay."

"Whew!" He pretended to wipe sweat from his forehead. "I wasn't sure. I've had a hard time reading you and don't want to mess things up between us."

I scrunched my eyebrows together. I thought I'd been clear, sending out signals like torpedoes. "What do you mean?"

He hesitated. "Like the other night. I thought it was a date, but then you wanted to leave early, so maybe I got that wrong."

That damn orgasm wouldn't stop haunting me. "Officially, it wasn't a date. I didn't think you wanted it to be."

Tom stopped dead in his tracks. "What? Why?"

I pulled him to the side so we wouldn't get run over by the other pedestrians. "Okay… I'm going to tell you something and I don't want you to freak out."

"Oh no! What? Did I have food stuck in my teeth?" He rubbed his finger viciously across his front teeth.

I pulled his hand down. "No. Nothing like that. It's... well... at the wedding..."

"Oh lord. Something weird *did* happen." He palmed his forehead. "I knew it. Dammit! What did I do?"

"Nothing bad," I assured him. "But you had a bit too much to drink and you... well... you kissed me."

"I kissed you? On the lips?"

I held up a finger. "Actually, it was more like a nuzzle. Right here." I pointed to my neck. "And you said some stuff. When you didn't remember and nothing else happened, I passed it off as drunken babble."

Tom blew out a breath as he ran a hand down his face. "Oh! My! God! I'm so embarrassed. What did I say?"

"I don't really remember," I lied.

"Aurora, tell me."

"Something about my eyes being so blue they were like puddles you could splash around in." I left out the part where he proclaimed his love for me. A man could only take so much humiliation.

He groaned. "That's one of the worst pickup lines I've ever heard. My sister is right; I've got no game."

I laughed and patted him on the chest. "It's okay, I've heard worse. So let's get this right, you are interested in me?"

"Since the first time I saw you."

"Then why didn't you want to dance with me at the wedding?"

Tom threw his hands in the air. "I did, but I didn't think you saw me as anything more than your nerdy neighbor. You looked so pretty, and I didn't want to freak you out by rubbing"—he pointed to his crotch—"against you."

I covered my mouth and giggled. "Hate to tell you this, but... hard-ons happen."

"Yeah, I know," he said with a roll of his eyes. "It's a perpetual problem around you."

Taking hold of his hand again, I held it up between us. "I'm glad we cleared this up. I've been going crazy thinking what happened at the wedding was fueled by alcohol and not genuine interest."

"Fucking Hunter and his expensive bourbon. This is his fault."

"He wasn't the one pouring shots down your throat. That was all you."

"Please! I'm going to blame Hunter for whatever I can. Don't take that joy away from me." He laughed, his eyes crinkling in the most adorable way. "To be clear, *you* are interested in *me*, right?"

"Yes, Tom. I like you."

He held up my hand and kissed the back of it. "Good, because I like you too." He looked down the street toward the pub and then back at me. "I need that drink now. This was both enlightening and stressful."

"No bourbon for you," I teased.

"No bourbon," he agreed. "Also, no more secrets."

Yeah, too late for that.

Chapter 13
Tom

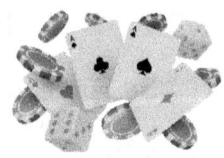

Once the sun set, the blistering heat of the day subsided. To protect Aurora from the slight chill in the air, I threw my arm over her shoulders on our walk back to the apartment. She snuggled into my side and a feeling of contentment settled in my chest.

This girl.

She had me laughing all night, recounting my stupid jokes from the wedding. It was embarrassing, but the most concerning part was the hole in my memory. That little niggling paranoia that'd been at the back of my brain for the past couple weeks was real. I knew I was missing something, but never imagined it was practically mauling Aurora and her putting me to bed.

If I could go back in time, I'd kick my own ass.

It explained why I continually thought she was keeping something from me. I didn't blame her for not telling me about my behavior at the wedding, but deception was not a good foundation to build a relationship on.

Little white lies had a way of steamrolling into bigger deceptions, and it was difficult to make informed decisions when you didn't have all the facts. My last serious girlfriend claimed she graduated from MIT, but the diploma I found in her nightstand drawer was from an online college in Pittsburgh. It wasn't that I looked down on her education, but if she lied about that, what other untruths was she telling me? Turned out there were many. She was a chronic liar, fabricating an entire life for herself that didn't exist.

Granted, Aurora had kept the information to protect me from embarrassment, which was warranted. But had I known, I would have been over it and she wouldn't have had to wonder if my feelings were real. Now that we'd cleared the air, I hoped things would move along a bit smoother.

When we got to our apartments, I took a tentative step forward and backed her against the wall, testing the waters of our new relationship. Instead of objecting, she looked up at me with those big blue eyes, a hint of excitement swirling in them. "I had fun tonight. Thank you for giving me a second chance and not holding my boorish behavior against me," I said, twisting a curl of her hair around my finger.

"I had fun too. And honestly... drunk Tom is funny and cute."

"I'm glad you think so. Are you open to another date?" I asked, dragging my finger down her cheek to her jaw.

She bit her lip and pulled it between her teeth, managing to look both innocent and sexy. "I would love that."

My heart pounded with excitement. "Me too." I took a chance and removed her glasses, something I'd been dying to do since we first met. Her eyes reminded me of the ocean, and I could easily get lost in them. "I must have kept some of my senses at the wedding because your eyes *are* like itty-bitty puddles. So beautiful. Have you ever worn contacts?"

She gulped. "I used to. What about you?"

"They make my eyes dry. So unfortunately, I'm stuck with the glasses. I wish I could ditch them."

"I don't. I think they look good on you. They make you look mysterious."

I laughed. "I'm probably the least mysterious person you know. What you see is what you get."

"I like what I see."

"Is it okay if I kiss you?" It seemed like I'd been waiting forever, and I couldn't wait any longer.

She nodded slowly as I took her face between my hands and lowered my lips to hers. When they met, it was like the first spark in a storm—sudden, breathless, charged with electricity that made the air around us hum. A live wire buzzing beneath our skin, zapping through nerve endings and lighting up everything in its path.

Her fingers curled into my shirt as though trying to ground herself, but there was no grounding this. I brushed my thumb against her cheek with agonizing slowness and swept my tongue along the seam of her lips. She opened for me, welcomed me in, and when the kiss deepened, it was like lightning struck twice.

A subtle tremble passed between us—a silent gasp and a needy moan—and the kiss pulsed with the raw, electric tension that'd been building for weeks. Every movement, every graze of teeth and tangle of tongues, was a spark leaping between us.

Time stopped, the world blurred, and for that moment, we were pure energy. Breathless and burning in the same current.

I pulled away and pressed a final kiss to the tip of her nose. "Thank you for tonight."

She stared up at me with those big, beautiful eyes. "Do you want to come in?"

"Not tonight. This has already been more than I hoped for. I don't want to rush into anything with you. You're the kind of woman that deserves to be savored, not snacked on."

Her cheeks turned pink. "That's the most romantic thing anyone has ever said to me."

"Then you've been dating the wrong guys." I held out my palm. "Give me your key." She dug around in her purse and handed it to me. I unlocked her door and pushed it open. "Good night, Rora."

"Good night, Tom," she said, looking up at me from under her eyelashes. "See you tomorrow."

I leaned in and pressed one last gentle kiss to her lips. "Tomorrow."

She backed away and closed the door, keeping an eye on me until the final click. I turned and punched the air. "Fuck yeah!" Finally. Finally, we'd made some progress. And god, her lips were so soft and her kisses so sweet. I was on cloud nine when I entered my apartment.

For about two seconds.

"What the fuck!" I nearly jumped out of my skin. Charli sat on my couch while Hunter stood in the kitchen munching on barbecue chips. My special chips I bought as a treat. "What the hell are you doing here?"

"I have a key, remember?" she said, holding it up.

I swiped it from her. "Not anymore. You were supposed to return it when you moved out."

"Technicalities." She stood and stomped toward me with her hands on her hips. "You've been keeping secrets. Was that Aurora you were making out with?"

"She was watching through the peephole. Apparently, my wife's a voyeur. Kinky," Hunter said with a waggle of his eyebrows, shoving more chips in his mouth. "Wish I would have known that sooner."

"Oh my god! You have a… a…" she said, gesturing toward my crotch.

"A boner. It's called a boner, Charli. You should know that," Hunter said dryly. "Good job, man." He held out his fist for me to bump.

I ignored his fist and grabbed the bag from his hand. "Stop eating my chips!"

"Rude." He wiped his orange fingers all over my clean dish towel.

"What's rude is coming home and finding the two of you hanging out in my apartment. And spying on me!"

"That's all her," Hunter said, pointing at my sister. "I didn't do any spying."

Charli rolled her eyes. "I'd hardly call it spying. You were standing in a public hallway."

I blew out a breath of frustration and stared at the ceiling, praying for patience. "What are you doing here, Charli?"

"You are keeping secrets from me. I. Don't. Like. It!" She poked me in the chest, punctuating every word. "Hunter told me about your security software. I can't believe you didn't tell me. I'm your sister, you're supposed to tell me these things."

I glared at Hunter, and he shrugged. "She's my wife. What did you expect?"

That's what this was all about? "I didn't tell you because there was nothing yet to tell."

"Obviously there's something to tell because he knows about it," she said, waving her arm toward her husband.

"Okay, fine. Sit down." Charli perched on the edge of the couch, and I sat on the coffee table across from her.

"Tell me everything," she said.

"Can I have my chips back?"

"No," I said, as Charli said, "Yes." She grabbed the bag from my hand and passed it to Hunter.

"She likes me better," he said with a smug smirk, diving back into the bag.

I was over it. He could have the damn chips. "Like I told you at your wedding, I had finished my secret project and was taking it to Brett as a possible investor. That secret project is a cutting-edge security software built with blockchain technology."

"I don't know what blockchain technology is."

"Ooh, I do!" Hunter raised his hand.

I ignored him. "That doesn't matter. What matters is Brett agreed. He's funding the project, but in three installments. I got a small up-front payment. The next installment of money hinges on Mystique's agreement to implement the software as a beta test. We haven't gotten confirmation yet. If they don't agree, we have to pitch it somewhere else. After successful implementation, I get the second payment. So honestly, until that happens, I'm still broke and there's nothing to tell."

"Oh," Charli said, biting on the nail of her thumb. "But it's still something, right?"

"It is something, but it's more potential income than actual income. I quit my job at Mystique, so the small payment will have to last."

She cocked her head to the side. "Do you need to borrow money? Because we can lend it to you."

And this was why I didn't want to tell her. The last thing I needed was my little sister worrying and her husband coming to my rescue. He'd never let me forget it. "I'll be fine. It's been tough, but I've been scraping by."

"Explains these crappy chips," Hunter said, holding one up. "I like a little more crisp in my chip."

"Yet you've eaten the whole bag."

He gave the bag a shake and peered into it. "Not the whole bag, but close. I'll buy you another one."

"I don't need you to buy me snacks."

"Don't be testy. I'm trying to help." He tipped the bag up, poured what was left into his mouth, and wiped his hands *again* on my once-clean dish towel. "I'm not supposed to tell you this, but"—he traced a triangle in the air—"we decided today to accept your offer. A formal notification is going out tomorrow."

My eyes grew into saucers. "Are you serious?"

"As serious as I am about exploring your sister's voyeur tendencies."

I gagged as bile rose in my throat. "Why can't you say shit like a normal person?"

"That would be boring." He scrunched up the chip bag and tossed it in the trash. "By the way, you're welcome. Try to act surprised tomorrow."

"I will. Thank you." This tidbit of news made his presence in my personal space more tolerable.

"You can thank me by buying some decent booze. All you've got is a half-empty bottle of cheap rum."

But still annoying.

Charli clapped her hands excitedly. "This is good news!" She leaned forward and wrapped me in a bear hug. "I'm so proud of you. I always knew you were destined for greatness."

Hunter frowned. "You should let Boy Genius prove this software is what he says it is before you start planning a parade."

"I believe in him. You should too, especially after he helped you with Leonard," Charli scolded.

Ah, the triangle of trust was even bigger. Not a square, but a pentagon. I should have known he would tell her.

"If I didn't, I wouldn't have been the one pushing for this," he said to Charli. Then to me, "Again, you're welcome."

It surprised me, but then again, it didn't. He'd been supportive in the meeting. I stood and held my hand out to him. "Thanks, man. I won't let you down."

He took hold of my hand and gave it a firm shake. "I know you won't. Next time we rendezvous, let's do it at our place. We have better snacks and better booze. Bring sweet cheeks from across the hall."

The words *hard pass* were on the tip of my tongue, but considering what he'd done for me, I bit them back. "We'll see." Nothing would make Charli happier than her husband and me getting along, but we weren't buying matching T-shirts anytime soon.

She gave me one last hug. "I'm so happy for you. Sleep well tonight."

"Oh, he will," Hunter said. "Considering that scorching kiss and the condition of his pants when he came in, I'm betting there's going to be a hand party in the shower after we leave."

I glared at him as my sister smacked him in the chest. "Stop it!"

A definite no *to the T-shirts.*

"What? I only peeked once, but it was the stuff porn is made of. Good job." He gave me two thumbs up.

I'd officially reached my limit and pushed them both out the door, then leaned back against it. Hunter aside, today was a good day.

I secured the deal with Mystique and made huge progress with Aurora. It took everything I had to walk away from her tonight. It was the right call, but my lips still tingled, along with other parts of my body.

As much as I hated to admit it, my brother-in-law was right about one thing; that kiss was scorching hot and there was definitely going to be a hand party.

Chapter 14
Aurora

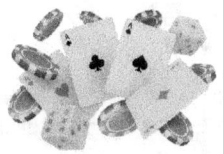

I couldn't stop thinking about kissing Tom last night. I'd been kissed hundreds of times, but none of them compared to his. A volt of energy had zipped from my lips straight down to my toes, electrifying every inch of me in between. My lady parts were singing a song. When he refused to come in, I heeded their call with my magic wand and quickly moaned out a filthy chorus. He may have wanted to *savor* me, but a little snack would have been nice too.

It was probably better to take things slow… well, slowish. If that toe-curling kiss was any indication, I had a feeling when we finally tangled in the sheets, we'd burn the place down.

I pushed the thought from my head, determined to stop daydreaming about Tom. It seemed inappropriate to walk into Helping Hands with sex on the brain when so many people depended on this place for basic needs. I'd rearranged my morning schedule to meet with Kendra. We needed to discuss the management information system, and I wanted to show her what I'd completed so far.

The shelter was practically empty. There were fewer volunteers at this time of day. I was used to the hustle and bustle, but only a couple people were in the main dining room, wiping tables and sweeping the floor. Breakfast was the least busy meal and consisted of things like cereal, protein bars, and fruit.

There was no need for Carl to be here this early, so I was surprised to see him. "What are you doing here?"

He gave me a big, toothy smile. "I could ask the same of you."

"Oh, I'm here to talk to Kendra." I looked at all the boxes piled in the hallway. "What are those for?"

"Today is community outreach. We're going into an encampment with supplies. Some people are leery of the shelter, so we go to them."

I bit my bottom lip as I thought about that. It would be another opportunity to find Aidan. "I want to go."

Carl gave me a stern look that reminded me of my father. "Nuh-uh. No way I'm taking you out on the street."

"Why not? I can help."

He gave me a once-over. "Have you looked at yourself? You're way too sweet to be out there. This isn't the same as serving food on the line."

I stomped my foot like a petulant child. "I want to help. Are you telling me you can't use an extra pair of hands?"

Another volunteer, Marcus, came up to Carl. "We have two no-shows. Gonna be a little short today. It's just us."

"See? You can use my help."

Kendra came around the corner, carrying her ever-present clipboard, and stopped short when she saw our standoff. "What's going on?"

Carl waved his hand at me. "Aurora here wants to go on the outreach run. I'm not sure she's ready for that."

I turned my pleading eyes on her. "I know we were supposed to meet, but I'd really like to go. I want to help."

Kendra pressed her lips together in a thin line as she considered my request. "I don't see any reason you can't, but stick close to Carl and do what he says. We can meet later to discuss the information management system."

I gave her a quick hug. "Thank you."

"Be safe," she said, patting me on the back before rushing off again.

Carl, still not convinced, crossed his bulky arms over his wide chest. "Fine. No wandering and only bring what you can fit in your pockets. People are desperate. And though they don't mean no harm, some tend to take things that aren't freely offered. Best to eliminate any temptation."

"Okay." It felt extreme, but I followed his directions, shoving everything into my pockets. "What do you need me to do?"

"Start taking these boxes to the van out back. Marcus is already loading up."

"Thank you, Carl. I promise you won't regret this."

He let out a huff. "I'm already regretting it."

Once everything was loaded, I hopped into the passenger seat of the van next to Carl. He continued his lecture as we drove the short distance across town. "The first time out here can mess with your head. Stay alert. Stay respectful. Don't make promises we can't keep. And most importantly, don't stare. You're gonna want to, guarantee it, but don't. They get judged enough. Don't need more of it from us."

Jeez, Carl acted like we were entering a war zone instead of doing a charity run. I'd been volunteering at the shelter for months, I knew what to expect.

Or at least I thought I did.

When the tires crunched over gravel and pulled into the shadow beneath a bridge, my heart fell into my stomach. I wasn't prepared. Not in the least.

God, my father would have a fit if he knew I was here.

Carl put his hand on my arm. "Take a minute to collect yourself. It's a lot to take in."

I nodded and rolled down the window. The smell hit me first—a cocktail of urine, mildew, and sweat. I put a hand to my nose to block the offensive smell, but it crept in anyway.

The encampment sprawled like a forgotten city: a patchwork of shelters constructed from blue tarps, scavenged plywood, and sun-bleached tents bound together with rope, duct tape, and desperation. A rusted shopping cart sat tipped over, its wheels spinning lazily in the breeze. Flies hovered around a black trash bag that had burst open, its contents spilling onto the ground.

I tried not to stare, but as Carl promised, my eyes were drawn to everything.

A man in a filthy hoodie crouched by a plastic basin, shaving with a shard of mirror and water that looked more muddy than clear. The razor scraped his flesh, and a thin line of blood beaded on his neck.

A barefoot and ragged woman sat on a flattened mattress, clutching a stuffed animal that had long since lost its color. Her lips moved silently as she rocked back and forth.

Everywhere, the sense of exposure was palpable. There were no real walls here. Privacy was a myth. Vulnerability hung in the air like fog, yet there was a rhythm, a fragile order beneath the chaos. A line of jugs filled with water. A handwritten sign that read *No Stealing*. A flower planted in an old soup can.

My throat tightened. I hadn't expected this. I thought I'd just *look*. But now, with the concrete groaning above, and the city's skyline visible between rusted beams, it felt like stepping into another world. So different from my life of privilege. The only way to describe it was the death of hope.

And the worst part wasn't the smell or the filth.

It was the eyes.

They looked at me—some guarded, some curious, some hollow.

All of them human.

Carl patted his hand on the door, making me jump. "You ready?"

I blinked and nodded.

"Here. Put these on." He shoved an orange vest and latex gloves through the window. "Safety first."

I shimmied into the vest, then wiped my hands on my jeans. My fingers were stiff and cold, like my body hadn't caught up to my brain yet.

By the time I joined Carl and Marcus, the boxes had been unloaded onto folding tables. It was quite the array: bottled water, toothbrushes, soap, first aid supplies, feminine hygiene products, food, socks, underwear, blankets, tarps... things most people didn't think about until they had none.

I snapped on my rubber gloves, ready to work. Word traveled fast here, and a loose line had already formed.

A tall man with a skeletal frame approached me first, face gaunt, eyes yellowed. He didn't speak, simply pointed at the socks. I handed him a pair, and the man's hand trembled slightly as he took them, nodding his thanks.

Next came a mother and her son, maybe seven years old, his Spider-Man hoodie two sizes too small. He clung to her leg but lit up at the sight of the granola bars.

I crouched and held one out to him. "You like chocolate chip?"

The boy snatched it, ripped it open, and was already chewing before I finished the sentence. His mother mouthed *thank you*, eyes glossy, voice caught somewhere between pride and shame.

They kept coming. A woman with open sores on her arms asked for wipes. A young guy wanted the empty boxes for his dog. A wiry man missing several teeth asked for soft food. At one point, a fight broke out—two men screaming over who stole whose blanket—but it fizzled as quickly as it flared. Everyone was trying to survive the day.

I found myself moving on autopilot. The smells no longer hit as hard, and the sounds faded into the background. I kept handing out what we had, making eye contact and listening to their stories of evictions, medical bankruptcies, abusive partners, lost jobs, and bad luck.

Near the end of the shift, as the supplies dwindled and the sun climbed higher, I stepped away to catch my breath. Leaning against a concrete pillar, I stared at the blue sky and puffy clouds—so clean, so quiet. A stark difference from life under the bridge.

Carl came over and joined me, cracking his neck from side to side. "You okay?"

I nodded slowly. "Yeah. I mean... no, but yeah."

He smiled. "It was more than you expected?"

"I knew it was gonna be bad but..." I motioned to the makeshift city. "Does it ever get better?"

He shrugged. "Sometimes, but not for everyone. Society has all but forgotten about them. But this, what we're doing, matters. Even if it's just socks and bottled water."

"Is it okay if I go talk to some of them?"

Carl hesitated then gave me a curt nod. "Don't sneak up on anybody and stay close to the van. I don't want you out of my sight."

"Thank you." I reached into my back pocket and pulled out a worn photo, the edges frayed and the corners soft from being handled so much. In the picture, Aidan stood next to his prized pickup truck with his arm slung over my shoulder. We were eighteen. We'd both changed since then, but his rugged good looks hadn't.

I'd been carrying the photo for months. Since the last rehab facility said *he checked out against medical advice*. Since the phone calls stopped. Since his apartment was left empty.

I approached a group clustered near a tarp shelter. Two men sat on overturned crates, passing a bottle wrapped in a brown paper bag. A woman with dreadlocks and a camouflage coat watched me approach with a guarded stare, her arms crossed tightly over her chest.

"Hi," I said, trying to keep my tone neutral and steady. "I don't mean to bother you. I'm looking for someone." I held the photo out, letting them see it without pushing it into their faces. "His name is Aidan. He's six foot two, mid-twenties, a veteran."

They all shook their heads, barely glancing at the picture. I thanked them and moved on to the next group. Then the next. And the next.

After making the rounds, I tried one last person—an older woman with stringy gray hair who looked about seventy but was likely much younger. She gently petted the cat curled up on her lap while talking to it.

"Excuse me. Have you seen this man?" I held up the picture.

She took it from my hand and inspected it through her cracked glasses. "Handsome fella. Probably has a beard now. Everyone's got a damn beard out here."

"He might." Aidan had always been clean-shaven, but who knew now? "His name is Aidan and he's a veteran. Mid-twenties."

She sighed and shook her head as she passed back the photo. "He don't look familiar. There're other camps though. Hope he ain't down by the tunnels. If he's there, he's in deep. That's rough territory, full of dealers and drugs." She took my hand in her tiny, dirt-stained one and patted the back of it. "I hope you find him, dear."

I thanked her for her time and headed toward the van, kicking gravel and feeling defeated. Another dead end. Another disappointment. No one had seen Aidan or remembered him. My heart sank thinking of the man I knew, who was once so vibrant, living in these conditions.

Supplies gone, boxes collapsed, and the camp already settling back into its grim routine, Marcus slammed the back doors of the van and jumped inside the sliding door. I climbed into the passenger seat, staring out the window as the van pulled away from the encampment. A lump stuck in my throat and my eyes brimmed with tears.

"You want to talk about it?" Carl asked.

I let the tears fall, then turned to him with watery eyes. "Tell me about the tunnels."

Carl's eyes went wide as he glanced in the rearview mirror at Marcus. "You wanna take this one?"

Marcus leaned between the front seats. "Right... the tunnels." He paused for a beat, like he was searching for the right words. "So, everyone comes to the Vegas Strip for the billion-dollar casinos, luxury nightclubs, and blackjack tables. What they don't know is right under their feet is an extensive network of storm tunnels."

I turned in my seat so I could fully face him. "One of the ladies I talked to said they were *rough territory*. What does that mean? How much worse could it be than where we were?"

Marcus blew out a rough breath. "Where we were is a garden party compared to the tunnels. They're dark, wet, and rat infested. The homeless there are called the mole people."

"Mole people?" *What an awful, dehumanizing name.*

"Yep. They live in the dark, hiding from the real world. It's a last resort, especially for those with drug addictions and mental health issues." He sat back slightly, his voice dipping lower. "It's its own society with no rules, no laws, and no police. If you enter their domain, there's a high risk of getting stabbed or worse."

Aidan had an alcohol addiction and PTSD. Hiding sounded like something that would appeal to him. "What about the outreach programs?"

"Most don't even attempt to go into the tunnels. It's dangerous as fuck."

"That answer your questions?" Carl asked.

I nodded as more tears fell, imagining Aidan living under those conditions.

"Hopefully whoever you're looking for isn't there," Marcus said. "If they are, don't count on finding them."

I swallowed down the lump in my throat. "I can't give up hope, even if he has. I need him to know that someone still gives a shit."

Carl patted my leg. "You keep that hope, Rora, but don't go lookin' in the tunnels. Won't do your friend no good if you disappear too."

Chapter 15
Tom

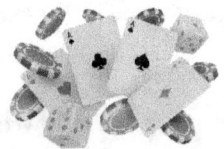

"Thanks for coming with me," I said to Aurora.

When Brett and I met with the Dorseys yesterday to finalize the deal, he showed me a hundred pictures of their newborn son. I later called Penny to check in on her, and she bluntly said, "Get your ass over here." So there I was, holding a powder-blue gift bag stuffed with rubber ducky tissue paper, standing in the elevator with my girl on the way to their apartment.

"I don't mind at all. I was wondering about Penny. We chatted quite a bit at the wedding, and she was super sweet. Plus, it gives me an excuse to spend time with you," she said, bumping me with her hip.

"You don't need an excuse. I love spending time with you." I leaned down and gave her lips a gentle kiss. I didn't know if I'd ever get used to kissing Aurora whenever I wanted, but I wasn't going to waste the opportunity.

She looked around the extravagant elevator with its mirrored walls and gold trim. "This place is swanky."

"You have no idea. My entire apartment could fit in their kitchen. They have more money than we could ever imagine."

"Mm-hmm." She hummed it like she didn't care, but I'd learned people always cared, whether they admitted it or not

"But hopefully, if this software takes off, I'll be able to bank some real bucks and take you to fancy restaurants or a show. You deserve more than a couple of drinks at a local pub."

Ever since the deal went through, I'd been dreaming about the money and what I would do with it. Once my bills were paid, I could get a new car with AC that worked reliably and an apartment that didn't overlook an alley.

Aurora and I had made it official a few days ago, but it felt longer, considering I'd been pining after her for months. Eventually, if things kept going the way they had been, maybe she would move in with me. We could be one of those couples who sipped coffee together in the morning and drank wine on the balcony at night. And I wouldn't forget about Ailuros. I'd get her the best cat tree money could buy.

I was getting ahead of myself, but it felt so right. I guess that's why they called it dreaming.

She put her hand on my arm. "Tom, you don't have to take me to fancy restaurants. I like you just the way you are."

I chuckled. "I bet you'd like me more if I were rich."

She scrunched up her nose, as if the words offended her. "Doubtful. Money is overrated."

"Said no one ever," I joked.

"So, I'm *no one* now?" She quirked one of her blond eyebrows, but it was the upturn of her lips that told me she was kidding.

"You could never be *no one* to me," I promised with a kiss on her forehead. We stepped out of the elevator into the vestibule and knocked on their penthouse door. "Prepare to be blown away."

Penny answered quickly and squealed. "I'm so happy you guys made it." She had shadows under her eyes, but other than that, she was her normal bubbly self.

I held up the bag. "Congratulations!"

She took it and peeked inside. "You didn't have to get me anything, but I do love gifts."

"Technically, it's for the baby, not you," I said, pushing up my glasses. Now I was wondering if I was supposed to get something for Penny too. I didn't know the proper etiquette for new moms.

"I'm teasing you. This is great! Thank you." Then Penny leaned in and gave Aurora a hug. "It's nice to see you again."

"Thanks for having me."

"I love your sundress. It's so cute." Penny rubbed her swollen belly. "It'll be a while before I can wear something like that again."

I cringed. *Dammit!* I should have been the one to tell Aurora she looked nice. She didn't just look nice; with dainty straps across her shoulders, her boobs pushed up, a flowy skirt, and wedge sandals, she looked smoking hot. I missed the opportunity to compliment her. If I did it now, it'd come out sounding contrived.

"You look fantastic," Aurora assured Penny. "You have that new-mom glow."

"Oh, you're too nice." Penny waved us through the door. "Come in, come in. Everybody is out back on the patio by the pool."

"Everybody?" I asked.

"Yup. We figured since everyone was anxious to meet Max, we'd do it all in one fell swoop."

"I love that name," Aurora said as we followed Penny through the foyer to the kitchen.

"We named him after Brett's dad. Maxwell passed away a few years ago and we thought it would be a great way to honor him." She picked up an open bottle of chardonnay from the counter. "Wine?"

"Please," I said. "Who all is here?"

"You know," Penny said as she poured the wine, "Trent, Gia, Hunter, and Charli. The whole crew." She tipped the last drops into a half-full glass. "Hold on. Let me grab another one."

Wow! That was more people than I expected. "I'm sorry. I thought it was just going to be us," I whispered to Aurora.

"No worries. I'm fine." Lifting her chin toward the patio, she whispered back, "They have a rooftop pool. *Very* swanky."

Penny returned with another bottle of chilled white wine, finished filling our glasses, and handed them to us. "We should join the others."

"Do you want to open the gift?" I asked, pointing to the bag on the counter and trying to buy us a few extra minutes before being immersed in a group.

"Definitely." She pulled out the tissue paper and dug around inside. "This is awesome, and totally true." She held up the blue onesie that said *I'm the Boss* for Aurora to see. "Brett's so good with Max, but he's going to have to go back to work to get a vacation. Between taking care of me and Max, we're running him ragged."

"I'm glad you like it." It was the first time I'd ever bought a baby gift and had no idea what to get. It seemed fitting.

"Awww… that was sweet." Aurora smiled at me.

A soft wail came from the sitting room. Penny went over and picked up baby Max from his carrier, which I hadn't even noticed when we walked in. She bounced him lightly, shushing his cries as we walked over to join her.

"He's so beautiful and so tiny," I said in amazement.

Penny harrumphed. "Didn't feel so tiny when I was pushing him out."

I obviously knew how babies were born, but I didn't need that image in my head, especially when it was about Penny.

Aurora giggled. "You should see your face right now."

"Sorry. I got a visual."

Penny rolled her eyes. "Men. They're all about the fun part, pounding their chest about their big achievement of planting their seed, but get all squeamish when the seed grows into an actual human and has to be pushed out. Trust me, it wasn't enjoyable for me either."

"Were you scared?" Aurora asked curiously.

"Petrified, but there's not really any turning back at that point. To be honest, I'm not sure who was more nervous, Brett or me. He wore grooves into the hospital floor with all his pacing. During the delivery, I was the one who had to tell him to breathe."

I chuckled at the picture she painted, imagining the man who I knew to be calm and collected losing his shit while his wife was in labor.

Penny rocked Max a bit more then held him to her chest, his green eyes big and bright. "Looks like somebody is ready to join the party. Come on." Penny waved for us to follow her to the patio.

When we stepped out, it was like being transported to a fancy resort. Overhead fans, shaped like palm fronds, cooled the area right outside the door, lowering the temperature by at least ten degrees. Beyond the overhang was the pool, which seemed an inadequate term, as it had a hot tub and rock-faced waterfall at one end, while the other end disappeared off the edge of the building. I'd never actually seen an infinity pool. The way the water blended with the horizon made me itchy, worrying that someone could go over the rim and fall to their death. To my relief, my sister and Gia were sitting on the steps with Carina as she splashed her feet in the water.

I admired the way Charli stepped into motherhood with Hunter's daughter. She fell in love with that little girl the moment she took the nannying job. I just never imagined she'd fall in love with Hunter too.

"Look what Tom brought us," Penny said to Brett, holding up the onesie in her free hand for him to see and bringing my focus back to them.

He was standing by the grill in more casual attire than I'd ever seen him wear. Sometimes it was hard for me to think of him as a regular guy and not a billionaire. "That's about right," he said, reading the lettering. "Thanks, Tom." He wiped his palm on his shorts and shook my hand. "Glad you could make it."

"This is Aurora," I said, then introduced her to everyone.

She gave a little wave of her fingers and smiled. "I know I only met you all for a short time, but I feel like I already know you from the way Tom talks."

Hunter sauntered over. "What'd he tell you about me?"

"Umm..."

"You don't have to answer that," I told her while scowling at him.

"We have a love-hate relationship," Hunter said with a wink. "I'm growing on him though."

103

I slung my arm around her waist and pulled her closer. The last thing I needed was Hunter harassing Aurora. She'd never want to hang out with me again.

"You're burning the burgers, man!" Trent yelled at Brett, redirecting everyone's attention.

"Shit!" Sure enough, flames rose through the grate on the barbecue, and the meat sizzled. Brett turned down the heat and flipped the patties.

Penny set the onesie on a chair and grabbed Aurora by the hand. "Come on. Let's go sit with the girls and leave the men to handle their meat." She slid out of my hold and giggled as she followed Penny and Max over to where the other women were gabbing.

"Does this mean you and Aurora are a thing now?" Trent asked, wiggling his eyebrows.

I stuffed my hands in my pockets, not happy to be the center of attention. "I guess we are."

"From the kiss I saw, I'd say they definitely are," Hunter added.

"Oh, fuck off! That was supposed to be private."

Trent put a hand on his brother's shoulder. "He has a way of making private things public. Be careful." He was referring to Hunter making a video of Trent and Gia having sex and sending it to the entire office staff at Mystique, which resulted in Hunter being fired. It took a lot of time and serious groveling for him to make amends with his family and be reinstated. That was one of the reasons I didn't like him married to my sister.

Hunter rolled his eyes and took a sip of his bourbon. "Jeez! Fuck up one time and that's all that anyone remembers."

Brett pointed at him with a spatula. "It was douchey. You're lucky I'm not your brother because I still wouldn't be talking to you."

Hunter smirked. "Good thing my brother and his wife are the forgive-and-forget type."

"We forgave. We didn't forget," Trent clarified. "If it wasn't for Carina coming into your life, you'd still be on the shit list. Gia's a sucker for babies."

"Well, I'll admit, my daughter is the best thing I've ever done, even if I didn't plan it. She snagged me Charli and got me in your good graces."

"Let's not overexaggerate."

"Anyway... that kiss was private. How was I to know you and Charli were in my apartment spying on me through the peephole?" I asked.

Trent palmed his face in exasperation, while Brett shook his head.

Hunter held up his hands. "That was all your sister." He bobbled his head from side to side. "Mostly."

"This thing with Aurora is new and I don't need you messing it up. I'm begging you, be on your best behavior tonight." I glanced over at the girls. She seemed to be getting along fine with them, although that didn't surprise me. The women of this group were fierce, yet friendly. It was the guys I worried about. One in particular.

Hunter lazily traced an *X* over his heart. "I'll try, but no promises. Sometimes it's too fun."

Trent came to my defense. "Hold your assholeness at bay. With this new software project, he doesn't need any more stress."

"How's it coming along with my team?" Brett asked. "Usually, I'd be more involved but..." He shrugged.

Glad to veer away from my personal life, I jumped on his question. "It's going great actually. Your marketing team are miracle workers. We've developed a product name with logos and a tagline."

"That's good," he said, slipping the burgers from the grill onto the buns. "What are we calling the software?"

"CyberSecure." I held up my hands and spread them wide like it was in lights on a marquee as I recited the tagline. *"Your information isn't safe unless it's CyberSecure. Hacker-proof technology for your peace of mind."*

Brett rolled it around on his tongue. "I like the concept, but it might need a bit more work."

I deflated. "Maybe. It's kind of long, but we really wanted to express the benefits of the product."

"How about *Keeping assholes out of your shit one block at a time?"* Hunter smiled proudly. "See what I did there? Block... blockchain. It makes perfect sense."

All three of us groaned.

"Best stick to finances, little bro," Trent said, clapping him on the shoulder.

He threw his hands in the air. "Whatever. I was trying to help."

"Tom, would you go tell the girls we're ready to eat?" Brett asked as he piled the burgers on a platter.

I gave him a two-finger salute. "Sure thing." I'd barely gotten ten feet before I stopped in my tracks. Aurora was rocking Max in her arms.

I'd never given much thought to having a family. My dreams of the future always revolved around creating a successful tech business, but seeing my girl quietly cooing at a baby turned my insides to mush. *That could be us one day.*

I shook off the feeling and approached the girls. Aurora looked at me with a dazzling smile. "Look who I've got."

Stepping beside her, I ran my finger along Max's chubby cheek. He had Penny's eyes and Brett's scowl. "Aren't you the cutest thing? You look good holding him," I told her.

"Oh, she's a natural," Penny said with a wink. Now that she'd found her happiness, she seemed dead set on me finding mine too. After all, she was the one who encouraged me to invite Aurora to the wedding.

Penny was a dreamer, but if she could marry a billionaire, why couldn't I have a happily ever after with the sexy girl across the hall?

Chapter 16
Aurora

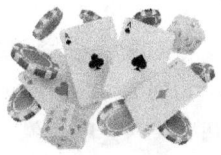

Max was so cute and warm and snuggly that I hated to let him go. It made me wonder what type of mom I'd be. I'd heard being maternal was instinctive, but I wasn't sure about that. Lately, my parents treated me more like a possession than their child. I vowed that when I became a mom, I wouldn't put restrictions on my son or daughter. They would be able to do or be whatever they wanted, whether I agreed or not. A parent's love was supposed to be unconditional, not a bargaining chip.

I reluctantly passed Max back to his mom. Penny talked to her baby softly as she set to tucking him into his carrier, his tiny baby feet wiggling.

The rest of us girls went inside to bring out the side dishes the catering company had delivered. Gia seemed perfectly at home in Penny's kitchen, taking things out of the fridge.

"My brother is different around you. More relaxed." Charli said to me as she leaned against the kitchen island.

"Yeah, as long as I've known him, Tom has always been way too serious," Gia added, handing me the potato salad.

I wasn't sure what to say to that, so I tried to brush it off. "It's still new. We made it official this week."

"You should have seen Tom's face when he saw you holding Max," Charli said, giggling.

"What? Was it a good thing or a bad thing?"

"Definitely good," Gia said. "He's got it bad for you."

Charli took a bowl of fruit from Gia. "I've been wanting my brother to find someone for a long time. I'm glad he's found a woman who makes him happy."

"I think you might be just what the doctor ordered," Gia said, setting the coleslaw on the counter and closing the fridge.

"Well, he makes me happy too. We have a lot in common. We're both tech nerds."

Charli looked at Gia and chuckled. "Honey, you're the furthest thing from a tech nerd I've ever seen. You're more like a tech-savvy little minx."

Gia waved a finger at me. "You've got the whole package going on. Guys think they have to pick between sexy and smart. We're living proof that a woman can be both," she said, flipping her red hair over her shoulder.

"Here! Here!" Charli agreed, raising the fruit bowl high in the air.

"What are we *Here! Here!-ing* about?" Penny asked, coming into the kitchen from the patio.

"That we're a bunch of sexy, smart bitches." Gia smirked.

"And that the guys are lucky to have us," Charli added with a nod of her head.

"Hell yeah, we are. And double hell yeah, they are." Penny raised her fist. "Woman power!"

I liked these women. I liked them a lot. Instead of ripping each other down, they thrived on building each other up. The world needed more of that.

Brett stuck his head inside the open slider. "You wanna bring some of that woman power out here? We're starving."

Penny turned over her shoulder. "Hold your horses. We're having a moment."

108

"You can have your moment, but I'm hungry and one way or another I'm going to eat, though plan B might be rude since we have a house full of company." Then he slid the door closed.

We all stood there silently, taking in the words he'd said. "Did he…?" Charli asked without finishing the question.

"Yep. The man is insatiable. Would probably make good on it too if it weren't for the no-sex-for-six-weeks rule." She grabbed the bowl of coleslaw from the counter. "Best not test it though."

We were a gaggle of giggling girls as we took the food outside and set it on the table.

"Finally," Brett said. Though he sounded annoyed, his smile betrayed him. The way he looked at his wife was damn near obscene; their love for each other clear as day.

I longed for that type of connection. Although things with Tom were edging that way, I knew it couldn't last, especially if I found Aidan. Our parents had our fates planned since we were sixteen.

He patted the seat beside him, and I plopped into it. "How is it going with the ladies?" he whispered.

"Great. They're a lot of fun." It was true. I'd laughed more with them than I did with my friends at home. Maybe because my girlfriends in California were more interested in appearances. The daughters of lawyers, doctors, and actors, they were a snooty crew who cared more about climbing the social ladder than making real connections. They'd turn on you as quick as a flash if it suited their agenda. I didn't have a true friend among them.

These women, on the other hand, welcomed me with open arms, though they barely knew me. They were smart and sassy and didn't give a fuck what people thought. It was refreshing and I was going to miss them when it was time for me to go home.

"Good." Tom pecked me on the cheek. "I felt bad letting Penny drag you off."

"No worries. They love talking about you." I chuckled.

Tom groaned. "Was my sister telling embarrassing stories?"

I put my hand on his arm. "Not at all. Everything was good. Nothing but admiration for you."

"Hey, you two," Hunter pulled our attention. "You wanna join the party or are you gonna make googly eyes at each other all night?"

Tom flipped him the bird as Gia smacked him in the chest. "Behave," she scolded.

I giggled again. The dynamics of this group cracked me up.

"What?" Hunter asked. "Maybe we want to get to know Tom's new chick too."

Tom narrowed his eyes at Hunter. "Don't call her my *chick*. It's offensive."

"Ignore him," Trent piped in. "Hunter's less domesticated than the rest of us. I'm pretty sure he was dropped on his head when he was a baby. Makes him a real asshole."

Hunter tugged on his collar. "I resemble that remark and I'm not even ashamed. It's not my fault I'm the only one who has the nerve to say what's on my mind."

Tom shook his head, but a small smile tipped his lips at Hunter's quick comeback.

Brett tapped his knife against his wineglass, and everyone turned their attention to him. "I want to thank you all for being here to meet baby Max and supporting us on this journey. We couldn't ask for a better group of friends."

The baby squealed from his carrier, which was set on a chair between his parents. Penny rubbed his little belly, "Max thanks you too. He's got the best aunties and uncles." She glanced around the table with tears in her eyes. "We're very fortunate."

Gia raised her glass of water. "I'm going to be a bomb-ass auntie." She rubbed her own tiny baby bump. "Oh... and we found out we're having a boy too. I hope they're best friends."

Hunter sighed. "Oh, goody. A mini Brett and mini Trent. Just what the world needs. They'd better keep their hands off my daughter." He protectively put a hand on Carina's tiny head, where she sat nestled between him and Tom's sister.

Charli patted her husband on the shoulder. "Don't worry, Carina's going to grow up fierce. She won't take any shit. If anything, the boys will be afraid of her."

"Damn straight," he agreed, giving her a searing, borderline inappropriate kiss with tongue and all.

Tom groaned and shielded his eyes. "That's enough. I don't want to see that crap."

"Turnabout is fair play." Hunter smirked at him, as if it was some sort of inside joke I wasn't privy to.

"Okay... back on track, everybody. Let's eat," Penny said, lifting the bowl of potato salad and handing it to her husband.

Food was passed around the table and everyone filled their plates. Conversation was relegated to small talk about their families. Seemed everyone liked to pick on Hunter, but he was a good sport about it and gave it right back. I didn't have anything to offer, so I sat and listened and stuffed my face with deliciousness.

"So..." Trent said as he plopped a second helping of fruit on his plate. "Hunter, Dad, and I were talking. We'd like to host a launch party for you, Tom. While this security system is fabulous, and we're thankful for the opportunity to pilot it, we feel even more connected because you're part of the Mystique family. We'd like to help build the hype."

Tom's forkful of coleslaw froze on the way to his mouth. I looked at Tom, who was looking at Brett, who was looking at Trent.

"Wow, you don't have to do all that," Tom said quietly. His throat bobbed and he looked like he wanted to crawl under the table. "I appreciate the offer, but it's really not necessary."

Brett pointed his knife at Tom. "Actually, I think it's a great idea. You may not want to be in the spotlight, but people want to connect a product with the person behind it. You, my friend, have a trustworthy face."

"It's just a face," Tom mumbled as he sank lower in his chair.

"It's a cute face," I whispered in his ear.

He grabbed my hand and squeezed it. A bit too hard. I could feel the anxiety oozing out of him. "I'm a computer guy. My comfort zone is behind a screen, not on a stage."

111

"Well, you're going to have to get over that. You can't launch a million-dollar product and stand in a corner," Brett said, turning to Trent. "I'll help fund it and we'll invite all the CEOs from the other casinos on the Strip. It'll be not only a meet and greet, but a show and tell. Tom can do a presentation on the software."

"A presentation?" Tom squeaked. He was growing paler by the second and I squeezed his hand back.

"On a stage," Hunter said, with a waggle of his eyebrows.

"Fuck."

"You can do it. I know you can," Charli encouraged. "You were on the debate team in high school and college. You won all kinds of awards."

"Yeah, but I wasn't trying to sell something."

"Don't look at it as selling," Gia said. "The best sales pitch isn't a sales pitch at all. Talk about all the benefits and how it'll improve business. Then Trent can follow up with why Mystique got on board."

"Basically, the same pitch you did for us, but without all the techy stuff and a lot more pizzazz," Hunter said, waving big jazz hands in the air.

I giggled at his antics.

"But..." Tom gulped. "I haven't even installed it yet. You don't know that you're going to love it. What if it flops?"

I'd never seen this side of Tom. I'd seen him nervous, but this lack of confidence was heartbreaking. Deciding I had to do something, I took both of his hands in mine and looked him in the eyes, blocking out everyone else. "By your own admission, you've been perfecting this security system for years. Would you have even pitched it to Brett if you weren't one-hundred-percent sure the software was amazing?"

"No, but what if there are glitches? This is a first run. It's a lot of pressure."

"There *are* going to be glitches. That's the nature of programming. You know that. But what I know is that when it comes to programming, I've never met anyone else who is more intuitive or capable than you. If there's a problem, you'll solve it."

Tom stared at me, rolling his lips between his teeth.

The table was quiet until Charli raised her hand. "I agree. I have faith in you, big brother."

"We all do," Penny chimed in.

Tom sighed and looked around the table at all the faces supporting him. "I promise I won't let you down."

Brett raised his glass and smiled. "I've got a million dollars that says you won't."

"When will this party be?" Tom asked, pushing up his glasses.

"How long do you think it'll take to get the security system up and running?" Trent asked back.

"Two weeks, give or take."

Trent took a sip of his wine. "Then we'll plan it for three weeks out. It's going to be great, Tom."

"Thank you. I didn't mean to sound ungrateful. It's a lot for a guy like me," he said humbly.

"I think we've all had our moments of uncertainty," I said.

Everyone nodded their agreement.

Gia put her napkin on top of her empty plate. "I'm glad that's settled. I'll get started on the planning, but while we're all here, I'd like to pick your brains."

"You're already missing me, aren't you?" Penny teased.

"More than you know," Gia said. "Penny and I had everything worked out for Mystique's next fundraiser, but there's been a *glitch*." She looked directly at Tom. "And I need some suggestions."

"What's going on?" Penny asked.

Gia scrunched her lips to the side. "I know you've been busy with Max, so you probably didn't see it, but the president of the charity we chose to support has been indicted for embezzlement."

Hunter let out a low whistle and Penny gasped.

"Thankfully, we haven't announced the charity to the press yet, so we're good on the PR front, but we're in need of a new one that isn't steeped in corruption. And we need it fast. The invitations are supposed to go out next month."

My ears perked up. What were the chances of something like this falling into my lap? I didn't hesitate to speak up. "Helping Hands."

Everyone turned and looked at me.

"What's Helping Hands?" Penny asked.

"It's a homeless shelter that I've been volunteering at. They provide meals, shelter, medical care, counseling, and employment resources. They're in desperate need of money and are at risk of having to shut down. Kendra, the director, is applying for a federal grant, but there's no guarantee."

Gia's eyebrows furrowed, forming two little lines between them. "And you can vouch for them? They're completely legit?"

I nodded frantically. "Absolutely. I've been helping with the grant application process. I can put you in touch with Kendra. She'll give you any information you need."

"That would be awesome. Thanks, Aurora."

Tom smiled at me. "Seems my girl has all the answers today."

My heart swooned when he called me *his girl*. It was possessive without being overbearing. It felt like being claimed, and I liked it.

My official address may have been in California, but my heart was making its home in Las Vegas. My time here was supposed to be short, an agreement I made with my father, but there had to be a way to stay.

The last thing I wanted to do today was think about my father and the hold he had on me, so I put him out of my head and pretended my commitments to him didn't exist. I was here today and what my father didn't know wouldn't hurt him. Yet.

I was more concerned about what Tom didn't know. This was all getting very complicated. I was supposed to be thinking with my head, but my heart was running the show. I was afraid in the end we'd both be shattered, and I'd have no one to blame but myself.

Chapter 17
Tom

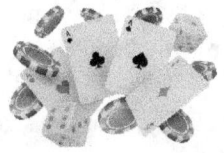

Our hands swung between us as we stepped out of the elevator and into the hallway of our apartments. "Thanks again for coming with me tonight," I said. It sounded like I was saying good night and the last thing I wanted was for this night to end.

"It was fun. Plus, Penny sent us home with strawberry cheesecake." Aurora's eyes lit up as she pointed to the white box in my other hand.

I'd almost said no when Penny offered for us to take home dessert, but now I was glad I didn't. Clearly, my girl had a sweet tooth.

Being with Aurora made everything better. What I thought was going to turn into an uncomfortable evening ended up being great. She mixed well with the ladies, like they'd been friends forever.

Since Charli and Hunter got together, I'd been included in the group more than I would have liked. I felt like a loser, showing up alone when everyone else was paired. A third wheel, along for the ride and completely unnecessary.

And although I tried to mask my anxiety, it was always there, bubbling beneath the surface. I was perfectly comfortable behind a computer screen, but put me in social situations and I was toast. They were my kryptonite. With Aurora at my side, all of that changed.

"Hunter aside, it *was* fun," I said.

She playfully smacked me on the shoulder. "He's not that bad. Honestly, he's hilarious and has a charm about him. I can see why your sister fell in love with the guy."

"Ugh. Not you too." I untwined my fingers from hers and threw the back of my hand against my forehead in mock despair. "He's invading every part of my life."

"You could have worse family," Aurora said with a shrug. "My father's up my ass all the time."

My head cocked to the side. "You don't really talk about your parents." It was more of an observation than a question, but I was curious.

She sighed. "My father and I don't see eye to eye and my mother backs him. I love them both, but they expect a lot from me. We have completely different ideas of what my future should look like. They're not happy I'm in Vegas."

There seemed to be more to that story. Whatever she wasn't saying dimmed her light. I didn't want to press her for details; she'd tell me when she was ready. "That's hard. Coming to Vegas wasn't my parents' first choice either, but they're happy I'm here to look over Charli. Had she not followed her dreams, I would have never followed her to Vegas, and I wouldn't have met you." I tapped her on the tip of her nose with my finger, trying to coax a smile out of her.

"I'm glad we're both here," she said, tilting her lips up, but the smile didn't quite reach her eyes. We stopped in front of her apartment, and she pulled out her key.

I couldn't let our night end with her being sad. "I feel like you need a joke."

Aurora held up her hand. "I don't think I can handle any of your jokes right now."

Undeterred, I pushed forward. "I promise these are good ones. What did the computer do during its break time?"

She stared at me blankly.

"He had a byte," I said with a chuckle. "Come on. It's like you're not even trying. Here's another one. What is a computer's favorite snack?"

Tapping a finger against her lips, she said, "I should be able to get this one." After a bit more thinking, she shrugged her shoulders. "I give up."

"Microchips. Ba-dum-dum!"

Aurora covered her face with her hands, hiding a hint of a smile. "That's terrible."

"It's not terrible. It's a great joke." I held up the small white box in my hand. "I might not have any microchips, but we can finish off this strawberry cheesecake." No one could be sad when cheesecake was involved.

That twinkle in her eyes returned and she put her hand on her flat belly. "I shouldn't, but it's too good. Let's do it!"

She pushed open the door and set her purse on the small table beside it. Ailuros ran to her and meowed. Aurora petted her softly on the head and scratched her under the chin. "There's my pretty girl."

When Ailuros saw me, her tail rose straight in the air, and she hissed. "Your cat hates me," I said as she ran under the beaded curtain of the bedroom.

"She'll come around. Ailuros hid from me for the first week I had her, but she's a lovebug once she warms up."

"I hope so." I'd read that if a woman's cat hated you, the relationship was doomed. I'd be damned if I let a cat determine my fate. I mentally added caviar treats and catnip mice to my grocery list for the finicky feline. It couldn't hurt.

Aurora kicked off her wedged sandals and sashayed into the kitchen. "Go ahead and get comfortable. I'll grab some forks."

I shuffled the pillows around and sat on the couch, strategically only leaving enough room for her to practically sit on top of me.

She returned with a smile on her face—a real one this time—and plopped down against the armrest with her legs across my lap, her soft thighs brushing against mine. "Do you care if we eat it right out of the box?"

"It's the best way," I said, taking a fork from her and opening the container. Dipping it into the creamy surface streaked with swirls of ruby red, I scooped some onto the fork and held it up to her mouth.

"You're going to feed me?" She smacked her lips like a baby bird. "Cheep, cheep."

"Open up, sweet cheeks." I didn't mean for the name Hunter had called her to slip out, but once it did, I didn't hate it.

"Sweet cheeks?" She giggled.

I shrugged. "I'm trying it out. Now, say 'ahh.'" She opened her mouth, and I teased her by holding it just out of her reach as she went to take a bite.

Her eyes narrowed, amusement glinting in them. "You're enjoying this too much."

"Yes, I am." When she opened her mouth again, I fed her the bite slowly, her pillowy lips closing around it. As I slid the fork out, her eyes fluttered shut. "It's so fucking good. It tastes like heaven." She hummed as she chewed.

My gaze locked on her lips, mesmerized by the slow, deliberate way they moved. When she swallowed, the subtle bob of her throat swelled my cock as I imagined her mouth around it. Goddamn, I swear she'd put a spell on me, and I was helpless against it.

Aurora opened her eyes and grinned. "My turn." She dipped her fork in the box, coming away with the perfect ratio of cake and glaze. "Open up."

"Nuh-uh." I shook my head. "I'm taking care of you, not the other way around."

She scrunched her lips up and frowned. "In case you haven't heard, it's the twenty-first century. If a woman wants to feed her man, she can."

She had a point. I chuckled and relented, opening my mouth. It felt ridiculous letting her feed me, but the joy taking over her face was worth it. Making her happy made me happy.

As Aurora lifted the fork to my mouth, I grabbed her wrist and held it there. Wrapping my lips around it, I slowly pulled the fork away and

118

savored the bite as the flavors exploded on my tongue. She stared at my lips as I chewed and swallowed. "This might be my new favorite dessert."

"Why is that?" she whispered, the sugary scent of her warm breath mingling with mine.

"Because of you," I answered, my eyes never leaving hers.

Her cheeks flushed. "It's my new favorite too."

We took turns feeding each other until there was one bite left. Aurora scooped the last bit on her fork and held it up, but instead of feeding it to me, she popped it in her own mouth with a smug smirk. A bit of strawberry dotted the side of her lips.

"You've got a little something…" My thumb brushed below her lip and smeared the strawberry glaze to the corner of her mouth. "Oops, I made it worse. I guess I'll have to clean it up." My heart raced, knowing what was coming next in my diabolical plan to seduce Aurora.

Her breath hitched. "Do you want a napkin?"

"Nope." Leaning in, I closed the last inches between us, kissing the corner of her mouth and swiping it with my tongue. A gentle sigh escaped her lips as my hand cradled the back of her head and my thumb brushed across her cheek. She tilted her chin up as I dusted kisses along her jaw and down her neck.

"Tom," she whispered. A plea that made my cock hard thinking about all the little sounds she might make when I made her come.

My lips traveled back up her neck to the soft skin right below her ear. "Yes?"

She dropped her fork, and it fell to the floor with a clatter as her hands found my chest, curling into the fabric of my shirt and pulling me closer. "Kiss me."

"I am kissing you."

"On the lips." My girl was greedy, but I was in no hurry. I'd waited so long for this and had no intention of rushing it. My lips brushed across her eyelids and down to the tip of her nose before meeting her mouth and those plump lips that my dreams were made of, though I usually imagined them doing other things to me.

My tongue swept along the seam, begging for entrance. She opened her mouth, and it was pure magic. The kiss deepened, slow and warm, like chocolate melting over an open flame. She tasted of strawberries and cream and something uniquely her that was totally addicting. We moved in sync, slow and deliberate, our tongues tangling together. Electricity hummed through my veins in a steady current, making my skin tingle and my mind hyperaware of her fingers unbuttoning my shirt and slipping inside.

A light rasping sound and quiet purr alerted me that we weren't alone. Ailuros had come out of hiding and was sitting on the coffee table licking the remnants of cheesecake, keeping one eye on us.

I pulled away enough to whisper, "Your cat is licking the box."

"It won't hurt her. She can have it," she said breathlessly. With a solid tug, she leaned back against the end of the couch and pulled me into her arms.

Hell yes!

We'd been dancing around our attraction for weeks. I felt like a little boy who'd finally been able to stick his hand in the cookie jar.

Time stood still as we devoured each other, not able to get enough. Teeth clashed. Tongues twisted. Breath mingled. So much, but not enough.

I'd never get enough of her.

The kiss turned frantic. Frenzied. Feral.

She groaned, the sound vibrating against my lips and going straight to my cock, which was definitely poking her in the leg. I braced myself on the arm of the couch and slid my other hand into her hair, fisting it enough to pull her head back and make her gasp.

My lips traveled down the column of her throat, across her chest, and to the soft swells of her breasts that heaved with every breath she took. "Absolutely gorgeous." I wanted so badly to pull the fabric away and finally get a peek at what was underneath, my patience growing thinner with every minute that passed.

"Touch me, Tom." Her voice hitched and her eyes fluttered. "Please."

My hands slid under the hem of her dress, caressing the smooth skin of her legs. I drew circles with my thumbs on the insides of her thighs as my hands crept higher to her hips, my fingers tracing the lace at the edge of her panties. Her soft flesh under my hands made me crazy, yet I wanted to respect her boundaries. We hadn't discussed any, but that didn't mean they didn't exist. "Is this okay?"

"So okay," she gasped. "Keep going."

Getting the green light, I ran the backs of my fingers over the silky material covering her most intimate parts. Her head fell back, and her eyes closed. My knuckles inched lower until they brushed over her pussy, the fabric warm and wet with her arousal. My cock strained in anticipation. He hadn't got the message that I wouldn't be fucking her tonight. Tonight was more about exploration and making her feel good.

"You're teasing me," she scolded.

"I'm not teasing you. I'm taking my time. Seeing what you like."

"All of it. I like all of it."

I moved my thumb over her clit and rubbed it in small circles, the silk a barrier between us. "You like that?" I asked, my eyes on hers.

Her back arched. "Yes!"

I increased the pressure and speed of my thumb while my fingers pressed into the wet fabric between her legs. It took everything I had not to pull her panties aside and push two fingers inside. Making myself wait to fully touch her was torture, but also a kind of savoring. It ramped up the anticipation for both of us and would make the moment we touched skin on skin that much better.

The more I rubbed, the more the muscles in her neck tightened. She let out a needy little moan and a full shiver racked her body.

I'd barely touched her for sixty seconds, yet all the signs were there. "Did you come?"

She bit her lip and nodded, then threw her arm over her face and turned her head to the side.

I felt like a king. It inflated my ego, making me want to pound my chest and shout it from the rooftop that I, Thomas Bently, made Aurora LeFleur come without hardly touching her.

"I'm sorry," she mumbled into the crook of her arm.

What? "You don't have to be sorry. You haven't done anything wrong." I peeled her arm away, revealing pink cheeks and dilated pupils, like the night at the bar when she claimed to be sick.

"I have a quick trigger. It's embarrassing," she said, not meeting my eyes.

Suddenly, the pieces clicked into place. I gently grabbed her jaw and turned her head to look at me. "Did you... come when we were at The Rabbit Hole?" My ego deflated and slyly stepped back into the crowd, realizing that maybe my achievement was not so unique. The flushed skin, the slight sheen on her forehead, the quiver... it all made sense now.

"I didn't mean to. We were watching the show, and you had your arm around me, rubbing my shoulder. You were so warm, and it was like we were in our own little cocoon. I started fantasizing about you touching me and the next thing I knew..." she rambled, then covered her face with her hands again. "I'm so mortified."

Mortified? I pried her fingers up one at a time until I could see her big blue eyes. "Don't ever be embarrassed with me, especially when it comes to sex."

"But that's just it, we didn't even have sex. There's something wrong with me."

I chuckled. "There's not a damn thing wrong with you. There are a lot of women who would gladly switch places with you."

She rolled her eyes. "That's because they don't know it's a curse. One little explosion and then nothing."

I raised an eyebrow. "Nothing? Ever?" That couldn't be true. Surely, some guy had taken their time with her. Had made her pleasure a priority.

Aurora shook her head. "Once I come, that's it. I've heard women talk about multiple orgasms, but I'm convinced it's a myth. At least for me."

Getting off the couch, I grabbed her hands and pulled her to her feet. "Challenge accepted. Let's disprove your hypothesis."

"What?" she asked, eyes wide and the flush spreading onto her chest.

I brushed a curl of honey-blond hair behind her ear. "I want you to enjoy every minute of the time we're together, so I'm proposing an alternative hypothesis. I don't think it's your body. I think it's the men

122

you've been with. I predict I can make you come several times before I'm ever inside you. It may take lots of experimenting and data analysis, but I'm nothing if not an overachiever."

"I don't want to be a science project," she refuted.

"It's not a science project. It's a pleasure project and, trust me, it won't be a hardship." I took her hand and led her to her bedroom, pushing the beads aside. "I think we should get started right away."

"Now?"

"Yes, now. Go sit on the bed." My instruction left no room for arguing. If Aurora and I were going to be together, I was determined to learn each and every one of her pleasure buttons. Master them.

She scooted into the middle of the bed, looking more innocent and unsure than a few minutes ago. "What do you want me to do?"

"You're going to count."

Her eyebrows nearly hit her hairline. "You sound mighty confident," she said as she lay back on her elbows.

In her white dress with golden locks falling around her shoulders, she looked like an angel. And I couldn't wait to dirty her up. "Oh, I am."

I wouldn't stop until I'd made her come at least three more times. She'd be begging me to give her a reprieve. And although I had no intention of fucking her, I was going to feel every inch of her... inside and out. By the end of the night, she'd know there wasn't a damn thing wrong with her.

Chapter 18
Aurora

"You're going to count." Oh *fuck!*

I'd always heard nerdy guys were better in bed. That they focused on giving a woman pleasure rather than taking it. That they were less selfish. That they studied sex like a puzzle and mastered it.

What I didn't count on was becoming an actual science project... or *pleasure project*, as Tom called it.

It made me both anxious and self-conscious. Failure was an absolute probability. I had years of experience that said it wasn't only a probability but a certainty.

As embarrassing as it was to orgasm so quickly, it would be even worse for Tom to be all up in my business and have nothing happen.

I'd learned how to fake it.

Most guys never noticed the difference, but I had a suspicion Tom would. He wouldn't be fooled by groaning and moaning and expletives. He'd be looking for all those little signs that let you know a woman was about to go off.

Tom stood at the side of the bed and stared at me like a specimen under a microscope, about to be prodded and examined in a not-so-clinical way. "I'm nervous," I blurted.

He ran a finger down the side of my face. "What are you nervous about? Do you not want me to touch you?"

"No, I do. It's just…"

He tilted his head to the side. "It's just what?"

"What if I fail?"

Tom chuckled. "This isn't a test, Aurora. There's no failing."

"Except there is. I don't want to let you down."

"Let me down? Angel, that would be impossible. I'm already the luckiest man alive," he said, brushing my hair over my shoulder.

My lips turned up. "Angel? I thought it was *sweet cheeks*."

"I'm not sold on it. I think angel fits you better, especially laid out in this white dress."

I quirked an eyebrow. "Is the dress staying on?"

His pupils dilated behind his glasses. "I think we'll get better results with it off."

Feeling a bit insecure, but determined to try, I sat up on my knees, freeing the material from beneath me, and moved toward the edge of the bed. "Then take it off," I said, looking at him from under my lashes.

His throat bobbed as his fingers danced along my shoulders. "If there's anything you don't like, tell me no."

"I don't think there's anything you could do to me that I wouldn't like. You promised me multiple orgasms, and I want to explore that."

A quiet *fuck* fell from his lips. Taking my face in both his hands, his thumbs traced my cheekbones. "I always keep my word. All I want you to do is enjoy it. Arms up."

I was still worried about failing, yet I raised them without hesitation. First, Tom removed my glasses, setting them on the nightstand. Then, he scrunched the hem of my dress in his fists and lifted the fabric from my body one agonizing inch at a time, slowly exposing my pink panties and bra. With one final tug, he pulled it up and over my head, gently placing it on the pillows behind me.

125

Starting at my temple, he ran the back of his fingers down the side of my face to my neck, then between my breasts, down my stomach, and over my belly button to the silk between my legs, leaving a trail of fire on my heated flesh. "You are perfection."

Goose bumps broke out on my arms and a shiver ran down my spine. He didn't have to say a damn thing. It was the intensity of his gaze. The gentleness of his hands. The little hum of appreciation. I'd never felt more adored.

"Your turn," I whispered. "I want to see you too."

"Will it turn you on?" he asked.

I bit my lip and nodded. The vision of him shirtless after running was burned into my memory.

He undid the last couple of buttons on his shirt and shrugged it off his shoulders. I ran my fingers over his chest and down to his abs, tracing every little crevice between his muscles. He was all lean muscle, toned and defined, with a sexy *V* at his hips that disappeared into his shorts and begged to be licked.

"These too." I reached for his belt.

He chuckled, letting me unbuckle it. "Someone's impatient."

Damn straight, I was impatient. With Tom standing in front of me shirtless, those little urges that usually disappeared after an orgasm returned in full force. The tingles on my skin. The desire in my belly. The involuntary clenching of my lady parts.

Tom grabbed both my wrists in his large hand and slowly pulled his belt through the loops, tossing it on the floor. It shouldn't have excited me, but he made the simple action titillating.

When I went for the button on his shorts, he took my hands and put them behind my back. "Greedy girl. Did I say you could touch my cock yet?"

Heat dampened my panties, and my body shuddered. I didn't expect Tom to be a dirty talker. Or his voice to drop two octaves. Or for him to be so dominant in the bedroom.

A mewl escaped my throat. "Not fair. You already touched me."

He pinned me with his steely blue eyes. "This is about your pleasure, not mine. Once I've fulfilled my promise, you'll get your turn."

This edgy, alpha side of him excited me.

My heart raced with anticipation. The pumping of my own blood rushed in my ears. I licked my lips as I watched him slowly undo the button on his shorts, as if we had all the time in the world and I wasn't standing on the precipice of being ruined. My impatience grew with every click of his zipper coming undone, knowing I'd finally get to see what was underneath.

With his shorts finally undone, Tom pushed them down his legs and kicked them to the side. His manhood strained against his boxer briefs, and my fingers itched to trace the outline of it. I knew he was packing some heat from the way I'd seen his pants tented, but my god... the man was very well endowed.

"You're big," I gulped.

He chuckled, his eyes crinkling at the corners behind his glasses. "I'm six foot two. All of me is big. Big hands. Big feet. Big—" He nodded to the bulge in his boxers.

"I want to touch it," I blurted.

That earned me another chuckle. "One hand and only a quick feel."

I reached for him, and he grabbed my wrist again, controlling my impulsiveness. He placed my hand on his length and held it there. My fingers explored and wrapped around it, my thumb rubbing over the bulbous head. When I tried to slip my hand lower to feel the rest of the goods, he stopped me, placing my hands behind my back again. "That's enough for now."

I pouted, pushing my lower lip out.

Tom leaned down and nipped it between his teeth. "Be a good girl and come for me, then I'll let you play with my cock all you like."

Yes, please!

"I'll be good," I promised.

"I know you will be," he said with a kiss to my temple. "Now, where to begin?" he mused, as he walked his fingers across my collarbone to the straps of my bra. He eased down one strap and then the other, letting them hang off my shoulders. "I've been dying to play with these beautiful tits." Hooking his fingers into the cups of my bra, he dragged them against my nipples, never once breaking eye contact.

Back and forth.

Back and forth.

Back and forth until my nipples were so hard they could cut glass.

"You're teasing me," I whimpered as my knees wobbled.

"Yes, I am. I'm getting you good and wet."

My pussy clenched. "I'm already wet."

"I don't believe you."

"Then check for yourself," I said, jutting out my chin and daring him to touch me where I wanted it most.

He pulled his fingers from my bra and wrapped one hand around my wrists behind my back, holding me in place. The other went right to my panties. Pulling the silk aside, he ran two fingers from my pussy to my clit, making me tremble. "Look at you, soaking your panties for me. Such a good girl." He brought those two fingers to his lips and sucked them inside as I watched with rapt attention. "Fucking sweet as sugar. I knew you would be. I can't wait to have my face between your legs."

I whimpered again, pulling at my wrists, wanting to touch him. "Please."

He tilted his head to the side. "Please, what?"

"Make me come," I begged, wanting to chase this feeling, but afraid it would disappear if he waited too long.

"So damn impatient." He dipped his fingers in my panties again, gathering more wetness and dragging it over my clit, where he teased the tiny nub in tight circles. It felt like heaven, and I knew, despite my earlier claim about not being able to come more than once, that it wouldn't take long.

I closed my eyes and let the pressure build, my muscles clenching with every rub of his fingers, like the click, click, click of a roller coaster ascending to its highest point. Every click wound me tighter, a spring coiled and ready to snap. "Tom... please."

He slipped his hand lower and filled me with his fingers. They crooked inside me and pressed on the magic spot no man had ever bothered to find. With his thumb rubbing my clit and his fingers massaging my G-spot, I was flung over the edge in a free fall that sent me soaring through loops and spirals on the most fantastic ride of my life. My body shook and fireworks exploded behind my eyelids in blinding bursts of color. All my synapses fired at once, turning my blood into white-hot lava. I quivered and quaked until my body gave out and I collapsed against Tom's chest, my breath ragged.

He lifted my chin and smirked. "That's one. Count for me, Aurora."

"One," I panted, though technically, it was two.

Tom picked me up and laid me in the middle of the bed. "You want me to stop?" he asked, straddling my legs.

I shook my head, still incapable of words. I couldn't remember the last time I came that hard.

"Good girl." He reached under my back and undid my bra. Pulling the straps down my arms, he lifted the lace away. He licked his lips as he pinned my wrists over my head in one hand and stared down at me. "So fucking gorgeous. I've dreamed about these tits. Jacked off to them. Imagined my dick pumping between them. You made me come so hard, you dirty girl."

His filthy words made me even wetter. The head of his cock peeked out from his boxers, a pearl of precum beaded on the tip. I bucked my hips, trying to get closer. Trying to get some friction. I'd never felt so wanton in my life. So needy. So horny. So filled with lust. "I'm waiting for number two," I gasped. "Or you could fuck me." It seemed like the quickest route to gratification for him, especially since coming again was highly unlikely for me.

Like he read my mind, Tom clucked his tongue at me in disapproval. "There will be no fucking tonight, angel. Tonight is about pleasure without penetration. You will come again."

Well, damn. Though I ached to feel him move inside me, the prospect of him fulfilling that promise outweighed my disappointment at not having sex.

He traced over my breasts with a featherlight touch, his fingers barely grazing my heated skin. "Let's see if I can make you orgasm from playing with your tits." He lowered his head and circled one hard nipple with his tongue, then blew cool air on the puckered tip, sending chills down my spine before flicking it with quick lashes. He squeezed and kneaded my breast, making my toes curl, before pulling the peak between his lips and grazing it with his teeth.

He gave my other nipple the same attention. Licking and sucking and nibbling. His mouth doing delicious things to me.

"Tom." I shuddered and moaned, arching my back and pushing my breasts toward his face. Wanting to touch him, I tugged at my wrists, but he wasn't letting go. The sense of having no control was both frustrating and erotic.

This dominating side of Tom was surprising, but it wasn't unwelcome. I trusted him implicitly to take care of me. Without worrying about having to fake an orgasm, I was able to let go and enjoy the experience. To get out of my mind and into the moment. To feel instead of think.

My head thrashed from side to side. "Please."

He continued his assault on my breasts and rubbed his cock between my legs. I was ready to combust from overstimulation and the need to have him inside me. His hard steel against my throbbing clit pushed me closer and closer to the edge. He gyrated his hips, grinding into me.

And that was it.

Game over.

I spiraled into another orgasm, my pussy wanting to be filled so bad, but clenching around nothing. It was sweet torture. Endorphins swam in my head, making my brain foggy. Every muscle in my body went as limp as a noodle.

Tom breathed in my ear, "Count, Aurora."

"Two," I gasped.

"Give me one more."

I shook my head. "No. I can't take any more. You proved your point."

"One more," he insisted. "Then I'll let you rest."

I was about to object when he scooted down my legs and pulled off my panties. I was too tired to be embarrassed about how wet I was and too turned on to care.

Starting at my ankle, he peppered kisses along the inside of my leg to the back of my knee and placed it over his shoulder. Then he kissed the inside of my opposite thigh and hooked that leg over his shoulder too. My ass was off the mattress, and my lady parts were inches from his face.

"You're dripping for me. I can't wait to taste you again. To fill you full of my fingers and feel you from the inside. Do you want that?"

Before I could answer, he buried his face between my legs and feasted. His tongue lashed inside me, licking up my release. I squeezed my thighs around his head and fisted the comforter. "Fuck! Oh god... more!"

I didn't think I could come again, but Tom was dead set on proving me wrong. He pushed my legs farther apart and set them on the mattress, his thumbs digging into my thighs. "I can't get enough of you."

Every lap of his tongue brought me closer to a third...yes, third... orgasm. My mind spun, my heart raced, and my body hummed. I was foolish to doubt this man could do whatever he put his mind to. Maybe he really did have superpowers.

"Tom," I gasped as he started working his magic on my clit, first flicking it with the tip of his tongue, then sucking it between his lips. He fucked me with two fingers while his mouth did unspeakable dirty things to me... nipping, licking, lashing. Eating me with the voraciousness of a hungry tiger.

The tingles began to build again, or maybe they had never gone away. I wasn't sure of anything except that I was helpless to stop them. I wrapped my legs tighter around his shoulders and dug my heels into his back. Tom was driving this pleasure ride, and I was a mere passenger, hanging on for my life.

He growled and it went straight to my core. My thighs shook uncontrollably. My back arched. My hands gripped his head. Riding a thin line between pleasure and pain, I wanted both to push him away and pull him closer. It was too much but not enough. My entire body pulled tight as a rubber band ready to snap.

He added another finger... stretching me, filling me, taking me to the brink as they pumped in and out of me faster and faster. His other hand slid up my body and pinched my nipple.

I detonated like a rocket, and filthy words flew from my mouth in an incoherent stream. Flames ripped through my body, sending tremors to my fingers and toes. A sea of stars blurred behind my eyelids as I soared, not just to the moon, but to planets far outside our galaxy. My body floated in both space and time, as I drifted on the waves of ecstasy that consumed me. Never had I experienced this kind of pleasure. I felt drugged—happy and dopey at the same time.

As I writhed with pleasure, I was barely aware of Tom's fingers still gently pumping inside me, coaxing out the last of my orgasm. My eyes fluttered open into thin slits, enough to watch him suck his fingers clean. "Count, Aurora."

"Three," I whispered, barely able to keep my eyes from closing.

He smiled like he'd won something sacred. "Good girl. I think that's enough for the night." Tom pulled back the covers and tucked me in, then crawled in next to me. With my head on his chest and his arms wrapped around me, I was warm and cozy. "You didn't get your turn," I said sleepily.

He brushed my hair away from my face. "Seeing you come for me was more than enough."

"You're too good to me. My own personal superhero."

He chuckled. "I think you're getting delirious."

The feeling of his touch was still on my skin as exhaustion pulled me under. I faintly remembered him kissing my forehead and saying, "Dream well, angel."

And for the first time in a long time, I knew I would.

Chapter 19
Tom

Everything in me wanted to stay in Aurora's bed with her wrapped in my arms, her cheek pressed against my chest, and the subtle scent of her coconut shampoo tickling my senses, but we hadn't discussed me spending the night and I didn't want to assume it would be okay with her. Besides, I had a hard-on the size of Texas in my boxers that refused to be ignored, and I'd rather take care of it in private.

When her breathing evened out and soft little snores filled the quiet room, I slipped out of her sheets and pulled on my shorts. Even though it felt a bit creepy, I stood and watched my angel sleep, admiring her beauty for a few more minutes before sneaking out. Being sure not to let the beads on her bedroom door rattle, I crept through her apartment, fighting my urge to stay and curl up next to her warm, soft body.

Ailuros sat on the back of the couch staring at me, as if she knew what I'd done to her mom and was judging me. "She liked it," I whispered.

Surprisingly, the cat didn't run away. I reached out with one finger and scratched her head. "You and I are going to be friends." She hissed and jumped down, making me roll my eyes. *Damn cat.*

Slipping out the door and into my own apartment, I went right to the bathroom and dropped my shirt into the hamper. I leaned on the counter and stared at myself in the mirror, my insecurities creeping in. My hair was ruffled, my eyes dilated, and there was a scratch on my shoulder where Aurora dug her nails. "Don't get full of yourself. She's too good for you, and you know it."

Tonight was everything I fantasized about. Seeing her fall apart over and over again under my touch made my chest puff up. Clearly, the men she'd been with before never bothered to take their time with her. I hated thinking about her past. She never talked about it, but I imagined a string of guys had shown up on her doorstep. How could they not? She was gorgeous and sweet and kind.

Every man's dream girl.

Looking down at my tented shorts, I quickly undid them and let my cock spring free. I could still feel Aurora's hand on it, gripping me tightly and rubbing her needy fingers over the head like it was her favorite toy. It took every bit of control I had at that moment not to pull it out and let her suck it right then and there. Now, I was paying the price. My dick was an angry purple color, and it hadn't softened a bit. So goddamn hard it actually hurt.

Turning on the shower, I pushed my shorts and underwear down my legs and dropped them in the hamper with my shirt before stepping in. All I could think about was her naked body. I could still see her luscious tits, her pretty pink pussy glistening for me, and that goddamn birthmark on the inside of her left thigh.

Squirting shampoo in one hand and leaning the other against the wall, I wrapped my fist around my cock as hot water sluiced down my back. My hand moved in lazy strokes. I pictured her long legs wrapped around my neck as I ate her pussy, making her come on my tongue. I imagined what it would be like to fuck her. To slide my cock in and out of her tight body. To have her clench around me when she came.

My hand moved faster, shuttling up and down my dick and squeezing so hard I thought I'd explode. I licked my lips, and the taste of her arousal damn near sent me over the edge.

I continued pumping my dick, jerking it harder and faster. My balls pulled tight, and the familiar tingle of an impending orgasm started at the base of my spine. Fire raced through my veins as long ropes of cum shot all over the shower wall and slid down the wet tiles.

Completely depleted and breathing hard, I leaned my head against the wall and let the water scald me. I was so fucking done for when it came to Aurora. She had me addicted in the best possible way.

I'd fallen for her hard and no other woman would ever suffice. She was it for me.

The next morning, I went for a run and stopped at the little café on the corner, picking up coffee and breakfast sandwiches for Aurora and me. I waited until after nine to knock on her door, figuring she might have slept in.

She answered, wrapped in a short robe and her hair still mussed. "What did you do to me last night? I slept like a damn rock," she said, pulling the door wide for me to come in.

"Good morning to you too. I didn't hear you complaining when my tongue was inside you." Her cheeks turned a beautiful shade of pink at the mention of our activities. Chuckling, I held up the paper bag and drink carrier in my hands. "I brought you nourishment."

Perking up, she reached out with grabby hands. "Thank you," she said, peeking into the bag and taking a whiff. "God, this smells divine."

Her stomach rumbled. "Sounds like I'm just in time. I bought us bacon, egg, and cheese biscuits. I hope that's okay."

"It's perfect," she said with a soft smile, carrying the bag over to the tiny kitchen table and taking the sandwiches out. "What's in the cups?"

I took her drink out of the carrier and handed it to her. "French vanilla latte with nonfat milk and three pumps of sugar-free French vanilla syrup."

She froze. "That's exactly my favorite."

I tapped my temple. "I told you I remember lots of things and that was an important one. Gotta make sure my girl gets what she wants."

She took a long sip of her latte and licked her lips. "Where have you been all my life, Tom Bently?"

I held my arms out wide. "Right here in Vegas, waiting for you. At least for the last few years."

Aurora giggled. "Well, I should have moved here sooner. Are you drinking a latte too?"

"Nope, plain black coffee for me. I never got into the fancy stuff. The town in Colorado where I grew up didn't have a big demand for lattes and cappuccinos."

"God," she said, holding her cup with both hands and taking another sip. "Specialty coffee is practically a religion in California."

"I've never been one to follow trends. I tend to stick with tried and true."

She quirked an eyebrow. "Like your bow ties?"

I frowned. "Don't go hating on my bow ties. They're classic."

"I'm not sure everyone would agree, but they suit you," she teased. Unwrapping her sandwich and taking a generous bite, she hummed her approval. "Thank you so much for this. I was starving."

"I figured you would be," I said, unwrapping my own breakfast.

Her cheeks flushed, her gaze dropping to the tabletop. "Speaking of last night... I feel bad."

"What? Why?" There was nothing she should have felt bad about.

"Because you didn't get to..." She waved her hand toward my crotch. "When I woke up, you were gone. I thought you might have been disappointed or mad that I fell asleep and didn't return the favor."

I put my sandwich down and took her hand in mine. "First of all, last night was about you, not me. Second, just because I didn't come, don't think that I didn't enjoy every second of it, because I did. Third, I didn't know if you would be okay with me spending the night, but I wanted to stay. Fourth, I took care of myself, so no worries. And most importantly, I couldn't ever be mad at you." I lifted her hand and kissed the back of it. "You're my angel."

Chapter 20
Aurora

I couldn't ever be mad at you.

Guilt swam in my belly.

"Pfft. I'm no angel." Being in Vegas, searching for another man who was slated to be my future husband made me the exact opposite. I was lying to him and lying to myself, thinking this could last.

He reached across the table and pushed a lock of my sleep-mussed hair behind my ear. "You're the sweetest, kindest woman I've ever met," he insisted. "Everyone here adores you. I'm pretty sure you were born with a halo, and nothing could convince me otherwise."

When he spoke like that, I wanted to believe him. Had we met under different circumstances, maybe…

But no matter what I wanted my future to look like, no matter how much I wanted Tom to be part of it, my future had been predetermined without my consent. I should have stopped him before we got too attached, but I was afraid it was already too late for both of us.

Unless I didn't find Aidan.

There was no guarantee I would find him, in which case I would be free.

I could have stopped looking once I met Tom, but Aidan had already sacrificed so much for me, and I owed him. To make sure he was safe and well and not living on the streets. Aidan was my ride or die. Always had been.

Tom deserved to know about him, yet it was a conversation I'd avoided. I stood and tightened the belt on my robe. My hands twisted together as I paced in front of the small table, my bare feet echoing on the wood floor while I tried to find the right words.

Tom stared at me like he thought he'd done something wrong. "What is it?"

"I have to tell you something and I'm afraid." Starting with honesty now seemed like a moot point, since I'd already told so many lies. Well, not so much lies as omissions of the truth. It was a technicality I was holding on to.

"Why would you be afraid to tell me anything?" he asked, straightening his glasses.

"Because you're going to be mad and I can't stand the thought of you being mad at me." Okay, that was a start. So far, so good... two truths, no lies.

Tom scrunched up his brows, confusion written all over his face. "Don't tell me you faked it last night, because then *I* would feel bad."

I stopped my pacing. "What? No." I slashed my hands through the air. "I didn't fake anything, though I was worried I was going to have to. But no, last night was amazing. You're amazing. No one has ever made me feel like that before. Thank you."

"Aurora, you never have to thank me for making you a priority. Making you happy makes me happy."

I rolled my eyes. "Ugh! Why do you have to say such sweet things and be so nice? It makes this even harder."

"In my experience, saying hard things is like getting a cavity filled. You sit around and agonize over it for days, when the actual experience is relatively painless and over before you know it."

I crinkled my nose. "I've never had a cavity, but I'll take your word for it." He was right. I needed to alleviate this guilt and that started with telling the truth… or at least some of it. There was too much. It was too heavy. So, I decided to start with the easiest deception, although none of this felt easy.

Shaking out my hands and taking a deep breath, I blurted, "I didn't move to Vegas for a job."

I stared at Tom and waited for a reaction. Anything… a downturn of his lips, a narrowing of his eyebrows, a flare of his nostrils. But I didn't see any of that. Instead, he leaned back against the chair, stone-faced, and took a sip of his very practical black coffee.

My nerves ratcheted to ten. I expected him to say something, anything but the silence I was getting. "Aren't you mad? I wouldn't blame you. I didn't tell you the truth."

He leaned forward and put his elbows on his knees, not giving anything away. "I'm not mad. I knew it was a lie. You were evasive about it, and it didn't make any sense. Nobody moves across state lines solely for a remote job, Aurora."

My brief bit of relief was overshadowed by confusion. "Why didn't you call me out on it?"

"Because I could tell you weren't ready to talk about it. That you'd tell me in your own time. Whatever you've been keeping from me, I'm sure you have your reasons. Are you ready to tell me now?"

My eyes welled with tears. "Yes." Not only did I hate lying, but talking about Aidan made me sad. I couldn't tell him everything, but I could give him this small piece of me.

"Then come sit back down, finish your breakfast, and tell me." He motioned to the chair I'd practically jumped out of.

Wrapping my robe even tighter around me like it could provide an extra layer of protection, I sat and stared at my folded hands in my lap. "Do you remember when I told you my best friend became homeless and disappeared?"

"Yes, that's why working at Helping Hands is so important to you. Why you dedicate so much time to it."

I nodded. "That's true, but there's more to it. I came here to look for him. Every day when I go to the shelter or on an outreach run, I hope I'll see his face or find some trace of him. It's why I didn't hesitate when Kendra asked me to help her build a database. He's got to be here somewhere." I peeked up at him, prepared to see disgust on Tom's face at my revelation.

His throat bobbed, but the rest of him was stoic. "Him?"

"Yes, him. His name is Aidan and he's been my best friend since I was five. We were inseparable growing up. He's everything that's good and right in this world. He made sacrifices for me that I can never repay."

Tom ran his hand over his lips, taking in my words. I could see the conflict on his face and the questions in his eyes. I wanted to answer all of them, but I couldn't... not yet.

"Say something," I begged.

He leaned his forehead on his hands, then dragged them down his face. "Do you love him?"

"Yes," I answered honestly. "I'll always love him, but I'm not in love with him."

"I see." He tapped his fingers on the table in a hypnotic rhythm. "Help me understand. Explain."

I took a deep breath, deciding where to start. I wouldn't tell him about our parents' insistence we marry, because I was still hoping we could convince them otherwise, but I could give him some truth. A story that wasn't laced with lies. "After college, Aidan enlisted in the military. It didn't take long for him to get sent to the Middle East. He'd always been upbeat, a jokester, the person who could capture the attention of an entire room with one of his stories. But when he came home, he was a different man. His eyes were blank and there was a sternness about him that I didn't recognize. He'd seen things no one should see and done things no one should have to do. He had PTSD and self-medicated with weed and alcohol.

"After a year of trying to push through on his own, he'd become a shadow of himself. The weed made him numb and the alcohol made him mean. He stayed holed up in his apartment, pushing away everyone who cared about him. When he finally went to rehab, it got worse. He hated the meds and talking about his issues. I went to visit him at the rehab facility, and we got in a big fight. I told him he needed to get his shit together and I didn't want to see him again until he did. Next thing I knew, he checked himself out of rehab, disconnected his phone, and disappeared. No one could find him. It was my fault. He was my best friend, and I turned my back on him."

Tom wiped the tears I didn't even realize were rolling down my cheeks. "I'm sorry. I wouldn't wish that on anyone, but that still doesn't explain why you're *here*."

I went over to the kitchen drawer and pulled out the postcard Aidan sent me with a picture of palm trees and casinos. Across the top, it said, *"Welcome to Fabulous Las Vegas."* I handed it to Tom. "Read it."

He flipped the postcard over. *"I'm sorry I couldn't be the person you wanted me to be and I'm even sorrier that I hurt you. I hope by leaving, it sets you free from the burdens I put on you. I'm not made for that life anymore. I have all I need, a backpack and a sleeping bag. Don't worry about me, I'll find my way. Love always~ Aidan."* Tom put the postcard down and pushed it back across the table. "That's why you're here."

"Yes. It was my fault he left, and I don't want him to think I don't care anymore. It breaks my heart to think of him living on the street. Yes, I was mad at him, but he deserves better than living alone among strangers. He deserves to know someone still gives a shit." I jutted my chin out in defiance, because although I was sorry I lied to Tom, I wasn't sorry I was trying to find Aidan.

Tom rubbed his lips together, his brows furrowing as he thought. "I have another question."

His inquisitive nature made me even more nervous than telling him about Aidan. Whatever he wanted to know, I had to be honest though. I'd already kept too much from him. "Okay," I said cautiously.

"What happens when you find your friend? Are you staying in Vegas or trotting back to California?" There was definitely a hint of aggravation in his voice, and I couldn't blame him.

This was a question I'd been dreading, because there was no easy answer until I found Aidan. I wrung my hands in my lap. "I don't know. My family—"

"You don't know?" he asked incredulously. "You don't know. Well, that's perfect. Here I am in a relationship—are we in a relationship?—with a woman who doesn't even know if she's sticking around. Fuck my life."

"Let me explain," I pleaded. Shit. I didn't want to tell him about my impending marriage, but...

"Let you explain? God, Aurora, this is a lot. I'm a bit overwhelmed to put it mildly. You should have told me," he insisted.

I threw my hands in the air. "How? How could I tell you I was here looking for another man, especially after I started having feelings for you? You would have never given me a chance."

"You don't know that." He stood and walked to the door. "I'm not mad. I'm disappointed you didn't trust me enough to share the truth with me. That you let me fall for you despite not knowing if you were going to hang around."

His disappointment stung more than anger. I had no one to blame but myself, but I took a cheap shot to assuage my own guilt. "I practically threw myself at you from the day I met you and the only time you showed interest was when you got hammered at the wedding. I figured, what did it matter?"

There was a slight tic in his jaw, but other than that, Tom showed zero emotion. "The truth always matters, Aurora."

"You're walking out on me too? Does this mean we're over?" Every fear I had about telling Tom about Aidan was materializing in front of my eyes. "I'm sorry."

He opened the door and looked back at me. "I know you are. I'm not saying we're over, but I need time to process. I hope you find your friend." Then he walked out, letting the door click softly behind him.

I fell to my knees and sobbed into my hands. I'd found the perfect man, and I fucked it up. Technically, I didn't owe him my life story. Technically, it wasn't his business if I wanted to find Aidan. Technically, I had no formal commitment to Tom. We'd gone on a few dates and messed around. That was all.

But none of those technicalities made me feel any better. I hurt him and that was the last thing I wanted to do. I couldn't stop hurting the people I cared about. It wasn't fair I had to choose between the man I loved and the man I was falling in love with. It was an impossible choice.

And at the end of this, there was a chance I'd get neither.

Chapter 21
Tom

I *was* mad. So fucking mad.

"Son of a bitch!" I smashed my hand through the bedroom wall and immediately regretted it. Pulling my hand from the drywall, I cradled it to my chest. It was stupid and impulsive. I never let my anger get the best of me, but I hated that she lied to me.

I knew there was more to the damn story about why she moved here. A dozen different scenarios had run through my head, but never did I think it was to look for a guy. A friend, she insisted. Who knew if that was even the truth? And if it was, she might not even be sticking around when she found him.

Ugh!

Going to the kitchen, I grabbed a dish towel and filled it with ice. The cold soothed the scrapes on my knuckles, but it did nothing for the scrapes on my heart.

I felt betrayed.

Deceived.

Foolish.

I knew she was too good to be true, yet I let my stupid heart fall for her anyway.

Pacing back and forth across my kitchen floor, I recounted everything Aurora told me.

Aidan. Fucking Aidan.

Her best friend.

When she told me about her best friend disappearing, I assumed it was a girl.

That was on me. You know what they say about assuming making an ass out of you and me? Well, that was true. I was an ass. A giant one.

And on top of that, she might not even be staying in Vegas. *What the fuck?*

My phone chimed with an incoming text. Hoping it was Aurora, but also hoping it wasn't, I pulled it out and checked my messages.

Charli: I'm downstairs. Can I come up? Trying to respect boundaries. ;)

I didn't need my sister all up in my business. I'd never shared details of my love life with her before, and I didn't plan on starting now.

Me: No, Charlotte.

I threw the phone on the kitchen counter, but it quickly chimed again.

Charli: Are you mad at me?

Rolling my eyes, I quickly typed out a response.

Me: No, Charlotte. Not everything is about you.

Charli: Okay that's two times you've used my formal name. I'm coming up... THOMAS

Tossing my phone back on the counter, I took the ice off my hand and stretched my fingers, testing the soreness. It wasn't awful, but my knuckles were red and angry. There was no way I'd be able to hide them from my sister.

Before I could even come up with an explanation, there was a knock on my door. "Thomas Bently, open this damn door!"

If I ignored her, she'd keep knocking. When Charli was determined about something, nothing would stop her, so I swung the door open and stepped aside. "Why are you here?" I asked gruffly. She didn't deserve my anger, but I had to channel it somewhere.

She marched inside and put her hands on her hips. "Why are you so fucking grumpy?"

"I'm not," I barked, shutting the door. My neighbors didn't need a show, especially the one across the hall.

"You sure as fuck are. You look like someone pissed all over your keyboard."

Usually, I could appreciate her sense of humor, but nothing about this was funny. "It's been a rough morning, okay. I don't really want to talk about it," I said, running a hand through my hair.

She grabbed my wrist and stared at my raw knuckles. "Who did you punch?"

"Nobody."

She pressed her lips together in a thin line. "The last time you punched someone, you were in third grade."

"Yeah, well, that kid on the bus wouldn't quit pulling your pigtails. He had it coming." I might not have ever been a tough guy, but picking on my sister crossed a line. Getting suspended for three days was worth it.

Charli crossed her hands over her heart. "You were my hero that day; Harold Trumble never bothered me again." Hands back on her hips, she asked, "So who picked on Aurora?"

"Nobody. I..." *Fuck it.* I'd reamed Aurora about telling the truth and I was contemplating lying to my sister. That didn't make me any better. "I punched a wall."

Her eyebrows went up.

"Don't judge."

"I'm not judging," she said. "I'm wondering what could have happened between last night and this morning that pissed you off."

Last night. Last night was a dream come true, and this morning was a harsh reality check that it was just that... a dream. "Aurora and I got into a disagreement."

"A disagreement? And how did punching the wall solve it?"

"It didn't," I said, rubbing my sore knuckles. "I'm still mad."

Charli pursed her lips. "I see. Want to talk about it?"

"Not really." I started pacing again, wearing a groove into the hardwood floor, and told her anyway. "You know how much I hate lying, and she lied to me."

Charli sat on the edge of the couch, waiting for me to elaborate. "About?"

"She told me she moved here for a job, but she didn't. Her friend became homeless and she's here looking for him."

Him.

Saying it aloud pissed me off all over again, but I recounted Aurora's whole story to my sister.

Charli's lips turned down. "That's so sad."

"It is, but that's not the point. The point is she lied about it."

"Actually, it's not. Her relationship with her friend is her business. You're not entitled to that. And if you want to get high and mighty, she betrayed her friend's trust by telling you anything about his life. You weren't entitled to that either."

I stopped dead in my tracks. What I was entitled to or not didn't matter to me at the moment. It was the lying that burned my ass. "She lied about why she moved here."

"Who cares why she's here? Does it change any of the things you love about her? If anything, it shows she has loyalty to those she cares about."

Still stuck on being right, I pointed out the most damaging fact. "It's a guy."

Charli tapped her fingers against her lips. "You're jealous."

"I'm not jealous." I was. I was so fucking jealous. All I could picture was a good-looking California dude, with a dark tan and a body built by beach volleyball. Some guy who could double as a romance cover model or star in the latest rom-com movie. Not some geeky guy like me, who spent his days behind a computer screen.

"Yes, you are. Let me put this in a different perspective. If something happened to Penny, would you want to help her?"

I rolled my eyes. "Doubtful that would happen. She has Brett."

Charli let out a huff. "You're acting like a child. Humor me. If Penny needed your help, would you help her? Even if you were in a relationship with Aurora?"

"Of course, I would. Penny's been my friend for years." I could see where this was going, but I wasn't ready to concede yet.

"And if Aurora broke it off with you because you wanted to help a friend? Would you still want to help Penny?"

Fuck. I ground my teeth. "Yes. I would owe it to Penny."

"There you have it," she said with a wave of her hand.

Digging my heels in deeper, I held onto my tiny bit of leverage. "She still lied about it. And when she finds him, she might... *might*, be moving back to California. What the fuck is that shit?"

"Oh, get the fuck over yourself. If you want to lose the best thing that ever happened to you over some perceived slight, be my guest. You're not entitled to her past. If she wanted to be with him, she never would have started dating you. And as far as her moving back to California, it isn't exactly a bad place to run a tech business. You could move with her. Security isn't only in Las Vegas... it's global. Who cares where the company is based?"

"Brett is here. He's the one I made the deal with."

"Pfft! Brett has businesses all over the country. It's a short flight. He might even like the idea of branching out."

Though I didn't want to admit it, everything Charli said made sense.

"And maybe, just maybe, she didn't want to tell you because she was afraid you'd act like this," she added. "It's quite unbecoming, by the way."

I sighed, letting go of some of my anger. "When did you get so smart?"

She stood and patted me on the chest. "It's in the genes. You're welcome." Charli walked to the door and opened it. "Make things right with her."

"Wait. Why did you even come here to begin with?"

"Oh," she said excitedly. "I came to talk about your launch party. You can't come being"—she waved a hand up and down my body—"well, being dressed like you. You're going to need to look classy. Hunter has volunteered to take you shopping and I'm going to take Aurora. Our treat, and no arguments. So put your big-boy panties on and fix things with her. Toodles." Charli tossed her hair over her shoulder and walked out the door, leaving me with my jaw hanging open.

I couldn't deal with the thought of going shopping with Hunter, but I mulled over everything else Charli said. It made sense, especially when I looked at it from a different perspective. I'd do anything to help Penny. Aurora felt the same way about Aidan. Who was I to make her feel bad about it? And how bad could it be to live in a state with white sand for miles? She hadn't asked me to go with her, but I could. Heck, I'd moved to Las Vegas for Charli without a thought. It wasn't that far of a stretch to do it for the woman I was falling in love with.

Damn it! I acted exactly the way she thought I would—like a jealous asshole.

I didn't create a safe space for her and that was on me.

Fuck!

Grabbing my keys off the counter, I headed out. I had some errands to run, least of all a trip to the hardware store to fix the fist-sized hole in my bedroom wall.

I prided myself on making rational decisions and every decision I'd made this morning was so far from rational, I'd embarrassed myself. I was being an entitled prick, and I didn't like that guy. He wasn't who I was.

I owed her an apology for not accepting her apology. For not fully listening to her. For not being a standup guy. For making her feel bad about her loyalty to her friend.

What a douchebag.

But a simple apology wouldn't do. It had to be something meaningful that would assure her I was in for the long haul. That I'd support her. Do anything for her.

I hoped it would be enough.

Chapter 22
Aurora

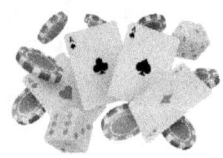

My father's phone call couldn't have been more ill-timed if he had planned it.

With my heart in ruins, I reluctantly pushed the green button on the screen and held it to my ear. "Hello, Father."

"What's your progress?" No *hello*. No *how are you doing?* Straight to business as usual.

Feeling brave, I couldn't resist being a brat. "I'm doing good. How are you?"

He sighed. "Please, Aurora, I don't have time for chitchat. What is your progress in finding Aidan?"

I curled myself into a ball on the couch and rubbed Ailuros's soft head as she purred by my side. It was amazing how much comfort a furry companion could give, especially when you were so far away from home with no real friends. "I'm working at Helping Hands today and going on another outreach run tomorrow. Also, I'm helping build a database for the shelter. I'm hoping that if he shows up when I'm not there, it will give me some clues. I'm definitely making progress." That was another lie. I was no closer to finding him now than when I first moved to Vegas.

"Hope in one hand and shit in the other, Aurora. See which one fills up faster."

"Dad!"

"I'm serious. We've given you the time you requested as a gift. Both Aidan's father and I are running out of patience. Senator Huxley doesn't need pictures of his homeless son popping up on the internet. We're hiring a private investigator. It's better if we find him first and clean him up. Then the two of you can get married and we can put this nonsense behind us." PTSD wasn't nonsense. My father acted as if Aidan could flip a switch and turn it off.

"We don't want to get married." We'd told our parents this a dozen times, but they never listened.

"Not this again. Stop being difficult, Aurora. You two are perfect for each other. The deal has already been brokered. It's done."

My tears started again. "What about what we want? Don't we get a say in our own futures?"

"I don't see the problem. What could be better for your future than the joining of two powerful families? Everything you want will be at your fingertips. I've sacrificed everything for you. Marrying Aidan is the least you can do for me, for this family, to secure our future."

It was always about money with my dad. That and public perception. He'd built his kingdom and instead of being his daughter, I was now a company asset to be traded and bartered. Partnering with the Huxleys would give him more power, more influence, more prestige.

"I met someone," I blurted. My relationship with Tom was tenuous at best, but I still hoped he could forgive my deceptions. That we would find a way to move past our argument.

He growled. "Break it off. It's bad enough you're hanging out with homeless people; now you're hooking up with some Vegas hoodlum looking to jump on our coattails. What is wrong with you? Do you care at all about this family and our reputation? The future your grandfather built for you? It's ungrateful!"

"He's not a hoodlum. He's a nice guy and he doesn't even know who I am." Another thing I'd kept from Tom.

"Aidan's a nice guy. If he'd never joined the military, you two would already be married and we wouldn't be having this discussion. We were able to overlook his defiance because who doesn't love a war hero? But this has gone on long enough. You find him and bring him home, or there will be consequences."

"Consequences?"

"Don't act naive, Aurora. You know what your grandfather's will stated. Think about if this guy is worth losing everything you've been given and everything yet to come. If you don't align your priorities you'll end up on the street with the homeless people you claim to care about, and so will your mother and I. The company will be out of our hands. Is that what you want?"

"No." I sniffed. I'd never actually seen my grandfather's will—I'd been too young when he died—but I'd been told about the marriage clause repeatedly.

"Then get your head on straight. You're smarter than this, Aurora. If you don't find Aidan soon, we'll have no choice other than to find him for you."

"Give me more time. Please!"

My father sighed. "I don't want to fight with you. One month. That's what I'll give you."

"Thank you," I practically sobbed.

The call ended with no *goodbye* or *I love you*. Just a click followed by silence.

I was more determined to find Aidan than ever. If for no other reason than to know he was okay. Once I found him, we could discuss our options, make our own plan. No one else had to know.

He could live his life, and I would be free to be with Tom, if he even wanted me anymore. I snuggled Ailuros to my chest and pressed my face into her soft fur. She was my only friend. I was more alone now than when I first moved to Vegas.

My world was crumbling around me, and I was helpless to stop it.

Even with makeup, you could still see the redness around my eyes. I looked like hell, but coming to Helping Hands kept me from replaying the morning's events over and over in my head. The monotony of mindless work was exactly what I needed. After loading the coolers and arranging the fresh fruit in the baskets, I put on a hairnet and apron and prepped for serving.

At ninety degrees outside, you'd think spaghetti would be a poor dinner choice, but it kept bellies full, and no one complained about that. The line wrapped around the building, and I was glad I was helping, not just for Aidan, but for all the people who depended on Carl's cooking to make it through another day.

Kendra tapped me on the shoulder. "We have a new volunteer today. Will you show him the ropes for serving?"

It always made me happy when someone new showed up. Most newbies were doing community service hours and didn't stick around for very long after, but the help was always welcome. "Sure thing." I looked past her and my eyes almost popped out of my head. "He's the volunteer?"

Kendra looked between Tom and me. "You two know each other?"

"We do," Tom confirmed.

"Then I'll leave you to it," Kendra said with a shrug, walking away with her clipboard clutched to her chest.

"What are you doing here?" I asked, a bit of unintended sharpness in my voice. I didn't need him to make a scene. Not here.

He approached me much like you would a cornered dog, with caution and apprehension. "Because you're here. And if this is important to you, then it's important to me. I was an inconsiderate ass today and I hope you can forgive me."

I twisted my lips to the side. "True, but I was the one who didn't tell the truth. I owe you an apology."

He stepped closer, running the back of his fingers along my cheek. "You already did. I'm sorry I made you feel bad about trying to find your friend. If things were reversed, I wouldn't give up looking either."

"I can't give up. I should have been up-front about why I was here, but—"

He put a finger to my lips. "Yes, I wish you were honest, but I understand why you kept it from me. We don't know everything about each other yet, but I want us to. In time, I hope you can find it in yourself to trust me."

The tears that I'd kept at bay ran down my cheeks. "I want that too. I'm sorry."

He pulled me into a tight hug. "I know you are and so am I. I don't want to lose you over this."

"I don't want to lose you either." I held on to Tom as a lifeline, hoping that I'd find some way to keep him. My father's words echoed in my head, and I held on tighter. I didn't want to have to choose between my family and the man I was falling in love with.

He held me by the shoulders and rested his forehead against mine. "I bought you flowers, but it didn't seem right to bring them here."

He shouldn't have spent his money on me. Things were tight enough for him as it was. "You didn't need to buy me flowers. Are you really staying? Here, I mean. Are you volunteering?"

"I'd kinda be an asshole if I didn't. Besides, I need one of these cool hairnets," he said, snapping the elastic on mine.

My hands flew to my head in embarrassment. I'd completely forgotten I was wearing the hideous thing. Say what you want, but hairnets weren't a fashion statement that looked good on anyone. "Oh god."

"Looks sexy on you." He chuckled.

I playfully swatted his chest. "Now who's the liar?" I went to the cabinet in the back of the kitchen and grabbed an extra hairnet and an apron for him, then pushed them into his chest. "Laugh it up."

Tom took the hairnet from me and stretched it to fit on top of his head. "How do I look?" he asked, holding out his arms.

"Ridiculous." I pulled it down so it covered all his hair.

He put the apron on and tied it behind his back. "Put me to work."

I glanced at the clock. "We open the doors in five minutes. Our guests will come in there"—I pointed to the far door—"and start the line there." I pointed to the end of the counter. "Everyone gets the same amount, but sometimes, I give a little extra if they look like they need it. I'll scoop the salad and you're in charge of the pasta. They'll get their own bread, drinks, and extras. We never comment on how much they take because this might be their only meal of the day. Also, try to make eye contact and smile, even if they're missing all their teeth or look like they crawled out of the gutter. These people get judged enough; they don't need us judging too. This is a safe space for them, and we want to keep it that way."

Tom stared at me.

"What?" I asked.

"You're passionate about this. I can tell how much you care. It's about more than finding Aidan for you, isn't it?"

I wiped my sweaty palms on my apron. "It wasn't when I started, but yeah, it is now."

"If I wasn't already proud to be your boyfriend, I would be now."

Considering the lecture I got from my father this morning, Tom's words meant more to me than he knew. My parents had expectations. I never got to hear they were proud of me when I met those expectations, but I sure heard about it when I fell short. Having Tom say he was proud made me warm and fuzzy inside. It was a testament that my work at Helping Hands mattered.

"Thank you. That means a lot to me." I lifted up on my toes and gave him a kiss on the cheek.

Carl came over with a huge pan of pasta and plunked it down in the warming tray.

"Carl, this is my boyfriend, Tom." It was the first time I'd officially referred to Tom as my boyfriend and it felt right.

He reached out to shake Tom's hand. "Good to meet ya. Aurora's one of my favorites. I hope you know you've got a keeper here."

Tom wrapped his arm around my shoulders and gave them a squeeze. "I do, sir."

"Sir? Ha! I ain't been called that since my time in the Marines." He looked at our bare hands. "Get your gloves on. It's gonna be a busy one today. Everybody loves my spaghetti," he said before going back to the kitchen.

I pulled two pairs from the box on the counter, handing a set to Tom. "Don't let him fool you. Everything Carl cooks is amazing. You ready?" I asked, pulling on my gloves.

"When it comes to you... always."

I hoped that was true, because when I found Aidan... *if* I found Aidan... shit was going to hit the fan.

Chapter 23
Tom

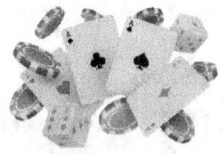

Watching Aurora interact with the people at the shelter made my immature response to her confession this morning even worse. Seeing her cry this morning over her missing friend had put me on the defensive, which was totally unfair. She'd done nothing but support me with my security software; the least I could do was support her too. I wanted to help Aurora find Aidan so she could put her worry to rest. I didn't know him, but that didn't really matter. If it was important to her, it was important to me.

And when... *if*... I met Aidan, I hoped he had a third eye, a horn growing out of his head, and gnarly teeth. Not gonna lie, that would make me feel a lot better. There was something intimidating about a man who'd practically known Aurora her whole life. He knew things about her that I never would. They shared a lifetime of memories. He took up a lot of space on her timeline; I was a mere blip.

Whatever this was between us, I needed to solidify it before Aurora found Aidan. That might have been selfish on my part, but regardless of the assurances she'd given me, there was still something niggling at the back of my brain and I'd learned not to ignore that feeling.

But with the start-up at Mystique, I would be lucky to spend quality time with her at all, let alone have time to spend with her at the shelter. It was a shitty situation, but I couldn't risk fucking up everything I'd worked so hard for. Not for Brett. Not for Mystique. And most importantly, not for myself.

There were long, grueling hours of work in my future and, hopefully, decadent nights with my girl. Somewhere in between, I'd find time to sleep, preferably with a head of blond hair on my chest.

With our bellies full of Carl's spaghetti, which he insisted we indulge in, I followed Aurora home. I pulled my car in next to hers and grabbed the flowers and gift bags from my front seat. Looking at my purchases now, I wondered if she'd think they were lame. Buying an *I'm sorry* gift was more stressful than I thought it would be.

"What's this?" Aurora said as she locked her car.

I handed her the bouquet of wildflowers. "An apology."

She held them to her nose and inhaled. "Thank you. You didn't need to buy me flowers."

"There's more." I held up the gift bags.

She took them and peeked inside. "I don't want to open these in the parking lot. Come up to my apartment?"

"I was hoping you'd ask." After the way we left things this morning, I wasn't sure where we stood. I'd seen the situation as black and white when really several shades of gray existed in between. It was embarrassing that it took my little sister to make me understand that.

When we got to her apartment, Ailuros danced around in circles, meowing at the top of her lungs. So desperate in her attempt to get fed, she didn't even hiss at me. It was progress.

Aurora laughed. "You'd think the little fur ball hasn't eaten in days instead of hours." She set the gift bags on the counter and emptied a can of food into the kitten's bowl, who happily lapped it up like it was her last meal. Then she turned to me and picked up one of the gift bags. "If anything, I should have bought you a gift. I was the one in the wrong."

"This one first." I took the bag from her and handed her the other one. "I'm the one who reacted immaturely. I should have stayed and talked to you instead of leaving in a huff like some teenage jerkwad. It wasn't fair and I promise to do better."

"True, but I didn't make it easy. I should have told you about Aidan from the start. And as far as me staying in Vegas, I—"

I put a finger to her lips. The last thing I wanted to discuss was her leaving. Instead, I wanted to live in this little bubble we'd created where the outside world didn't matter. "Let's not talk about it. There will be plenty of time to figure out logistics later. We're together now; that's what matters."

"Are you sure?" she asked skeptically.

"Positive. Now open your gift."

Did I know I was in avoidance mode?

Absolutely.

Did I know it might bite me in the ass later?

Abso-fucking-lutely.

Did I care at the moment?

Not a bit.

She pulled out the tissue paper and tossed it aside. "Is this what I think it is?" Removing the spa basket from the bag, she set it on the counter. "This is amazing. I've barely pampered myself since I've been here." The basket contained lotions and shower gels, bath bombs, a candle, some mitt thing that I didn't know what was for, and a bunch of other girlie stuff the lady at the boutique assured me she'd love. Aurora kissed me on the cheek. "Thank you. It's very thoughtful of you."

"You're welcome." I slid the other bag toward her. "Now this one."

She held a hand to her chest. "It's already too much."

I rolled my eyes. "Open it. It's not really for you anyway."

Her face scrunched up. "Okay." Reaching in, she pulled out a long plastic wand with foil streamers on the end and started laughing. "Are you trying to bribe my cat?"

"Yes, I am. I want her to like me." I took the toy and shook it close to the floor. "Come on, Ailuros. Come see what I got for you." She poked her head out of the bedroom where she'd snuck off to after eating. "Come on, you know you want to," I said, shaking it some more. She sank low and eyed it suspiciously before creeping over and batting the steamers with her paws. Then she jumped and grabbed the toy with her teeth and paws, pulling it out of my hand, and ran into the other room with it. "Whoa!"

Aurora patted me on the shoulder. "Your cat play needs some work, but you're making progress."

"Yeah. I didn't think she'd go crazy like that." I reached into the bag and pulled out my other purchases: catnip mice, plastic balls with bells inside, and a variety of flavored treats... salmon, chicken, turkey. "I didn't know what she liked."

"She's going to love all of it," Aurora said with a laugh. "You're spoiling her."

I wrapped my arms around her hips and cupped her ass with my palms. "I want to spoil both of you."

"You already did," she said, putting her arms over my shoulders. "Between last night, the flowers, the gifts... I want to do something nice for you."

"Yeah? What did you have in mind?" I asked, pressing soft kisses right below her ear while my fingers danced along her spine.

She tilted her head to the side and gasped. "A continuation of last night."

"I would love that."

Our lips met in a slow, searing kiss. "And I'm going to take care of you," she whispered.

"Even better." My cock swelled with every word she said.

She fisted my shirt and began walking backward, pulling me with her until her back hit the wall with a thud. "And you're going to wake up in my bed."

"I can agree to that." I scooped her up, and she wrapped her legs around my waist as I pinned her to the wall.

She looked into my eyes and slid her hand through my hair. "And I don't want there to be any question about what I want. I want you to fuck me."

"Understood." Jesus Christ, this woman had me hard as a rock. I sealed my mouth to hers, lips and tongues moving in desperation, fed by a hunger we'd both been denying. She gripped the back of my head and tugged at the short strands, causing a sting of pain I didn't know I longed for. With a growl, I turned us toward her bedroom and blasted through those dangly beads, not bothering to turn on the lights.

We devoured each other with a passion that set us both on fire, bumping into the dresser and laughing breathlessly between kisses that grew into an inferno. She tasted like every fantasy I'd ever dreamed about in the dead hours of my lonely nights behind a keyboard. Her hands were in my hair, digging into my shoulders, and tugging at my shirt like she needed me *now*, and every inch of me burned in response.

With my lips sealed to hers, we crashed into the bed, and I fell on top of her, leaving no space between us… just heat and need. "Are you sure about this?"

She licked her bottom lip and pulled it between her teeth in a sexy tease. "What part of *I want you to fuck me* isn't clear?"

Goddamn! Aurora tugged at the bottom of my T-shirt, pulling it up my torso. Grabbing the collar behind my neck, I pulled it up and over my head and threw it to the side. Aurora's shirt landed next to mine in a heap on the floor.

Our mouths met again, all tongue and teeth and aching want. My heart thundered and blood pounded in my ears as I fumbled to get her bra off. Once her tits were free, I took one in my mouth and sucked her nipple into a hard peak.

"Yes," she moaned.

I gave the other the same attention. She gasped and arched her back, pressing her breasts up into my face. "Don't you dare come yet," I scolded her.

"Then hurry," she snapped back.

She didn't have to tell me twice. I quickly undid her pants and yanked them down her legs, throwing them with the rest of our clothes. Her panties were next. The restraint I had last night flew out the window the minute she said she wanted to fuck, but that didn't mean I wouldn't make her come at least once before we had sex. I spread her legs wide and set her feet on the mattress, putting her pretty pink pussy on full display for me. Goddamn, she was wet, and I couldn't wait to have her all over my lips and tongue again. I took a minute to appreciate the perfection that she was before diving in.

"Wait!"

My head snapped up from between her legs.

"Get naked," she ordered.

I wasted no time shucking off my own pants and boxer briefs in one fluid motion. My cock sprang free and pointed in her direction as I kicked the clothes into the pile on the floor.

She sat up on her elbows and stared at it with lust-filled eyes. "Finally. Now, come here. Straddle my shoulders. I want to suck you."

Not one to deprive a woman of what she wanted, I crawled up her body. "Someone's bossy."

"I'm matching your energy. You refused me last night, but I won't be denied again," she said, beckoning me forward with her wiggling fingers.

I leaned over the top of her and flipped us over, making her squeal and giggle. "I didn't want to squish you."

"Such a considerate boy." Having her lay on top of me without the barrier of clothing was heaven. The warmth of her soft skin seeped into mine and I decided this was my favorite place in the world. She and I, together with my impossibly hard cock sandwiched between us. She removed my glasses and gazed into my eyes. "Has anyone ever told you that you look like Clark Kent?"

"A time or two. And right now, I'm definitely the Man of Steel," I said, chuckling as I lifted my hips and pressed my hard-on into her.

"Yes, you are." She took off her own glasses and set both pairs on the nightstand, then crawled down my body, running her hands over every inch of me as she went… my nipples, my abs, my happy trail. Taking my cock in her hand, she stroked it from root to tip and ran her tongue over the head, lapping up the bead of precum.

I growled. "Now who's teasing?"

"Not teasing. Taking my time," she said, repeating my words from last night with an evil glint in her eye. "I'm seeing what you like."

"What I would like is my dick in your mouth."

She licked a line up the underside and wrapped her lips around the tip, working me slowly. "Like this?"

"Just like that," I hissed. It was sweet torture, but it wasn't enough. I bucked my hips up and held the back of her head. "More. Swallow me down. See how much you can take."

Never one to back down from a challenge, she widened her lips and took me to the back of her throat, her hand wrapped around the base of my cock. It was pure heaven, her mouth wet and warm. And then she started to bob. "Fuck! That feels amazing." It'd been a while, but of all the blow jobs I'd ever had, this one was the best. She sucked my dick like it was her favorite flavor popsicle, her tongue lashing and lips suctioning tight as she worked me over. When she bottomed out and swallowed, her throat squeezed my dick. The tingles at the base of my spine started and I was ready to explode. But I didn't want to come in her mouth; it was her pussy I wanted.

I pulled out of her mouth, and she released me with a pop of her lips. "You're going to make me come."

Aurora wiped the saliva dripping down her chin with the back of her hand. "That's the point."

Flipping her over again, I lifted her higher on the bed. "I will when I'm inside you." I reached for my pants, then realized my mistake. "Shit," I grumbled. "I don't have a condom."

"Nightstand drawer." She motioned with her chin. When I raised an eyebrow, she added, "I bought them for us, you goofball."

Thank god one of us had been thinking ahead. I opened the drawer and pulled out a brand new box of XL condoms. I should have known she'd be totally prepared. But it wasn't the condoms that were most surprising; it was the pink vibrator sitting there in plain view. I held it up. "You dirty girl. I'm going to have to put this to good use."

A beautiful crimson crept up her chest. "You weren't supposed to find that."

165

"Yet you didn't hide it. Do you think about me when you use this?" I turned it on, and it began to vibrate in my hand. The thing had some power behind it. "Do you?"

"Yes," she admitted.

"Good girl." I kneeled between her legs to keep them open and held the toy to her clit. "Do you like that?"

She fisted the sheets and arched her back. "Yes."

"And what if I do this?" I slid it inside her and let the rabbit ears tickle her clit. "Do you like that?"

A moan was the only answer I got as she squirmed beneath me. I turned the power to the highest setting, and her eyes rolled back. With her quick trigger, it didn't take long to see the signs of an impending climax. The slight sheen on her forehead. The rosiness in her cheeks. The rounding of her lips. The gentle gasp. And then a full-body shiver racked her from head to toe.

"You're so beautiful when you come," I said, turning off the toy and setting it aside.

"I need you. Now."

"You don't have to ask twice." I was still hard as a rock, but the tingles had subsided. The last thing I wanted to be was a two-pump chump. Ripping the box open, I pulled out a condom and rolled it over my length. "Are you ready for me?"

"I've been ready."

I grabbed a pillow and slid it under her hips to get the perfect angle. It was simple geometry if I wanted to hit her G-spot, and I definitely wanted her to come when I was inside her. It would make it better for both of us. Inserting two fingers, I checked to see if she was wet enough. *Soaking.* I pulled them out and painted her lips with her own arousal, then sucked them clean. "So damn good."

Lining up my cock with her entrance, I leaned over her, my face a breath away from hers, and threaded our fingers together on either side of her head. This wasn't just about sex; it was about connecting on a deeper level. Cementing the bond we'd formed. There'd be plenty of time for crazy, untamed sex later, but I wanted our first time to be something she'd remember.

Slowly, so slowly, I entered her an inch or so. She was soft and warm and wet. Then, another inch as she stretched to accommodate me. Aurora let out a tiny yelp as her body adjusted to mine. "You okay?"

"I'm perfect," she said with a contented sigh. "Keep going."

Inch by inch, I filled her until I was fully seated. I wanted to stay there forever, tucked inside her perfect body that was meant for mine. Two puzzle pieces that fit together.

Nothing had ever felt so right.

Etched into my soul.

Sacred.

With the bright Vegas lights as a background through the open blinds and the dim beams coming in through the doorway, they cast her in an ethereal glow. Her golden hair falling around her and those pouty lips mere millimeters from mine, she was pure perfection.

Our eyes met, and the feelings I had for her shone back at me. We hadn't said the words, but we were both there.

Our hearts raced.

Our breaths shallowed.

Our souls connected.

I pulled out slowly, then pushed back in and the sensation was indescribable. She let out a moan and whispered, "Tom." Her voice was breathy and low, like she couldn't believe this was happening. And I was right there with her. She was my fantasy come true and there was no stopping us now.

Not when it was this good.

Not when she was made for me.

Not when all I wanted to do was keep going.

To love her.

To kneel at her altar.

To worship her.

Tonight, I was all in, the risks be damned. If I lost her someday, at least we'd always have this. This moment in time where nothing else mattered but the two of us. Our future might have been unknown, but the present was too damn good to care.

Her legs wrapped around my hips and her heels dug into my ass, pulling me in on every downward pulse. She let go of my hands and gripped my shoulders, digging her nails in and scratching my skin. I cupped the back of her head and brought her lips to mine. Our tongues tangled and I cherished her, sinking into her over and over again. Each stroke, each gentle kiss, each whispered plea—an unspoken promise.

"Oh god. I'm going to come again."

I picked up the pace, wanting to fall over the edge with her. My thrusts became harder. Faster. Deeper. The tingles were back, and my balls pulled tight. She shattered beneath me, her pussy gripping my dick like a vise as I chased my own release.

It hit me like a tsunami. Wave after wave of pleasure coursed through my body. Fire raced along my spine. Neurons zapped every nerve ending.

As I came down from the high, my hips slowed. I pushed a strand of sweat-soaked hair from Aurora's face. "Hi."

She smiled up at me. "Hi."

Sex had never been so good before. This intense. And it had everything to do with her.

I wished that it could last forever.

Chapter 24
Aurora

Tom rolled to the side, and I immediately missed the heat and pressure of his body against mine. Sex with him was everything I imagined and more. I'd never orgasmed during sex before. It usually happened before and then I pretended to enjoy the rest of it as a man pounded in and out of me to get his.

But not with Tom.

He was slow and steady, making sure to stroke me in all the right places. I was surprised I lasted as long as I did. Every pulse, every breath, every kiss had brought me closer and closer to the edge until sweet ecstasy blossomed inside me like I'd been touched for the first time. Like everything else was a prelude.

Resting on his elbow with his hand supporting his head, he asked, "How do you feel?"

"I feel... invigorated. Alive."

"Me too. Are you sore?"

I shook my head. "You were so gentle with me. I expected your bossy side to come out."

He chuckled. "I can't promise I'll always be that gentle. I've got a spreadsheet of all the ways I'd like to fuck you, but I wanted our first time to be special."

I rolled on my side, matching his pose. "I appreciate that. It was amazing, but know that I'm up for anything on that spreadsheet of yours."

Tom groaned. "You're killing me in the best possible way." He looked down at his now-soft cock with the used condom hanging on it. "I need to go take care of this. Do you want anything? Water?"

"Water would be great." I rolled to my back, enjoying the view as he left the room, and threw an arm over my face. There had to be a way to keep him. To sidestep my father and all his plans for me. There had to be something I was missing. I needed to get my hands on my grandfather's will and read it for myself. Surely there was a loophole.

I wanted to tell Tom everything tonight, but he'd shushed me. He didn't want to hear it any more than I wanted to tell it. We were living in a fantasy world where my demanding father didn't control my life. Soon that bubble would burst, and we'd have to face reality. The question was... what was the reality?

The will was the key.

My father would protect it at all costs if it gave me an out, so my mother was my one hope. Surely she would empathize with me. What mother would want their daughter stuck in an arranged marriage? I had no doubt she loved my father when she married him, but that was before his pursuit of power and prestige turned him into a tyrant.

Tom returned with a bottle of water for each of us and a hand towel. He set the bottles on the nightstand and held up the towel. "Figured you'd need a little cleanup too."

"Thanks." I went to grab it from him, but he pulled it away.

"Let me. I'm the one who got you all dirty."

The idea of him wiping between my legs embarrassed me. "I can do it."

170

He smirked. "Don't get shy on me now. I've already been all up close and personal with your private parts."

That was true, but him cleaning me seemed more intimate. I reluctantly spread my legs a few inches and let him tenderly rub the towel between them. "Thank you."

Tom tossed the towel into the hamper, then handed me a bottle of water. I drank it down greedily and handed it back. He got in bed, his back against the headboard, and patted his chest. "Come here."

Shimmying over, I snuggled into his side and rested my head on his firm chest. His arms wrapped around me in a warm embrace. We were both still naked, but neither of us cared. Our hearts beat in sync as we basked in the afterglow of the best sex I'd ever had. It felt like more than sex… it felt like love. I wouldn't say the words though. If I did, it would make it ten times harder if I had to leave.

He carelessly ran his fingers through my hair. "You're still keeping things from me, aren't you?"

And there it was. "Yes."

"It's going to break my heart, isn't it?"

"It could break both our hearts," I answered.

He tugged on my hair, tilting my head back so I had no choice but to look him in the eyes. "I don't want to know. If it breaks my heart, we'll forever have this."

A tear ran down my cheek. "I'm sorry. I don't want it to be this way."

He brushed it away with his thumb. "How much time do we have?"

"A month. Maybe less."

"Then I don't want to waste a minute of it. Your nights belong to me." He pulled me closer and pressed his lips to mine.

I crawled into his lap and kissed him back with all I had. It was an apology. A plea for forgiveness. A prayer that somehow we could make this work.

We devoured each other with a hunger neither of us could deny. His hands fisted my hair. My fingers scratched down his back. Our bodies so close there wasn't a breath between us. "I need you again," I said, as I pressed my wet center against his growing cock.

171

We broke apart only long enough for him to grab another condom and sheath himself. I lifted onto my knees and slowly sank down on him until he was fully inside me. We both groaned, loving how we connected. That, in this moment, nothing could separate us.

With my hands braced on his chest and his on my waist, I rode him. With a gently rocking motion, I slid him in and out of me. There was no hurry. No need to rush it. No urgency. With each undulation of my hips, the tension coiled. The pleasure was so intense that my eyes closed, and my head fell back. I let myself drift away to another world. One where no one could stop us from being together.

"Eyes on me, angel."

Tom's commanding words had them snapping back open. "I'm so close."

"Right there with you." He tightened his grip on my hips and pushed up into me. Repeatedly. It wasn't gentle. It was fierce and frenetic. I held on to his shoulders for balance, digging my fingers in. My boobs jiggled from the crazy pace he set. My heart thundered faster and faster. And that little inkling of a climax swelled and swelled.

Fireworks exploded. Ecstasy burst through every cell in my body and rocketed me to the heavens. I flew so high I never wanted to come down. I swore I could touch the stars as they rained down around me in a brilliant display of light and color.

With a grunt and a moan, my name was a prayer on Tom's lips. And then he stilled, pressing me down onto him and squeezing out every last drop of his orgasm.

I collapsed onto his chest, my breathing ragged and my heart erratic. A sense of peace washed over me, and I knew I was exactly where I was supposed to be.

Chapter 25
Tom

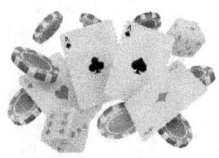

Strolling into the conference room at Mystique, I was on cloud nine Monday morning. My weekend with Aurora was one I'd never forget. It was unlike me to bury my head in the sand, but when I was with her, all I could think about was the here and now. And the sex... chef's kiss... phenomenal... the best I'd ever had.

"Someone got laid," Hunter said as I sat next to him.

"Hunter!" Edward chastised his son.

"What? It's written all over his face."

Trent glared at his brother. "Try to be somewhat professional."

Not even Hunter could ruin my mood today. "Things are going well with Aurora. That's all I'll say."

"Totally got laid," Hunter mumbled. "You've grown up so quickly." He pretended to wipe a tear from his eye, then patted me on the back. "I'm so proud of you."

I rolled my eyes and tried to snap back with a witty remark, but I seriously had nothing. Not one snarky comment came to mind.

Hunter stared at me. "What's wrong? Pussy got your tongue?" He laughed at his own joke.

My lips curled up without my consent and a chuckle spilled out. "Something like that."

Trent and Edward tried to hide their amusement behind closed fists, but the moment had taken on a life of its own. Despite my animosity toward Hunter, once you got past his cocky and crass exterior, the guy was a hoot. I hated to admit it, but he was growing on me. A bit like poison ivy, but still...

Edward picked up the stack of papers in front of him and tamped them down on the polished table to straighten the pile. "Back to the business at hand."

Edward decided to delay his retirement until the new security system was up and running. I couldn't blame him. It was an exciting yet scary change for Mystique. Although they had other properties around the world, this was their flagship.

"Are you ready to start the install?" Trent asked.

"As ready as ever. I want to thank you all for allowing me to run the beta test at Mystique. You won't regret it."

"Although I have total confidence in you, Tom, I would be lying if I said this change wasn't giving me heartburn and indigestion," Edward admitted.

Hunter pulled a roll of Tums from his suit pocket and handed them to his father, who greedily chewed and swallowed two.

I understood his anxiety. Being this was my first large-scale install, my stomach was a bit queasy as well. There were so many things that could go wrong, including a total system failure, but I couldn't let them know that.

"So, I know the words 'blockchain' and 'technology upgrade' might sound a bit intimidating, but I promise we're not reinventing the wheel here. We're just making it turn a whole lot smoother and more efficient."

"What kind of disruption should we expect to our current system during the changeover?" Edward asked.

"Minimal. Once installed, we'll run your current system in parallel with the new system for a while. Your staff will keep using the old system and

174

I'll be watching the blockchain in the background. Once we confirm the sync is clean and the data flows correctly, I'll switch over the live operations to the blockchain."

Edward took a breath and relaxed back into his chair. "I swear this is giving me more gray hair than I already have."

I chuckled. "I get it. I really do, but rest assured, I won't switch anything until I'm confident everything is working properly."

"And if something fails?" Trent asked, tapping his fingertips together.

"We roll it back. No harm done. That's why we'll be testing in shadow mode first. Plus, we're not getting rid of your current system. It'll still function as a backup for at least a week. Once we get through the heavy traffic on the weekend, it'll give me a good idea of any tweaks that need to be made."

Edward nodded. "Good. Good. How will the interface change for our employees?"

"Visually, the dashboard won't change much, but in the background, the blockchain will be logging everything. The transition should be seamless, but I'll put together some cheat sheets and troubleshooting guides. I can also run a few training sessions for the staff."

"Perfect."

"What do you need from us?" Hunter asked.

"I'll need admin-level access to your current software that handles property management, payment processing, and the loyalty program. I'll also need to get into the control room where the servers are housed."

"I'll contact Tony, our IT coordinator. He can get you everything you need." Hunter scribbled a note on the pad in front of him.

"Great." I clapped my hands together. "I'll train Tony on the system so he can do any minor troubleshooting without calling for help."

That made me start thinking about hiring staff. One hotel was doable, but once I started getting more clients, there was no way I'd be able to handle everything on my own without going crazy. I'd need a reliable crew of tech nerds like me. I added the item to my never-ending mental list of things to talk to Brett about.

"There's one more thing you'll need," Trent said.

"There is?" I asked.

"There is," Edward confirmed. "We've got a surprise for you."

"What the hell is the surprise?" Hunter asked, clearly annoyed he wasn't in the know.

"Follow me," Trent said, standing from the table.

The three of us walked behind Trent down the hallway until we got to the large storage room that was Hunter's temporary office when he first returned to Mystique. Trent motioned to the door and opened it. "An office. A home base. A control center. Whatever you want to call it. Dad and I figured you'd need a workspace."

I peeked into the room. The walls were covered in fresh paint, and the floor was newly carpeted. An oak desk sat in the center with an executive leather chair behind it. Three monitors sat on the desktop, along with a cup full of pens and a small plant. The room was totally unrecognizable compared to when Hunter used it. "Wow! This is really nice. Thank you."

"What the fuck is this?" Hunter griped, plopping into one of the two padded chairs in front of the desk. "Where are the cracks in the wall and the ink-stained carpet?"

Trent stuck his hands in his pockets, a smirk on his face. "You were on probation. You hadn't earned fresh paint yet."

"Whatever."

It was more than I expected and way bigger than the cubicle I was used to working in. "You shouldn't have done all this for me. I'm not going to be here that long. Once the install is done, I'll only come by to check the systems are all running correctly."

Edward clamped his hand on my shoulder. "We're aware, but you're family. You'll always have a place here at Mystique."

"What am I? Chopped liver?" Hunter asked.

"Dog food," Trent said dryly. "Tom has never screwed us over, unlike you."

"One fucking mistake!" Hunter exclaimed.

A lump stuck in my throat at their generosity. "Thank you. This means a lot to me." I'd always viewed myself as an outsider, but I was beginning to see that maybe I wasn't as far on the outside as I thought. I was appreciated. I was *family*. And maybe it wasn't because of Charli and her marriage to Hunter. Maybe along the way, I'd earned their respect.

My chest filled with pride. For a kid from a small town in Colorado, I was doing alright. I was making something of myself.

A man Aurora would be proud to have standing next to her. *If we made it that far.*

I stood in the control room, tucked behind the front desk of the hotel. Racks of blinking servers hummed quietly, and cables snaked through ports connecting them all together. In the corner was a tiny desk covered in spreadsheets and sticky notes with a half-eaten sandwich wrapped in wax paper on top of the pile. It was a far cry from the office I'd been granted upstairs. I had a feeling when Tony got his tech degree, this wasn't what he had in mind.

He rocked back on his heels in his cargo shorts and Iron Maiden T-shirt, motioning to all the machines. "This is it. This is where all the magic happens." He eyed me skeptically. "So you're the blockchain guy?"

"I am."

"Weren't you Trent's assistant?"

Yeah, I could see how that position didn't give me much credibility for installing a million-dollar security system. "I was, but it wasn't my passion. My nights were spent working on this."

Tony nodded his head. "I hear ya. I'm a bit of a programmer myself. Gaming is more my thing though. Nothing cooler than designing a dragon that can burn down an entire village with a single flame. Add in the screaming peasants fleeing their huts with their faces melting off and it doesn't get much better than that."

Okay, maybe I jumped the gun with the office envy. Maybe this cave of a room was exactly up his alley. Wouldn't be surprised if he still lived in his mom's basement. "Cool. Yeah, I know exactly what you mean," I said, attempting to build a rapport with him. I tried to hold my judgment at bay. The Dorseys wouldn't have hired Tony if he was a total loose cannon, but he did give me creepy vibes. One of those guys who sat in the dark, surrounded by a dozen screens spying on his neighbors after hacking into their home systems.

A shiver ran down my spine. *Stop it!*

He clapped his hands and rubbed them together, bringing my attention back. "What do you need from me?"

I opened my folder and handed him a piece of paper. "Everything I need is listed here. Let's start with whitelisting our blockchain node server on your firewall and getting me admin credentials for everything. After that, I'll need the API documentation for any third-party vendors—booking sites, payment processors, room service apps. Also, any guest loyalty program data, preferably in a CSV file."

Tony scanned the list. "Most of this will be easy. I should have everything you need emailed within the hour."

"Secure email?" I asked, then chastised myself for being condescending.

"Of course. Don't let the clothes fool you; I know what I'm doing," he said with a scoff.

"Never doubted that. If the Dorseys trust you, then I do too. Once this is all up and running, we'll sit down and go over the monitoring and maintenance." It was hard to think that I would be giving up control of my baby, but it was something I'd have to get used to. Once the software was installed, it belonged to the hotel and, hopefully, I'd be at another site doing this all over again.

Now that I'd had time to think about it, the launch party was a genius idea. What better way to sell CyberSecure than by having my beta testers sing my praises? Well, not me personally, but the security software.

"Sounds good," Tony said. "You gonna run this parallel to our current system for a while?"

"A whole week. That should give us an idea of how it runs during peak hours and allow me to fix any issues."

"Smart, man. Smart." He walked over to his desk and shoved what was left of his sandwich in his mouth. "I'll get started on this right away," he mumbled around the food in his mouth, which, from the smell of it, was tuna.

My phone rang and I used the opportunity to deftly sneak away from Tony. I held up my phone. "Gotta take this."

Tony gave me a wave with the tuna-covered wax paper still firmly in his grip. "Talk later, blockchain guy."

I gave him a thumbs-up and went to the lobby to answer the call from my sister. "What's up?"

"Did you make amends with Aurora yet?" she demanded.

I sighed. She was nosy, but I owed her for making me see that I was being unreasonable and a bit asshole-ish. If she hadn't stuck her nose where it didn't belong, my fantasy weekend with Aurora wouldn't have happened, so I cooled my agitation. "I did."

"Yay!" she squealed into the phone, making me have to hold it away from my ear.

"Are you trying to make me deaf?" I asked when the sound subsided.

"Don't be dramatic. I'm happy is all."

"Is that why you called? To get into my business?"

"Yes and no. I called to set up your shopping trip with Hunter. We're meeting you guys for dinner on Wednesday and then I'll go with Aurora, and you can go with Hunter."

Charli exasperated me. "Was there a question in there? Maybe asking if I was available or if we even wanted to go to dinner?"

Now she sighed. "Let's not pretend you have an active social life. I have the night off work, and we need to do this pronto. It's not like you just walk into a store and walk out with a perfectly fitted tux or dress, for that matter. You need to leave time for alterations."

I gritted my teeth. "Fine, I'll check with Aurora. She might be scheduled at Helping Hands."

"No worries. I'll call her next."

"Wait! You have her number?" I knew damn well I hadn't given it to her.

"Of course, silly. I got it at Penny and Brett's the other night."

"Charli!" My sister had boundary issues.

"What? Why shouldn't I have my future sister-in-law's number?"

It was a nice thought, but a bit premature. "You're getting ahead of yourself."

"I call it being optimistic. You should try it."

If our relationship wasn't a huge Jenga tower waiting to tip over, maybe I would.

Chapter 26
Aurora

I really liked Charli. She had a take-no-shit attitude and a generous heart. It made me an awful person that I was deceiving her. Deceiving them all.

It wasn't just Charli and me on this shopping trip. Penny and Gia decided to join us.

"I'm going to tell you now," Penny said. "Don't look at the price tags. The first time I came shopping here, I nearly passed out from shock."

"Same," Gia added. "If I wasn't married to Trent, there is no way I'd be able to afford to shop here."

"Time-out!" Charli held her hands up in a *T*. "I'm not going to listen to this self-deprecating talk. Let's face it, none of us were born rich, but we've worked damn hard to get where we are. None of us are gold diggers. It's not our fault that we fell in love with rich men. The only fault we have is that we are so damn irresistible that they fell in love with us."

"Damn straight," I said, thrusting my fist in the air. Not all of that was true about me, but I got caught up in Charli's woman-empowerment proclamation anyway.

"You're right," Penny said. "I can't help that Brett loves my quirky personality and plump bottom."

"And I'm proud that Trent loves my brilliant mind." Gia nodded. "He likes my boobs too."

"And Hunter, he loves a good fight. He craves my sharp tongue in and out of the bedroom. Also, my flexibility. I can put my legs behind my head."

I cringed because that was too much information about Tom's sister.

"Eww! Nice visual." Gia gagged. "I almost threw up in my mouth."

Charli put her hands on her hips and clucked her tongue. "Don't act like you're married to monks. I've heard stories about Brett and Trent. I'm more than positive you all have thriving sex lives."

"True," Penny conceded, and they all burst into a fit of giggles.

I kept my mouth shut and suddenly became very interested in the fancy light fixtures hanging from the ceiling. Tom wouldn't like me gossiping about his bedroom prowess. He was a private person, and I respected that.

His sister bumped me with her hip. "What about you?"

It was weird to be questioned by his sister, so I kept staring at the ceiling. "Do you think those are real crystals on that chandelier?"

She glanced up and then shrugged her shoulders. "For what these dresses cost, probably, but who cares?"

"Wait!" Penny gasped. "Have you and Tom not"—she dropped her voice to a whisper—"had sex?"

"Umm."

"Oh, my! You're turning into a tomato," Gia shrieked.

Damn my telltale cheeks.

"So, you have." Penny's eyebrows practically wiggled into her hairline.

"Yes, but he wouldn't want me talking about it," I said in a low voice.

"Why are you whispering?" Charli asked.

My head swiveled in every direction, like someone might be eavesdropping and jump out from behind a potted plant. "Because it's private."

All three women cackled. "Girl, you've joined the wrong group of gals. There's not much that's off-limits between us, except maybe Charli's mattress gymnastics," Gia said, waving a hand at her sister-in-law.

"She's jealous," Charli clapped back, hiking her thumb at the redhead.

"Here we go again." Gia rolled her eyes.

Penny snapped her fingers at them. "Focus, ladies. We're talking about Aurora and Tom."

Charli scrunched her nose. "He doesn't use technical terminology in the bedroom, does he? Because I could totally see him doing that."

All the naughty things he'd said to me ran through my brain. *Greedy girl. Did I say you could touch my cock yet?* "Uh, no. He's got a dirty mouth. Filthy actually." I looked around again to make sure the space behind the potted plant was clear. "And he's bossy."

Gia's eyes went wide. "Our sweet Tom?"

"Are you saying he's a freak in the sheets?" Charli gasped. "My brother?"

I nodded but put a finger to my lips. "You didn't hear it from me."

"It's always the quiet ones you gotta watch out for." Penny giggled.

I'd been harboring so many secrets I couldn't carry any more. So, although I shouldn't have said anything else, I whispered, "He made me come three times in one night. And he demanded I count them."

Gia put her fist to her temple, then exploded her fingers out. "Mind blown."

Charli crossed her arms. "Guess we shouldn't be too surprised. He's always been an overachiever."

"You can say that again." I giggled so hard, a very unladylike snort—which would have mortified my mother—slipped out. Sharing with these ladies felt better than it should have. Liberating. Cathartic. Invigorating.

They brought out my true self. I didn't have to watch my *p's* and *q's* or pretend to be the perfect daughter. I could just be me.

With our fits of laughter under control, Gia got us back on track with a clap of her hands. "Okay, girls, let the shopping commence."

An attractive blond saleswoman approached us. "Ladies, nice to see you again."

"Vivian!" Penny stretched up on her toes and gave the woman a hug. "I'm so glad you're here. I'm going to need your expertise today." She rubbed her hands down her curvy hips. "I haven't quite got my prepregnancy body back."

Vivian smiled at Penny. "Nonsense, Mrs. Kingston. You look wonderful. I've already pulled some dresses that I think will be fabulous for you." Then she addressed the rest of us. "If any of you need anything, I'm happy to help. As always, champagne is by the dressing room." She took Penny by the hand and led her away.

"She's a miracle worker," Penny said over her shoulder.

"Wow! You guys must come here a lot," I said, as the two of them walked away.

"Only for special occasions. It's the best boutique in Vegas. Every designer you can think of is right under this roof. And you should see the shoes! It's like a dream," Gia said, spinning in a circle with her hands raised above her head.

Charli grabbed one of her arms, bringing the spinning to a halt. "Okay, shoe queen, get to the shopping. We have two hours until they close."

"Yikes! I'd better get looking." Gia said, taking off toward a rack of classic Chanel gowns.

"It's a good thing that one married rich. She loves her designer clothes," Charli said with a chuckle.

"What's not to like about Gucci and Prada?" I asked with a shrug.

"They're constricting. I like clothes I can move in, and if I spill a bit of wine on them, I throw them in the washing machine. These dresses are totally impractical, but"—she held up a finger—"I'm doing it for my brother. And because I know Hunter will want to rip it off me as soon as I put it on and I'll be able to torture him all night."

"You two have a *unique* relationship," I said with a shake of my head.

Her lips turned up in a grin that had all the makings of an evil mastermind. "It's fiery. As a matter of fact, I think I'll wear red. That ought to get his blood pressure up." She skipped away in search of the perfect dress and a tiny bit of me actually had pity for Hunter.

Left alone, I browsed through the racks. I had a dozen dresses like these back home in my walk-in closet. Chanel, Dior, Versace… I owned them all, thanks to the company my grandfather built, and my father now ran. Mine was a life of privilege I'd taken for granted. Something my father liked to remind me of and hold over my head.

No one here knew my connection to LeFleur Media, and I liked it that way. These women assumed I came from humble beginnings, like them. I wondered what they would think of me when they found out I wasn't forthcoming with them. I never lied. They assumed. There was a difference.

I plucked several dresses from the racks, going for understated yet classy. The launch party was Tom's big night; I was simply supportive eye candy. I was a master at this role… smile and schmooze… easy peasy.

Taking my dresses to the fitting room, along with several pairs of shoes, I glanced at the price tags of each one. It was highway robbery. The cost of one of these dresses would feed a family for months. And not for the first time since starting at Helping Hands, I was disgusted by the gluttony of society, mostly because I was a product of it. The glitz, the glam, the overindulgence… it made me feel slimy when the people at the shelter just wanted decent meals on a regular basis.

Gia stepped out of the dressing room in a sleek black gown that fit her perfectly in all the right places. I gave a low whistle. "You look hot."

She cupped her breasts. "You don't think it shows off the girls too much? They've gotten bigger since I got pregnant."

"Nah. It's the perfect amount of cleavage to give every woman in the room boob envy."

"Tell me about it." Charli plopped down in one of the velvet chairs with her arms full of dresses. "I wish I had cleavage to show. I'm going to have to wear a padded bra just to get a little shape."

"Actually…" Vivian appeared with a tray of champagne and set it on a side table. "Our seamstress can sew pads right into the lining of the dress. They'll look totally natural. She's the true miracle worker around here."

Charli raised her eyebrows and swiped one of the glasses from the tray, downing it in a single gulp. "Really?"

"Yes, ma'am." Vivian took the dresses from Charli and hung them in a fitting room. "In you go."

"Gia?"

"Hmmm," she hummed while looking in the mirror, her hand on her tiny baby bump as she turned this way and that.

"Have you talked to Kendra at Helping Hands yet? They could really use the assistance of a fundraiser."

She bit her bottom lip and bowed her head sheepishly. "I have not, but I'll do it first thing in the morning. I promise."

"Thank you." All I could think about was how much the amount of money the four of us were spending tonight could benefit the shelter.

"No, thank you for the suggestion. I looked at the website and did a little digging. I needed assurance they were on the up and up. It's a terrific charity."

"It really is." Knowing that Helping Hands would be the beneficiary of hundreds of thousands of dollars assuaged my guilt about the luxury gowns draped over my arm. "Where is Penny?"

"I'm in here!" she shouted from behind one of the curtains.

"We're still working on it." Vivian gave me a gentle nudge and took the dresses from me, hanging them on a hook inside a stall. "These are all excellent choices, but with your hair and coloring, I'm partial to the sapphire blue. It'll be stunning on you." Then she pulled the curtain closed, leaving me in one of the most opulent dressing rooms I'd ever stood in.

After trying on all five dresses, I had to admit the blue off-the-shoulder gown with the thigh-high slit was the one. I loved the way it fit my curves, and the shimmery fabric caught the light. Tom would fall to his knees when he saw me in it.

"Are you coming out, Aurora? You haven't shown us shit," Charli grumbled. There was a slight *oomph* from the other side of the drape. "I mean... you haven't shown us any of your dresses."

Pulling back the curtain, I stepped out in the Manolo Blahnik stilettos and blue gown.

"Stunning. Just as I predicted," Vivian said, pressing her hands together. The girls, all in their own dresses, concurred.

"Wow!"

"Beautiful!"

"Are you trying to kill my brother?"

I did a little twirl. "I'm in love with it. You all look great too. Penny, that plum color is fabulous on you."

She gave me a shy smile. "It's really this asymmetrical ruffle that makes it look good."

"Nonsense. Nothing is more beautiful than a new mom," I assured her.

"You ladies are going to knock them dead at the gala," Vivian raved. "Now, let's have Vessa pin you all for your alterations and I'll meet you at the counter when you're ready for payment."

As if on cue, a woman who must have been seventy, with the lines on her face to prove it, pointed at Gia. "You first. Step up."

Vessa measured and pinned each of us in rapid succession, with a speed I wouldn't have thought possible. She hacked away with a large pair of sewing shears and ripped at the fabric with her bare hands. The woman was a force to be reckoned with.

Once back in my regular clothes, I made my way to the counter with Charli hot on my heels. "Aurora, wait! I told Tom I would pay for your dress."

Yes, Tom had mentioned the generous offer from his sister, but I reached into my purse anyway. "I've got it."

She put her hand on my arm. "Please, Tom would kill me if I let you go into debt because of his launch party."

I pulled out my black credit card and handed it to Vivian. "I appreciate the offer, but it wouldn't be right."

187

As Vivian passed the card back to me, Charli swiped it from my hand and turned it over, reading my name on the back. She slapped it against her open palm. "Does my brother know about this?"

I shook my head. "No. He assumed because we live in the same building that I didn't have money. He was so hellbent on proving himself that I didn't have the heart to tell him otherwise. He never outright asked, and I never volunteered the information."

She looked me up and down, noting my basic jeans and white T-shirt with the word *Meoow* splashed across the front. "You don't look rich."

I quirked an eyebrow at her and gave her the same appraising look, taking in her purple leggings and black tank top. "Neither do you."

Her lips pursed like she'd sucked on a lemon. "Touché."

"Look, Charli, I'll tell Tom when the timing is appropriate, but right now it's not relevant. Having money doesn't change who I am. Can you please keep this between us?"

"He wants to take care of you."

"I know, but I don't need someone to support me financially. That's not why I'm with him."

She seemed to roll that around in her head. "I'll keep your secret, but you better not hurt him."

My heart leaped into my throat, making my words come out sticky. "I'm doing my best not to."

Making Charli an accomplice to my deceptions was a low I never thought I'd sink to, yet I'd done it anyway. This web of deceit was getting more twisted with every passing day.

I owed Tom another piece of the truth.

Chapter 27
Tom

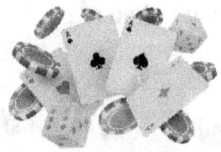

I would rather have been skydiving without a parachute than standing on a pedestal while an overzealous tailor measured my inseam and stuck pins precariously close to my balls, and Hunter stood watching with a smug smirk on his face. "Are you enjoying this?"

"Immensely. The look on your face is priceless." Hunter chuckled.

"Excuse me for...ouch!" I glared down at the man kneeling between my legs who'd stuck a pin in my thigh.

"Sorry. You're moving too much. Stand still."

I straightened my shoulders and stood stiffly, trying not to get poked again. "Are we almost finished?"

"A few more pins and you'll be set." He patted my butt and tugged on the material. "You're good. Take them off carefully, we don't want to do this again."

We certainly didn't. I went to the fitting room and gently took the pants off, careful not to snag my socks on the pins. The coat and shirt came off next. I hung the clothes back on their hangers and got dressed.

Exiting the fitting room, I found Hunter leaning against the wall, typing on his phone. "Now what?"

Hunter glanced up at me. "You act like I'm torturing you instead of doing you a favor."

He wasn't wrong. "I'm sorry. It's not that I don't appreciate this, but I don't understand why I can't rent a tuxedo instead of buying one."

Slipping his phone into his pocket, he clapped me on the shoulder. "Because that's for the ordinary man and you're not ordinary. You, my friend, are a budding millionaire. And as so, you must dress the part. People are not going to take you seriously if you show up in a generic tux that hangs on your body like a potato sack. If you want corporate executives to spend their money on your product, you must look like you're worth the investment."

It made sense, but it still seemed excessive. "They're buying a security system, not me," I refuted.

"That's where you're wrong. No one's going to buy your product, no matter how good it is, from a schmuck."

"A schmuck?"

"No offense," he said, as if the words erased the insult he threw my way.

I sighed. "Fine. What's next?" In all honesty, I was glad Hunter was with me, and I wasn't left to bumble through this shopping trip on my own.

"Ties and pocket squares. Charli said Aurora's dress is sapphire blue. Go check out the options and I'll be over in a minute." He pulled his phone back out and started texting again.

Glad to have a minute to myself, I perused my choices. It was like bow-tie heaven, so many patterns and different fabrics. It made me giddy. Bow ties were my trademark, even if they garnered a few side-eyes. They were classic.

I quickly selected the ones that made me happy, keeping in mind the color of Aurora's dress. I wondered what kind she got. Would it be low-cut, showing off her beautiful tits or something more conservative that showcased the slender slope of her neck? Tight on her hips or flowing? Would she wear regular underwear underneath or a thong, or no panties at all? I didn't know how I'd make it through the night if she didn't wear panties.

My cock thickened thinking about our last few nights together. The swell of her breasts. The curve of her hips. The sweet paradise between her legs. I hadn't slept in my own bed since Saturday. Every minute with her was sacred.

"What'd you pick, Boy Genius?" Hunter swiped the ties from my hands and narrowed his eyebrows.

"What?"

One by one, he tossed them back on the table. "Garbage. Trash. More Garbage. Jesus Christ, it's a launch party, not a clown convention."

I scowled at his description of my choices. "Fine, what would you suggest, Mr. GQ?"

"Cute. I like it," he said, tugging on the cuffs sticking out from his suit coat. "You're so lucky I'm here to save you from yourself. When Charli said you had no fashion sense, she wasn't kidding. I thought what you wore to work was a quirky habit, but I can see now that you're completely fashion deficient."

"My sister said that?" I mean… it didn't surprise me, but still.

"What she actually said was, 'Make sure my brother doesn't look like a nerd.'"

I threw my hands in the air. "I am a nerd."

"I realize that, but we're going more Clark Kent than *Bill Nye the Science Guy*."

"Why does everyone keep comparing me to Superman?"

"Seriously? Have you looked in a mirror lately?" Hunter rearranged the discarded ties on the table. "The point is, you need something classy, not a mishmash of crazy colors." He picked up a solid blue tie with little paisleys a shade deeper embroidered on it. "Something like this."

I took it from him and examined the details. It *was* nice. "Fine. I'll get this one."

Hunter clucked his tongue at me. "It's like you don't care at all."

That wasn't true. "I do care. I want to look nice for Aurora."

"That's admirable, but you should want to look nice for yourself. I'm not going to be here to hold your hand through every shopping trip."

"For fuck's sake, I'm not a child."

"Then quit dressing like one. Up your game, Tom. You need to start thinking like a Vegas millionaire instead of a guy from Bumfuck, Colorado."

My nostrils flared and a spurt of hot air burst out. Unfortunately, not hot enough to light Hunter's ass on fire. "Are you going to insult me the entire night?"

He casually looked at his watch. "Only for the next half hour, then I'm going home to screw your sister."

Grabbing the matching pocket square, I headed toward the register. "I think we're done here."

Hunter followed behind me. "But we were having so much fun. I think we're really bonding."

"How was your shopping trip with Hunter?"

I plopped on Aurora's couch, kicked off my shoes, and put my feet on her coffee table. "Fucking awful."

She gave me a chaste kiss and sat beside me. "It couldn't have been that bad."

"I was the bulls-eye, and he threw darts at me all night. Dude's got great aim too. Ping, ping, ping... they kept on coming."

"Awww... I'm sorry. You know he does it because he likes to ruffle your feathers." She rested her head on my shoulder.

My arm went around her, pulling her tighter to my side. I'd gotten addicted to the feel of her skin against mine and the smell of her coconut shampoo. "I know. It's so damn hard though. The guy is an expert at needling my biggest weak spots."

She chuckled. "I didn't think you had any weak spots."

"Everybody does," I said with a kiss to the top of her head.

She crawled onto my lap, straddling me. "What's your kryptonite?"

Between Aurora and Hunter, I wasn't sure who was more obsessed with superhero references. When Hunter did it, it was annoying and mocking. But when Aurora made them, she looked at me like I might actually be able to save the world. Granted, my power didn't come in the form of superhuman strength; it was more about preventing people from becoming victims of crime in the first place. That was the whole point of CyberSecure.

I grabbed her hips, loving her weight on top of me. "Tonight, he poked at my nerdiness and lack of fashion sense."

She puffed out her bottom lip in a dramatic pout. "You poor thing. I thought you had better self-esteem than that." With a pat to my chest, she asked, "What else?"

Maybe I was being a bit sensitive, but it was more than the snide remarks about my bow ties. "He keeps talking about having sex with my sister. It's weird."

"Actual details or implications?" she asked with a quirk of her brow.

"Implications, but it's enough. I don't need those pictures in my head," I said with a huff. I wasn't under any illusion that my sister was a virgin, but it wasn't something any brother wanted to think about.

"I might not know Hunter well, but he's the kind of man who likes a reaction." Aurora ran her hands through my hair, her fingernails sending goose bumps down my spine. "Don't let him into this brilliant mind. What else?"

"Money." It always came back to this. Yes, I was on my way, but the lifestyle and privileges that came with having millions of dollars were still a mystery. No matter how much I made, I'd always feel on the outside of an exclusive club, bumbling my way through high society and ignorant of the unspoken rules. "He makes me feel... inadequate," I admitted.

"Oh, Tom, you're more than enough. Money doesn't define who you are. It's what's in here"—she tapped my temple with her finger—"and in here"—she patted my chest—"that counts. Everyone sees it but you."

"Maybe," I conceded. "I hate knowing Hunter and Charli paid for our shopping sprees tonight. And let's face it, it's Hunter, because my sister doesn't make that kind of money as an aerial performer. It feels emasculating. I'm going to owe him."

Aurora worried her bottom lip between her teeth. "About that…"

Chapter 28
Aurora

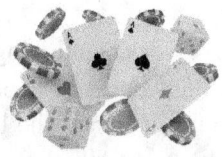

I worried my lip, because if Tom found it emasculating for Hunter to pay for his tuxedo, I dreaded what he'd think about me paying for my own dress and shoes.

"About what?"

Instead of tiptoeing around it, I blurted it out. "I didn't let Charli pay for my dress."

His eyes bulged out and his hands tightened on my waist. "What?"

"Hear me out. With our... *situation*... I didn't think it would be right. If I have to leave Vegas—"

He closed his hand over my mouth. "We're not talking about that. Remember?"

I pried his hand away. "Just because we're not talking about it, doesn't mean the possibility doesn't exist. It wouldn't be right to let her pay, only for me to leave. Besides... I can afford it."

His lips twisted to the side as he absorbed that information. "You can afford it?"

Swallowing the lump in my throat, I admitted, "Yes. I'm sure you have questions about that."

He looked up, preferring to focus on the ceiling rather than on me. Finally, his eyes found mine. "I do have questions."

"I'll tell you what I can."

"How much money do you have? I mean… obviously I don't want exact numbers, because that's not my business, but are we talking comfortable wealth or extreme wealth?"

I bit my lip. "The latter."

"Why didn't you tell me? I've been thinking you and I were in the same boat, but it seems I'm in a dinghy and you're on a yacht."

"You didn't ask. My bank account is the least interesting thing about me. Would it have changed how you felt about me?"

He sighed. "No…. maybe. It would have probably intimidated me at first. Is this from your job?"

"That's a complicated question. I make good money at my job, but I work for the family business. My grandfather started the company and it's been successful. I have a trust fund and get a monthly stipend in addition to my salary. The real money comes from there."

"Jesus Christ. All this time, I've been talking about rich people this and rich people that. You must think I'm an idiot."

"I don't think you're an idiot." I smoothed back his hair. "Actually, I have a lot of respect for you. I've done nothing to earn my money except be born into a wealthy family. You've worked your ass off to get where you are. That is so much more commendable."

"I still don't understand why you wouldn't tell me."

I crawled off his lap. "My whole life, people have befriended me because of my family connections. It's hard to tell who is sincere and who thinks I can do something for them. My friendships have been precarious to say the least. This was my chance to be anonymous. For people to get to know the real me without money being a factor. It was refreshing, so I ran with it. No show. No expectations. No unrealistic standards. I hope you can forgive me."

Tom rubbed his chin as if he was mulling over my confession. "I forgive you, but I'm disappointed you didn't feel secure enough to tell me."

"Let's be honest. This relationship is new. We're still learning about each other."

"True."

"Besides, my father uses it as a weapon. Threatening me that everything can be taken away like that," I said with a snap of my fingers.

"Is that why you don't get along with him?"

I nodded. "That's part of the reason." It was the truth, but not the whole truth. My father's insistence that Aidan and I get married drove the wedge deeper between us. My resentment grew with every passing day. The more I fell in love with Tom, the more I hated my father.

"Wait!" Tom exclaimed. "Does this make me a gold digger? Are you my sugar mama?"

Despite the serious expression on Tom's face, I laughed. His thought process was absurd. "This! This is why I didn't want to tell you." I held his face between my hands. "You, Tom Bently, are the furthest thing from a gold digger I've ever met. If anything, you've spoiled me to your own detriment. I'm definitely not your sugar mama."

"Whew!" He pretended to wipe sweat from his brow. "I want to spoil you, but does it even count if you can afford it yourself?"

"It counts," I assured him. "When you spoil me, it shows me your heart, not your wallet. Besides, you've given me plenty of *gifts* in the bedroom that didn't cost you a dime."

His face lit up. "Oh, have I now?" He grabbed me around the waist, and I squealed as he put me back on his lap. "Those are my favorite gifts to give."

Tom's fingers dug into my sides, hitting a ticklish spot and making me squirm. "What a coincidence. They're my favorite gifts to receive."

Burying his nose into the sensitive spot between my neck and shoulder, he growled. "Ask and you shall receive, my angel."

"Please," I begged.

"Please, what? What do you want, Rora?"

"Please take me to the bedroom and ravish me. Fuck me hard and long. And, oh…" I held up a finger. "If you could do that trick with your tongue, I would really appreciate it."

"Such a dirty girl. I love it."

In one fell swoop, he stood and tossed me over his shoulder, giving my butt a hard smack. It stung, but was surprisingly enjoyable, sending shivers down my spine. It may have taken a while to get Tom to notice me, but now that he had, he couldn't take his eyes off me.

I think I unleashed a beast.

The information management system for Helping Hands had been up and running for a week. Every day, I looked at the client input, hoping to see Aidan's name. Hoping that somehow we'd simply missed each other with my volunteer schedule, and he'd been here all along.

And every day I was disappointed.

His name was nowhere on the log.

Today wasn't any different.

Kendra scrolled through the backend information that the program gathered. "This is amazing! We've never had this kind of data before. Not only will it help us get the grant, but it'll improve our services. I don't know how to thank you."

I waved off the compliment even though I was glowing inside. "I'm happy I could help. By any chance, did you get a phone call from Gia Dorsey?"

Kendra tore her eyes from the computer screen, her face beaming. "Yes, I did! She told me you recommended us for their charity fundraiser. Eeek! I'm meeting with her tomorrow. Between this and the grant, Helping Hands will be financially stable."

My hands flew to my chest in relief. Although Gia had said she would follow up, I wasn't sure if it was for my benefit or if it was genuine. "That's such great news."

"I want you at the event as one of our representatives. You've done so much for us since you've been here. I don't know where we'd be without you."

I gave her a tentative smile. "I'd be honored."

The truth was, I probably wouldn't be in Vegas for the fundraiser. My father would have carted me back to California by then to live a life that suited his needs. What I wanted didn't matter.

Everything hinged on finding Aidan, getting him the help he needed, and creating our own plan. A way to change our destiny.

I just didn't know what that was yet.

Chapter 29
Tom

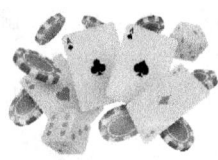

Sitting in my office at Mystique, my fingers froze over the keyboard of my laptop. *Do it*, I told myself. *You would have already if it were anyone else.*

It was true, no doubt about it, but still I hesitated. It felt like an invasion of privacy. A trust broken. An intrusion.

But I needed to know. My mind wouldn't rest until I did. Arguing with myself wasn't helping.

Fuck it!

I was pulling back the damn curtain.

Before I could change my mind, I typed *Aurora LeFleur* into the search bar. My fingers tapped restlessly while the blue loading indicator spun on the screen. Within seconds, dozens of results popped up, the first of which was a damn Wikipedia page.

What?

Ignoring Wikipedia, I clicked on her Instagram first. Her most recent post was almost four months ago. A picture of a younger her and a guy. He had his arm slung over her shoulder and they stood in front of a black pickup truck. The caption read: *Missing my best friend @Aidan Huxley.*

I enlarged the picture and squinted my eyes. So, this was Aidan. The guy Aurora crossed state lines to find. Unfortunately, he didn't have a third eye, a horn growing out of his head, or gnarly teeth. He was a good-looking dude, objectively speaking. I inspected the picture more thoroughly, looking for... I didn't know... a twinkle in her eye that told me he was more than a friend?

Finding nothing, I scrolled through more of her page. Her on the beach. Her standing by a new convertible Corvette. Her holding a glass of wine at a vineyard.

Interesting. In not a single picture was she wearing glasses. I remembered asking her if she ever wore contacts. *I used to.* That was all she said. Now, I wondered if it was part of the anonymity she cherished.

Clicking into her other social media pages, I found many of the same pictures. Aidan wasn't among any of them. She didn't post often, and not once since she'd been in Vegas.

Having put it off long enough, I moved the cursor to hover over the link for the Wikipedia page. I knew it would give me the most information. Part of me was afraid to find out the truth; the other part was desperate to know it.

Quit being such a wuss. Do It!

I closed my eyes and pressed my index finger on the mouse. Cracking one eye open, I began to read.

Aurora Adele LeFleur is an American socialite. She is the great-granddaughter of Gerard LeFleur and sole heiress of the LeFleur Media empire. She is the daughter of Gerard LeFleur II and Serina LeFleur.

"Holy shit!"

Everything she told me was true; however, she neglected to tell me the *family business* was LeFleur Media. No wonder her father wanted her back in California.

I skimmed down the rest of the page.

The approximate net worth of LeFleur Media is $53 billion.

Taking off my glasses, I leaned back in my cushy leather chair and rubbed my eyes. I couldn't believe what I was seeing. Aurora wasn't wealthy; she was swimming in an ocean of money.

Or at least her family was.

There was no way they would approve of us dating. I was a nobody. A guy from Bumfuck, Colorado, as Hunter so eloquently stated. A guy who'd been living off ramen noodles and caffeine for the last few months. A guy with a pipedream who hadn't made a single dollar from it yet.

I had no business dating a woman like Aurora.

"Fuck! Fuck! Fuck!" I banged my head against the back of the leather chair.

"Is there a problem with the software?" Trent leaned against the doorjamb with his arms crossed and a concerned look on his face.

Putting my glasses back on, I watched the data of the old system and the new system flow across my screens, embarrassed he'd seen my outburst. The data was all in perfect sync. "No issues. It's honestly going smoother than I expected. We had a slight glitch with check-ins at first, but that's been corrected. Your staff followed the protocol for manual backup perfectly. Since then, no issues. I'm getting ready to install the loyalty program. We'll be ready to go live next week."

"That's excellent." He pushed off the jamb and sat across from my desk. "You seem stressed."

Was he kidding? "Of course, I'm stressed. I don't want to let anyone down. There's a lot on the line. Just because it worked in my closed system at home didn't mean it would work here."

His brows furrowed. "But it is, correct?"

"Perfectly." With each glitch-free day, my blood pressure dropped, and my confidence soared. The real test would be when we shut down the original software and CyberSecure was running on its own.

"Then why the head bashing?"

My lips twisted. "Are you asking as a friend or my boss?"

"I'm not your boss anymore. Remember? You ditched me," he said with a chuckle.

"I didn't ditch you. I moved on to bigger things. I thought you were over it."

His lips pressed together in a thin line. "I am. My temp PA is fine, but losing you was like losing a limb. This new guy is a golden retriever puppy." He held his arms up like paws and let his tongue hang out, panting. "What's next, sir? What's next, sir?" Trent folded his arms across his chest. "Maybe I never told you, but I appreciated your ability to anticipate my needs and get shit handled. Made my life a hell of a lot easier."

Better to hear it late than never. "Thank you. I did my best. Give the new guy a break. He's still learning, and you can be a bit intimidating."

"Naw. Since marrying Gia, I'm more bark than bite." He leaned forward and rested his elbows on my desk. "Back to your question. I'm asking as a friend, not your boss. We're practically related now, me being your brother-in-law's brother and all."

"And is the triangle of trust still intact?"

He lifted an eyebrow. "Always."

"You can't tell Hunter."

"Okaaay. What's up?"

"I found out some stuff about Aurora and I'm not sure how to feel about it," I admitted.

His lips pursed. "Good stuff or bad stuff?"

"Neither really. She mentioned her family had money, so I Googled her."

"That was mistake number one, but I had you background check Gia when she first started working here, so I don't have much room to talk. What did you find?"

I turned my laptop around so he could see the screen. "Read for yourself."

He pulled it closer, and his eyeballs moved side to side as he read, growing wider and wider. Finally, he pushed the computer back at me. "LeFleur Media? Wasn't expecting that. She's the sole heiress?"

"Apparently."

"So what's the problem? Looks like you've hooked yourself a good one."

I cringed. It was the exact reaction I didn't want to receive. "I'm a nobody. People are going to think I'm with her for the money. Her family will never approve."

"First of all, you didn't even know about the money. Secondly... fuck anyone who thinks you two don't belong together. You're perfect for each other."

I laughed. "A perfect mismatch. She comes from a world of wealth and power and legacy. According to her Instagram page, she has a convertible Corvette back in California. I drive a Honda with shitty air conditioning that needs a prayer to start."

"Who cares? You're compatible in every way that counts. I've never seen you smile so much. Did you think any less of Penny when she started dating Brett?"

"Besides the fact that I wanted her to pick me and he broke her heart? No."

Trent jumped out of the chair and pointed at me. "I knew it! I knew you had the hots for her. Why didn't you make a move?"

"Shhh! Sit down." He reluctantly sat with a smug smirk on his face. "By the time I got the nerve, she was already googly-eyed over Brett. I didn't want to be anyone's second choice. It worked out better this way. She's happy and we're still great friends."

He tsked a finger at me. "Don't let anyone snag Aurora away from you. You fight for the one you love."

"Nobody said anything about love." Yes, I was desperately in love with Aurora, but saying it out loud would make it hurt more when she left.

"Pfft! You don't have to. Everyone sees it."

I turned to my computer again and pointed to the screen. "But this! This is a problem."

"It's only a problem if you let it be a problem. Man up! You're not the same guy you were before."

No. No, I wasn't, but that didn't mean I wasn't still afraid of losing her.

Chapter 30
Aurora

Since I'd been in Vegas, I'd spent most of my time either in my apartment or at the shelter. This wasn't a vacation for me. I came with a mission, not a travel itinerary. But now that Tom and I were running out of time, I wished I had.

Time was a funny thing.

There were moments when it crept at a snail's pace, every tick of the clock agonizingly slow.

But when time was limited, it was like being in a cyclone, everything spinning fast and blurring together in a kaleidoscope of colors.

Tom insisted on taking me on a tour of the Strip. Yes, I'd driven by, but I hadn't experienced it. I'd be lying if I said I wasn't excited.

Our rideshare pulled to the curb in front of Mystique. Tom stepped out, then took my hand and helped me. The sun dipped behind the mountains, turning the Strip a watercolor blend of pinks and golds. "I thought we'd start here, do a little gambling, and then walk. There is so much I want to do with you."

I stood there for a moment, taking everything in… the bright neon lights, the music and laughter, and the people. So many people. Some were dressed in casual attire, like us, but others were ready to hit up the clubs in short dresses and sky-high heels. A showgirl covered in sequins and feathers passed out fliers for a music revue. An Elvis impersonator shook hands and posed for pictures. A lady with a guitar, who had to be at least seventy, wearing cowboy boots and a tiny, saggy bikini, sang. It was almost obscene, but I couldn't look away. "Is it always like this?"

Tom chuckled. "Usually. Some nights are crazier than others." He tugged on my hand. "Let's try our luck in the casino."

We walked through the sliding doors and an elaborate lobby to the gaming area. "This is where you work?" I asked over the hum of whirring slot machines, clinking chips, and dinging bells.

Tom held up a finger. "Technically, I'm not an employee anymore. I'll only be at Mystique until the security software is up and running, then hopefully it's on to the next hotel. I don't spend much time down here. I'm up on the second floor where the administrative offices are."

The room was full of gaming tables and hundreds of slot machines. "I don't even know where to start. I've never been to a casino."

"Anywhere you want. Let's hit the bar and you can think about it."

We took the stairs to an elevated bar in the center of the room, where Tom ordered us both a fruity concoction.

One sip and I was in heaven. "Oh my gosh, this is so good!"

"Easy there, killer. They look innocuous, but they're potent. At least the first one is. They keep you coming back for more. People tend to gamble more recklessly with a little liquid courage. It's all part of the game. And I don't want you to get too buzzed because I have a lot planned for us tonight."

"Understood." I took another tiny sip. "What's your favorite game?"

"I'm partial to blackjack," he said, cracking his neck from side to side.

"Then let's do that. I want to watch for a bit."

"Alrighty." He led me over to the blackjack tables and traded a hundred-dollar bill for chips. We stood on the outskirts and watched. Tom's eyes followed the dealer, paying close attention to the cards that were dealt.

After a few hands, he took a seat and began to play. I didn't know much about blackjack, but Tom ordered the dealer with expertise, clearly comfortable. Twenty minutes later, he had a whole pile of chips in front of him. Thanking the players, he bowed out and scooped his chips from the table.

"You're really good at that," I said as we walked to the cashier.

"Too good. People like me have to be careful."

"Were you counting cards?" I whispered with a gasp.

"I plead the Fifth." Taking his winnings from the cashier, he held out a few bills to me. "What do you want to try?"

"Slots?"

Tom slung his arm over my shoulder. "Okay, let's give the one-armed bandit a try. Pick your poison."

We wandered toward a machine with sevens emblazoned on it and I sat on the little stool in front of it. Feeding the money into the machine, it came to life. "How many credits should I bet?"

"Up to you. The more you bet, the bigger the winnings."

Feeling cautious and not wanting to waste Tom's money, I bet one credit and pulled the arm. The reels inside spun, landing on a cherry, a seven, and a dollar sign. "How much did I win?"

"Nothing yet." He laughed. "Try again."

After a few more pulls, the machine started to ding. I didn't win anything big, but it sent a little thrill of excitement through me. Pushing the button to cash out, I said, "I can see how this is addicting."

"You're finished? You didn't play long."

I wrapped my arms around his waist and looked up at him with a smile. "I want to see all the sights, so we should move along." Plus, spending Tom's money at a casino didn't sit right with me.

"Your wish is my command." He twined our fingers together and we headed back to the Strip. We hadn't walked too far when we stopped in front of a large pond and Tom checked his watch. "Perfect timing. It should be starting any minute now."

As if on cue, water shot out of the pond in colorful arcs and Frank Sinatra's voice crooned "Fly Me to the Moon" from invisible speakers. The jets danced and swirled in a choreographed routine, the lights and water perfectly synced to the music. "You planned that," I said, as I leaned against the railing and watched in amazement. I'd seen videos of the Bellagio fountains, but they couldn't hold a candle to the real thing. "It's so beautiful!"

Tom stood behind me, his hands on the railing next to mine. The warmth of his body seeped through my thin blouse, making me feel protected and cherished. He pressed his lips to my cheek. "You're what's beautiful."

When the show ended, we crossed Las Vegas Boulevard to the Eiffel Tower replica at the Paris. "I've been to the real one," I blurted and immediately regretted shoving my money in his face.

Tom took it in stride. "That may be, but you haven't seen the view from this one." He purchased two tickets, and we waited in line for the elevator.

Once tucked inside, I realized it was made of glass. As it started to ascend, I buried my head in Tom's chest to keep my stomach from doing flip-flops. "Oh god!"

He wrapped his arms around me. "I would never let anything happen to you. Wait 'til we get to the top."

When the elevator stopped, I cautiously stepped out onto the observation deck. It wasn't as scary as I thought it would be, as we were caged in.

Tom stepped up to the railing, and I followed. The city was alive and bustling beneath us, yet we could barely hear it. He pointed out the half-scale Statue of Liberty at the New York-New York Hotel & Casino, the Sphere, the High Roller Observation Wheel, and the Luxor's pyramid with its massive skyward beam cutting through the darkness like a sword. The city seemed almost magical, bold and glittering. "I'm glad I waited to do this with you."

"I'm glad I'm getting to show it to you. I wasn't born here, but it feels like home."

"It's beginning to feel like home to me too. Not because of the glitz or glam or neon lights, but because of you."

Tom cupped my face between his hands. "Then stay." He looked over my shoulder in thought and then back at me. "I have a confession, and I hope you're not upset. I Googled you. I know who you are and what you have waiting for you in California."

I wasn't surprised. The only shocking part was that it took him so long to do it. My whole life was public information. When people found out who I was, they looked at me differently. It's why I enjoyed the anonymity of living here. For the first time in forever, I could be myself. "I'm not upset. You know the real me, not what some society page says. LeFleur Media is my family legacy, but it's not what I want. My father doesn't understand that."

"All I know is I want you. The real you. I don't care about anything else, and I'll do whatever I can to convince you to stay. To take a chance on us."

A lump caught in my throat. "I wish it were that easy. That what I wanted mattered."

He rested his head against mine. "I'm in love with you, Aurora LeFleur."

Those were the words I'd been dying to hear since the night of Charli's wedding. Not some drunken proclamation, but a sober declaration. Standing at the top of the Eiffel Tower with the lights of Vegas shining around us, it was the most romantic night of my life. "I'm in love with you too, Tom Bently."

His eyes closed and a smile spread across his face. "I've been in love with you since the day we met, but I've been too afraid to tell you."

"We could have had so much more time together." Thinking about what could have been, it was hard to keep the sadness out of my voice.

"Tell me what I can do," he begged.

"I wish I had an answer for you, but I don't. I've been turning it over and over in my head."

"I'm not going to give you up without a fight. Whatever happens… you're mine. I'll move to California if I have to."

I shook my head. "You've just built a new company. I won't let you risk it. You need to be here."

"We'll figure it out. We'll make it work," he promised.

It sounded good in theory, but he had no idea the lengths my father would go to. Gerard LeFleur II was ruthless when it came to getting what he wanted. This was bigger than Tom and me.

Not wanting to ruin our night, I agreed. "You're right. We'll figure something out. I don't want to let you go either."

His lips crashed into mine in a searing kiss as his hands grabbed my waist, sending a jolt of desire straight to my core. I slung my arms over his shoulders and buried my fingers in the hair at the nape of his neck, tugging at the short strands. Oblivious to the other people on the observation deck, our mouths opened, and our tongues tangled. We devoured each other with passion and desperation.

This spark. This chemistry was what had been missing my entire life. All the clichés about knowing when you'd found "the one" were true.

He pulled me closer with his hand on my back, pressing his hard length into my belly. My panties became useless, soaked with my desire for him. We should have stopped, but I refused to let him go. Being in his arms felt too damn good.

"Get a room!" someone yelled.

We broke apart and laughed. I felt like a teenager all over again, caught making out in the back seat of a car at the high school football game. Except here, I didn't have to worry about someone reporting me to my father. There was freedom in that. "We should get going."

Tom straightened like some random stranger hadn't chastised us. "We should. So much still to see and do." He took my hand and led me to the elevator.

Back on the ground, Tom took me to the Venetian, where we rode in a gondola through the streets of Venice under a painted sky.

He checked his watch again as we exited the boat. "Shoot! We need to get moving. We have a dinner reservation in fifteen minutes." We practically ran to the curb as Tom raised his hand in the air, hailing a taxi. When the yellow checkered cab pulled over, he opened the door and ushered me inside. "STRAT hotel, please."

"You got it, mister." The driver merged into traffic, cutting off a party bus. The taxi dodged and swerved around other cars, honking and barely missing a group of pedestrians.

I gasped. "Please don't kill us or anyone else."

The driver chuckled as he looked at me in the rearview mirror. "Been doing this twenty-seven years and haven't lost a tourist yet." I wished he would keep his eyes on the damn road. And what was that smell?

When he stopped in front of another hotel, I quickly opened the door to escape while Tom handed the driver some money. "That thing was a death trap."

"I usually close my eyes and pray. You'll forget all about it during dinner," he promised. "I've never been here, but I've heard it's a must-see."

Another long elevator ride later, we stepped out into a restaurant that could only be described as magical. Every wall was made of windows, giving a spectacular view. As we stepped to the hostess stand, I could have sworn the floor shifted. "Is it me, or do you feel like we're moving?"

The hostess smiled. "You are indeed moving. Top of the World rotates a full three hundred and sixty degrees every eighty minutes, giving you the best view in Vegas." She led us to our table, right next to the glass. "Enjoy."

"Tom!" I whispered. "You shouldn't have. This place probably costs beaucoup bucks."

"Why do you think we hit the blackjack table first? Don't worry. Let me take care of you," he said with a wink.

I'd been to a lot of fancy places, but nothing as unique as this. The food was divine and the wine even better. Tom and I talked about everything except the trajectory of our relationship. It was as if we mutually decided that if we didn't talk about it, then the possibility of my leaving didn't exist. I liked that fantasy world and wanted to stay in it forever.

With my belly full and my brain a bit hazy from the wine, we strolled back down the Strip hand in hand. I leaned into Tom's side. "Thank you for tonight. This has been so much fun."

"You're not pooping out on me, are you?" he teased.

"Not yet."

"Good, because I have one more thing I want to show you and you're going to love it." He stopped and grabbed my shoulders, turning me to face a building that looked straight out of Morocco with its exotic architecture and huge neon palm trees, aptly named *Oasis*. "This is my favorite show in Vegas, though I might be a bit biased."

The marquee read *Indulge Your Deepest Desires*. I slapped a hand over my mouth. "Is this one of those nudie shows?"

Tom laughed. "No. No nudity, although it is sensual and erotic. This is where Charli performs. She snagged us two tickets." He pulled them from his back pocket and held them up.

The sluggishness I'd been feeling after dinner evaporated as I grabbed the tickets from his hand. "I've been dying to see her perform. It seems so dangerous, yet exciting," I said with a shimmy.

"I've been watching her for years and it still gives me heart palpitations. I'm afraid those silks won't hold, and she'll go spiraling to her death. She says I'm ridiculous, but it's my right as her brother to worry. She may be a pain in my ass, but I kinda like that girl."

Although he tried to sound nonchalant, I could hear the affection in his voice. He'd left Colorado to make sure his sister was safe as she followed her dreams. It was admirable and endearing.

I knew as I listened to him that although he'd said he'd move to California, this was his home. I wouldn't take that away from him.

Chapter 31
Tom

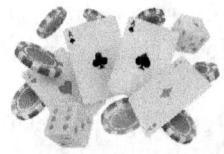

"Oh my god! Charli is amazing!" Aurora gushed. "When she did that flippy-do thing, where she unraveled and free fell… my heart jumped out of my chest." She was so animated as she waved her hands all over the place, trying to mimic the move. "I understand the palpitations now. You must be so proud of your sister."

"I am. That girl has determination in spades. She doesn't let anything stop her." If she were in my place, she'd do whatever it took to make things work with Aurora. I'd foolishly offered to move to California on a whim, but my job was in Vegas—at least for now. It would be reckless to start a new business and then move, especially when Mystique was hosting a launch party and my potential clients were here.

Maybe Aurora could stay.

Maybe her father would see how happy she was.

Maybe I could convince Gerard LeFleur II that I wasn't some *schmuck*, as Hunter said.

Maybe.

Maybe.

Maybe.

I'd lived my whole life on facts and certainties. The maybes made me crazy.

Shaking my head of the thoughts, I focused on the here and now and the beautiful woman on my arm. Risking our lives in another taxi wasn't on my agenda, so I ordered a rideshare to take us home. When it pulled to the curb, I opened the door for Aurora and ushered her in.

She snuggled into my side. "This is so much better than the cab. Smells better too."

"That it does," I agreed, cupping the back of her head. Pressing my lips to hers, I caressed the seam with the tip of my tongue, begging her to open for me. She kissed me back, our tongues moving in tandem as she crawled onto my lap and straddled me. I pressed my growing erection into the soft space between her legs, and she moaned as she rolled her hips against my length.

We moved in perfect rhythm. Her soft against my hard. No hurry. No rush. Just two bodies synced to our heartbeats, lost in a moment. My inhale was her exhale. A single breath shared between us.

I grasped the perfect globes of her ass and pulled her down harder against me. She had to be close. My girl had a hair trigger, and I wasn't against using it to my advantage.

Within moments, she gasped and shivered.

"Did you?" I whispered.

"Yes."

"No sex in the car!" the driver yelled, making us break apart.

She buried her head in my chest and giggled.

"No worries. All our clothes are on," I assured the driver, although that wouldn't be the case for long.

He pulled up in front of our building and I rushed Aurora through the lobby and up to her apartment. She may have gotten a release, but my dick was painfully hard behind the denim of my jeans. It needed inside her perfect pussy. Right now!

214

Once through the door, we were a mess of lips and tongues and teeth, hands groping and clothes flying. We clawed at each other, feral animals succumbing to instinct.

Want.

Need.

Lust.

A shot of adrenaline straight to the heart and I was drunk on her.

"On your knees," I demanded, as I picked her up and tossed her on the mattress, her tits bouncing.

"Bossy."

"Damn right." I gripped my dick in my hand and gave it a hard tug. Precum dripped from the tip and spilled down my shaft.

Her pupils dilated. "If you want it, come and get it." Refusing to obey, she spread her legs and ran a finger through her drenched center, bringing it to her lips and sucking it clean.

I nearly came right then and there, with my dick in my fist instead of buried inside her. "You're a bad girl." With a groan, I kneeled between her spread legs and captured her mouth with mine. She tasted like every fantasy come true.

Filling her with my fingers and curling them to hit her G-spot, I pressed the heel of my hand against her clit, teasing out another orgasm. Her head fell backward, and a needy moan escaped her lips. "You're so fucking gorgeous when you come, but you're going to look even more gorgeous when you come all over my cock."

She licked her lips. "Yes, please."

That was it! My restraint snapped. I flipped her over and pulled her up on all fours. "Tell me you're on the pill," I growled as I ran the head of my cock through her arousal.

"I am."

Thank god! I'd never fucked without a condom, but I didn't want anything between us. I needed to feel her.

All of her.

I slid in an inch, her warm heat hugging me tight. Heaven. Pure heaven. I took a deep breath, trying to fight the orgasm already crawling up my spine. "Goddamn, Rora, you're so fucking wet. So ready for me."

"More, Tom," she begged with a wiggle of her hips.

"Stay still." My palm came down with a hard smack on her ass. She moaned as a beautiful pink handprint bloomed on her skin. My dirty girl liked being spanked and, fuck, that was sexy. Two more smacks, and her ass was bright red. Her pussy pulsed as another orgasm rocked her.

"Greedy girl, that's three for you." I couldn't take any more. With a thrust of my hips, I buried myself balls deep in her pussy. So wet. So tight. So fucking perfect. "Fuck. You feel too good."

"Oh god!"

I wrapped one hand around her hair and pulled, making her back curve and her ass stick up in the air. With my other hand holding her hip, I drove into her at a punishing pace, our skin slapping together loudly. I'd never experienced such pure ecstasy. With every thrust, it brought me closer and closer to the edge.

She clenched again and her walls fluttered around my dick. It took everything I had not to explode inside her. "That's four."

I let go of her hair and wrapped my arms around her waist, bringing her back to my chest. Kissing her shoulder, I slowed the pace, loving the position. I didn't think I could get any deeper, but I did. Deeper than I'd ever been before.

Her head fell back, exposing the slender column of her neck. I started at the base and worked my way up, covering her in kisses. "I love you."

I didn't know how badly I needed to hear those words. How those three little syllables would make me serve my heart up on a silver platter. It was hers… to love or destroy. Either way, she owned it.

"I love you too, angel." I kneaded her breasts and rolled her nipples between my fingers, giving them a gentle pinch before doing it all over again. She gasped and sighed as I fucked her slowly. Every nerve in my body was a lit fuse, ready to detonate. "Need to come now." I quickened my pace, snapping my hips faster. It was too much and not enough. *Fuck the tingles.* A trail of fire shot down my spine in an explosion of pure pleasure. My vision blurred and my brain short-circuited as endorphins filled every cell in my body. I was high on them.

The world tilted and blood rushed through my ears.

Up was down and down was up. It was complete and utter euphoria. Nirvana.

Nothing could ever be as perfect as this.

Chapter 32
Aurora

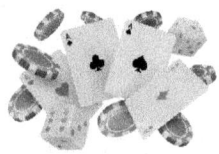

My index finger hovered over the green icon on the screen. It needed to be done. It couldn't be put off a minute longer. Before I could talk myself out of it, I pushed the button.

The phone began to ring. Once. Twice.

I tapped my short nails against my thigh.

Three times.

"Hello, my beautiful girl. It's nice that you're calling me for a change instead of me calling you."

"Hi, Mama. How are you?"

"I'm good. Your father is driving me crazy, but what else is new?"

They'd been married for almost thirty years and the last ten had been miserable. He wasn't always such an insufferable human. When I was little, we used to go to the beach. He'd play in the waves with me, and we'd have sandcastle-making contests. He'd been happy once. Everything changed when my grandfather died, which was the reason for my call.

"I was hoping you could do me a favor," I said.

"Of course. What do you need?"

Nervous to ask, I hemmed and hawed before spitting out my request. "Could you email me a copy of grandfather's will and trust?"

There was a sharp intake of breath on the other end of the line and then silence.

I tapped on my phone screen as if that would get her attention. "Mom?"

"Aurora, please don't ask me to do that," she begged quietly.

"Why?"

"Because it's your father's business, not mine or yours."

"*Bzzt!* Wrong answer, Mom. Dad keeps threatening me by saying I need to marry Aidan. Saying it's because of Grandfather."

"Yes, that's the plan."

"No! That's *his* plan. It's never been mine or Aidan's. I need to know exactly what's in that paperwork."

She sighed. "Aurora, please know that your father wouldn't insist unless it was in our family's best interest. There's a lot to be gained on both sides by Senator Huxley's family joining ours. You and Aidan are a perfect match."

I ground my molars in frustration. "Except we don't love each other that way. I'm in love with someone else, and if there's any loophole in that paperwork, I need to know about it." There was no question of whether I was going to find Aidan; it was more of a *when*. Because if I didn't find him first, then surely the private investigator would. I'd come to realize that looking for him on my own was only putting off the inevitable. He would be found. The fathers would make sure of it.

"I don't know where it is, Aurora."

That was a lie. We both knew my father kept all his important documents locked in the safe behind the Monet painting in his home office. "You do. The combination to the safe is your wedding anniversary."

"You're not supposed to know that," she huffed.

"Well, I do. Dad isn't as sneaky as he thinks."

"And what are you going to do with this paperwork?"

"Read it. Analyze it. Find the escape clause. Take it to a lawyer if I have to." There was no sense in hiding my intentions. She would find out soon enough anyway.

"You're playing with fire. Whatever your father wants, your father gets. That's the way it works around here. You know that."

Even though she couldn't see me, I jutted out my chin in defiance. "I'm willing to take the risk." If it meant a chance to build a life with Tom, I'd happily go down in flames.

My mother let out a loud sigh. "Is this boy really worth losing everything over? Think with your brain, Aurora, not your heart."

That pissed me off. She sounded exactly like him. "My brain *and* heart are telling me yes. Let me at least read the paperwork myself. I can't make an educated decision without knowing all the details. I'm not a little girl anymore. I'm a grown woman capable of making her own choices."

"You've always been headstrong with fierce determination. Like it or not, you get that from your father. You're more like him than you know."

I didn't want to be like my father, but you couldn't fight genetics. We may have both been stubborn, but I would never treat my children as assets to be traded. "Then you know I'm not going to drop this. If you care about my happiness, you'll help me." It was my Hail Mary. A guilt trip I hoped would work.

"You're putting me in an impossible situation by asking me to go against my husband."

"I'm not asking you to go against him. I'm asking you to support your daughter. There's a difference."

"Fine. I'll get you the paperwork, but he can't know you got it from me. I hope you find what you're looking for."

The tightness in my chest dissipated. It was a step in the right direction. "Thank you, Mama."

"And Aurora?"

"Yes?"

"Be careful. Your father is a powerful man. He'll stop at nothing to get what he wants."

It was an ominous warning I had no intention of heeding. "I understand. I love you."

"Love you, too."

I hung up the phone and sagged against the couch.

Step one was in progress, but I had a feeling it was only the beginning of a long and curvy road with a fork in the middle. Whichever route I chose was bound to have consequences. The question was, what were they?

Chapter 33
Tom

It was hard to believe the first time I came to Brett's office, I came with an idea and an offer. I'd changed my shirt three times and eaten half a container of mints on the drive over. Everything about it intimidated the shit out of me.

And here I was, a month later, and my entire world had flipped upside down. My dream wasn't a dream anymore. It was a full-fledged tech start-up, with one successful implementation under its belt.

Brett looked out the window overlooking the city, his hands shoved in his pockets. "I'm impressed with you, Tom. What you've done at Mystique is remarkable. I have to admit, I had my doubts, but you've delivered on every promise you made. The Dorseys are ecstatic. They're already seeing the benefits of CyberSecure."

"Thank you. I'm not quite finished there yet. I want to monitor the program and make a few upgrades based on the data I've received." My to-do list was never ending, but I wanted this software to be great, not good. The perfectionist in me demanded it.

"That's what I like about you... good is never good enough. That's the mindset of a successful man." He pulled open the drawer of his desk and pulled out an envelope. Handing it to me, he said, "You've earned this."

I peeked in the envelope and nearly lost my lunch. "This isn't what we agreed to."

"I'm aware."

"So why?"

He walked around the front of his desk and leaned against the edge, crossing his ankles. "I was hesitant to invest in this project, and to be honest, if it weren't for Penny, I would have passed."

I'd done the same thing to Brett that Aurora said people did to her. I used him and Penny for their money and influence. But to be fair, I was friends with Penny before she became a billionaire's wife. If it weren't for her, I'd still be coding in my living room. She believed in me, but Brett didn't. "You did pass," I said, pushing my glasses up with one finger.

He chuckled. "I did, but I underestimated you *and* my wife's power of persuasion. Letting this opportunity go would have been a big mistake on my part."

I beamed with pride. Brett's approval meant more to me than I'd admit, but I was still confused. "That still doesn't explain the number of zeros on this check."

Brett blew out a ragged breath. "I offered you a shit deal and you took it. Making you wait for the entirety of the money was a power play on my part. I liked seeing you sweat. Does that make me an asshole?" He shrugged a shoulder. "Probably, but you don't get where I am without being a little ruthless."

"So what changed?" I asked.

"I've had my ear to the ground. Vegas is buzzing about the new CyberSecure software Mystique implemented. Every single Vegas CEO we invited to the launch party has RSVP'd. They're dying to get their hands on it. No one wants to miss out on the next big thing."

There were at least thirty casinos on the Strip and even more off it. That didn't even count the hotels that weren't marketed as casinos. The number was staggering. If even ten percent purchased CyberSecure, I'd have more money than I knew what to do with. "That's awesome and a little frightening."

"Exactly. This software isn't just creating a spark; it's a goddamn rocket ready to launch and Vegas is only the tip of the iceberg. This has the potential to blow the fuck up. Hence, the million-dollar check in your hand. We need to start talking about the next steps."

"I've been thinking about that too. I need to hire some tech guys."

"Ya think?" He raised an eyebrow. "And not just tech guys. You'll need a personal assistant, an assistant to the assistant, an accountant, a marketing professional, a contract lawyer." He counted each one off on his fingers. "Not to mention a dedicated office space. There's a lot to do and you're going to need that million dollars to do it."

With every item he mentioned, my palms sweated a little more and my knee bounced a little harder. "Are you abandoning me?"

"What? Fuck no! However, this is going to get too big to use Kingston Enterprise's resources. You're going to need a dedicated team of people who work directly for you. I'll help you find them, but it's going to be up to you to manage them."

"Fuck." It was overwhelming to say the least. I was a computer nerd, not a business manager. I'd probably have to hire one of those too.

"Welcome to the big leagues, kid. You wanted it, you got it."

I swallowed down the lump in my throat. *Aurora.* More than anything, I wanted her. "What if... what if I wanted to move the company to California?"

His eyes bulged. "You're kidding me, right? Why the hell would you want to do that?" he asked, throwing his hands in the air.

"Ummm..." Saying it was for a girl sounded lame. Not to mention immature and stupid. "Personal reasons," I settled on.

He paced in front of his desk, his lips in a thin line as he tapped his fingers together. Finally, he stopped and squared me with a disapproving stare. "This personal reason wouldn't happen to be about five foot six with blond hair and blue eyes, would it?"

"It might."

"Jesus, Tom! Forget every compliment I gave you. You're an idiot!"

Ouch! That was it! Done with his power stance, I stood and faced him. I was neurotic, obsessive, and quirky, but I was not an idiot. "I'm not!"

"Correct me if I'm wrong, but you're considering moving a business, which isn't even fully established yet, because you're getting laid. That sounds idiotic to me!"

When he put it that way, it did sound idiotic, but I refused to back down. "You're saying that because you don't know who she is," I insisted.

Brett loosened his tie, yanked it off, and threw it on his desk. "And who is this woman with the magical pussy that has you throwing away the best thing that ever happened to you?"

"She's the heiress of LeFleur Media," I blurted. "And if you mention her pussy again, I'm not above knocking you the fuck out!"

He burst into laughter and looked around his office. "Where are the cameras? Because now I know I'm being punked."

I pulled up her Wikipedia page on my phone and shoved it in his face. "You're not being punked."

Brett ripped it from my hand and began reading. "Well, I'll be damned." He slumped against his desk. "So, not only have you created a multimillion-dollar product, but you're dating one of the country's most eligible bachelorettes. Do you shit golden eggs too?"

My anger subsided and I couldn't help but laugh. The entire situation was preposterous. "I wish. Just regular shit. It stinks the same as yours."

He rubbed a hand over his face and tugged on his short beard. "Explain to me your reasoning for wanting to move the company."

How could I explain something I didn't quite understand myself? "It seems Aurora's father wants her back in California. I don't know all the details, but he sounds like a dick." I held up a hand. "I know you're going to say I haven't known her that long, but I've never met anyone like her. I'm telling you... she's the one."

Brett sighed. "I get it. I really do. Not quite sure what I'd do without Penny. But... there's a lot on the line here. A lot of money invested. A market here that wants this. Now is not the time to move. Give it a year. If you two are still together in a year, then move the company. However, I can't support moving it now. If that's what you want to do, I'm going to have to pull out of our deal before you cash that check. I'm also going to remind you there's a launch party this weekend. If you're leaving, you should tell the Dorseys so they can cancel it."

Brett stared at me with a blank look on his face. I got the message: the ball was in my court. I could leave with the original ten thousand that was almost gone, move to California, and try to find a new investor or... I could cash the million-dollar check, fulfill my obligations, and hope Aurora would wait for me.

It should have been an easy decision.

A no-brainer.

My heart tugged me in one direction and my head in the other.

Aurora was my future, but what kind of future could I give her without my own financial security?

I wouldn't freeload off her.

I wouldn't be *that* guy.

We could travel back and forth.

A year wasn't *really* that long.

This was *my* dream and I'd sacrificed everything for it.

I peeked in the envelope and looked at all the zeros on the check. It wasn't simply money; it was opportunity.

"I'll give it a year," I finally said.

Brett clapped me on the shoulder. "Now you're thinking like a businessman. It's the right decision. Now let's talk about the future of CyberSecure."

I should have been happy as a nerd with color-coded spreadsheets. My head knew it was the right decision, but my heart disagreed.

Looked like I didn't have to worry about Aurora breaking my heart; I was already doing it to myself.

Chapter 34
Aurora

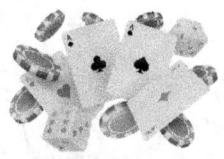

My mother followed through on her promise. The will and trust were dozens of pages long, with so much legalese it made my head spin. I was a smart cookie, but I also knew when I was in over my head.

Penny gave me a recommendation for an estate lawyer and that's how I ended up in Conrad Wyse's office. Nibbling on my already short nails, I waited for him to decipher it for me.

Finally, he set the papers down and looked at me over the edge of his wire-rimmed glasses. "I've never seen anything quite like this."

That sounded ominous. "What do you mean?"

Mr. Wyse took off his glasses and rubbed his forehead with the back of his hand. "I'm thinking your grandfather was an angry man when he had this drafted. There are a lot of conditions and side notes. He was very specific on how the company was to be structured after his death and the consequences for not following his demands."

"I don't understand. What is there to structure? My father is the CEO."

He leaned on his desk. "That's not exactly true. He's the interim executive steward, meaning he has *temporary* control until the next eligible heir has met all inheritance requirements. And that's you."

"I always knew the company would eventually be passed down to me. I'm the *only* heir."

He shook his head. "You're not understanding. It's not an *eventually* situation." He handed over a document with a section circled in red. "Read this."

Article VI- Disposition of Business Holdings

I hereby bequeath all my ownership interest, rights, and controlling shares in LeFleur Media, Ltd., not to my son, Gerard A. LeFleur II, but to my granddaughter, Aurora Adele LeFleur, upon the fulfillment of the following conditions:

1. *That she shall have reached the age of twenty-five (25) years, and*
2. *That she shall have entered into lawful matrimony with a man of sound moral character and established reputation, as determined by the appointed trustees herein (see Article VII), who shall have full discretion in evaluating said character and reputation.*

This couldn't be right. "Wait! So all I have to do is marry a man of moral character and the company is mine?" Tom was a man of moral character. It was a little soon to think about marriage, but nobody could dispute he was a good guy. Everyone loved him.

"Yes and no. This is where things get sticky." He shuffled through the stack of papers. "The trustees include your father and the board of LeFleur Media. They have to agree."

My heart sank. My father would never agree that Tom was a suitable husband. "And what if they don't agree?"

"If you haven't satisfied the requirements by the time you're thirty-five, then both you and your father get diddly-squat. All rights, titles, and

228

interests in LeFleur Media will be transferred to the LeFleur Family Trust, with your father serving in an advisory role and no executive control. You'll both get one percent of net profits instead of ownership."

What? This is what my father had been going on about. Why he said we'd end up on the street and the company would be out of our hands. One percent wouldn't sustain the life we'd been living.

Everything depended on me. The good news was technically, I had until I was thirty-five. There was no hurry to get married.

My brain swam with questions. Lots of them.

"Does it say why my father was passed over?"

"Yes." He shuffled through the papers until he found the one he was looking for. "There's a lot here, so I'm going to summarize. When your father first started working at LeFleur Media, he made some poor financial decisions for the company. The stocks crashed and the company almost went bankrupt. LeFleur Media used an outside investor to get back on its feet again. Your grandfather vowed that your father wouldn't have complete control of the company due to his financial recklessness."

"Who was the investor?"

He looked at the document again. "Senator George Huxley."

My eyes bulged. That was Aidan's grandfather. Things were starting to make sense.

I pressed my fingers to my temples. "Please tell me he didn't promise my hand in marriage as part of the deal."

Mr. Wyse scratched his head. "Not specifically. There's a copy of a handwritten letter from Senator George Huxley to your grandfather." He flipped to the next page. "It says here, and I quote, *'If our families have the chance to unify through marriage, it will be done as final payment of the debt, with each family retaining fifty percent of the controlling interest of LeFleur Media.'*"

My insides burned with rage. All this time, I'd been upset with my father, when it was my grandfather who set it in motion. My father wasn't blameless... he was the catalyst with his shitty decisions. But my sweet grandfather, who took me for ice cream every Sunday, was the man who condemned me to a future I didn't want.

Memories of Aidan and me as kids spun through my head like a movie. Trips to the zoo together with our grandpas weren't a coincidence. They were matchmaking. Days at the beach, impromptu picnics, birthday parties… every memory I had was now tainted.

"This can't be enforceable. Arranged marriages are antiquated." I crossed my arms in defiance, but before he could answer, another thought popped into my head. "What would my father get out of it?" He'd been the one pushing for the marriage ever since my grandfather died.

He held up the copy of the handwritten letter. "This is what would be called a *gentleman's agreement*. There's no way to legally enforce it. However, you're correct in assuming your father would benefit from a marriage to the Huxley family." His eyebrows knitted together, and his lips pursed as he passed me a page from the trust. "There's another clause."

"Of course there is," I said as I took it from his hand. Every word I read served to fuel the anger that already burned inside me.

In the event that Aurora LeFleur enters into legal matrimony with a member of the Huxley family—specifically, a direct descendant of Senator George Huxley—a secondary transfer shall be executed wherein Gerard LeFleur II shall be granted a lifetime Executive Advisory Position, complete with board voting rights, immunity from removal by the CEO, and ten percent (10%) controlling interest in the company's parent trust, separate from Aurora's holdings.

It explained so much.

This was my father's quest to right his wrongs and seize the control that'd been stripped from him.

I was caught in the crosshairs.

A casualty of power-hungry men.

A pawn on a chessboard.

An asset to be traded.

And I wanted nothing to do with any of it.

Yet, knowing that I would be removing my father from LeFleur Media didn't sit right with me. It was his birthright before it was mine. As mad as I was at him, he was still my father. "Is there a way to contest the trust? A way for my father to retain some ownership in the company without me marrying a Huxley?"

Conrad Wyse blew out a breath. "Maybe? Since your father is one of the trustees, his approval of your marriage is required. You could appeal to the board and seek its approval, but you would still have to legally contest the trust in court to change the corporate structure. In my experience, the court is reluctant to get involved. You need to understand that a trust is a legally binding document. They don't generally undermine how a settler, especially one as renowned as your grandfather, wants their assets managed."

"But there's a chance?"

"Yes. A small one. You're going to need a California attorney who is well versed in estate law. I can recommend someone if you'd like."

I stood and shook his hand. "Thank you for your time and expertise. I'd appreciate a recommendation."

"Good luck, Ms. LeFleur. You're in for a battle."

A small chance was still a chance, and it was worth fighting for.

Chapter 35
Tom

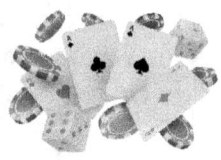

I didn't tell Aurora about the agreement with Brett to keep my company in Vegas for a year. She still hadn't told me the reason her father wanted her back in California, and until then I was justified in doing what was best for me.

Keeping the information from her made me a hypocrite. I gave her a lot of shit about keeping secrets, but when push came to shove, I was no better.

If our relationship was meant to be, we'd figure out how to make it work long distance. It was an hour flight and with all the zeros in my bank account now, I could afford it.

Tonight was about me and securing a future for my company. There would be plenty of time for difficult conversations later. After the launch party, I'd insist that both Aurora and I lay our cards on the table and figure out the way forward. The avoidance game we'd been playing would need to end.

Ignorance was bliss, but it wasn't reality.

As I walked into the party with Aurora on my arm, I felt like a king. She'd spent all day at the salon with the other ladies, insisting she wanted to look her best for me. Her honey-blond hair hung down her back in loose curls, and her makeup, though a bit darker than I was used to, made the color of her eyes even more prominent without her glasses. The sapphire-blue gown hugged her curves and accentuated her beauty. She was stunning. My girl looked every bit the wealthy heiress she was, commanding the attention of the room.

And for once, I deemed myself worthy of her.

I was no longer a personal assistant working for a millionaire boss. I was the millionaire boss. And although CyberSecure was a budding baby, tonight I was going to blow away the casino owners of Vegas with what it could do for them.

"Have I told you how gorgeous you look tonight?" I whispered in Aurora's ear.

She threw her head back and laughed. "About a dozen times." Grabbing two flutes of champagne from the tray of a strolling server and handing one to me, she clinked her glass with mine. "Congratulations! No matter what happens tonight, you deserve to be celebrated. I'm so proud of you."

"Here, here!" My sister and Hunter approached, carrying their own flutes of champagne. Charli wrapped me in a tight hug. "I'm so proud of you, big brother."

"Thank you," I said, hugging her back.

"And thanks to me, he doesn't look like a schmuck," Hunter added.

Charli gave him a playful smack in the chest with the back of her hand. "Be nice. Tonight is Tom's big night."

"What?" Hunter looked offended. "I said he didn't look like a schmuck. That *was* nice."

Not even my brother-in-law could ruin my mood with his unnecessary comments. "He's jealous because I look better than him."

Hunter scoffed. "You wish."

"I think you both look very handsome," Aurora said.

Charli wrapped her arm around her husband. "Agreed. Have you seen the others yet?"

"If you mean the Bobbsey Twins, they're by the bar," Hunter said with a jerk of his head.

The four of us joined Trent and Brett at the bar, along with Gia and Penny. They greeted us with handshakes and hugs. "Are you ready for your speech?" Trent asked.

"Got my notes right here," I said, patting the pocket inside my coat. My speech was well rehearsed, but standing at the podium, tongue-tied, was my worst fear. I hoped I wouldn't need the cue cards, but it never hurt to be prepared.

"You'll do great. I have every confidence in you," Brett assured me with a hand on my shoulder. "Come on, I'll introduce you to some people."

For the next hour, I shmoozed with the Vegas elite, cataloging names and faces in my mental Rolodex. With every person I met, my anxiety about giving a speech rose. By the time I sat down for dinner, sweat trickled down my back.

Aurora put her hand on mine. "It's going to be fine. You got this."

I pulled out my cards and reviewed them. "I don't want to fuck up."

"You won't," she said, pushing the cards down. "You know your speech inside and out."

She was right. I'd practiced in front of her dozens of times, yet by the time the servers arrived with our meal, my stomach was full of butterflies. I barely tasted the Chicken Marsala or garlic roasted potatoes. It all turned to sawdust in my mouth.

After dinner, Edward Dorsey got up on the stage to introduce me. I couldn't tell you what he said because the butterflies turned into a swarm of bees buzzing in my gut.

I ran a finger along Aurora's exposed thigh and under her dress up to her hip. She gave me a quizzical look as I hooked her underwear. "Take your panties off," I whispered in her ear.

Her eyes went wide. "What?"

"Take them off."

"Tom, everyone will see."

I looked around our table and the tables surrounding us. Everyone's eyes were glued to Edward. "No one's paying attention. Please. I want part of you with me when I give my speech."

"This is crazy." She wiggled them down her hips, covertly slid them off under the table, and balled them into my waiting palm.

Aurora gasped as I slyly lifted the scrap of fabric to my nose and inhaled her essence. The swarming settled to a low buzz and my anxiety melted away.

Applause filled the room as Edward said, "It's my honor to introduce to you the genius behind CyberSecure, Mr. Thomas Bently."

It was showtime. I slid Aurora's thong into my pants pocket and strode to the stage with the confidence of Bill Gates. I channeled his determination and ambition, knowing I'd created something truly groundbreaking. As I took the stage, my fingers slid over the silk in my pocket, harnessing Aurora's calming energy.

"Thank you, Edward. I'm honored to be standing here at Mystique, knowing they put their faith in me to deliver something incredible. CyberSecure is an innovative approach to hotel and casino security, assuring impenetrable protection for your business and its guests." I went on for the next fifteen minutes to explain the benefits of the software through a carefully curated slideshow and followed up with a quick Q and A. The goal was to create excitement and intrigue, not bore the CEOs to death with logistics.

After thanking the Dorseys and Brett for taking a chance on me, I stepped off the stage feeling like a two-ton brick had been lifted from my shoulders. With the speech out of the way, I could relax and enjoy the rest of the evening.

As music drifted through the speakers and the dance floor opened, Aurora strode toward me with open arms. "You were amazing."

I held her a little longer than necessary, burying my nose in her hair. "I couldn't have done any of this without you."

"Sure you could have, Tom Bently, you were destined for greatness long before you met me."

I pulled her underwear from my pocket, enough to give her a peek. "It was the magic panties."

She burst out laughing. "I can't believe I did that."

"You're a naughty girl who will do whatever I ask. Admit it. You can't say no to me," I said, running my hand down her backside.

She tugged on my lapels. "It's not that I can't, it's that I don't want to."

I groaned. "I can't wait to get you home."

Letting go of my coat, she pressed her hands to my chest. "There will be time for you to boss me around in bed later. Right now, there are people waiting to talk to you. Go work the crowd. It's what this whole party is about."

She wasn't wrong, yet I didn't want to leave Aurora alone for the entire night. I looked between her and the men clamoring for my attention.

"Go," Aurora said, giving me a gentle shove. "Don't worry about me. I'm gonna hang out with the girls and I'll come find you later."

"Save me at least one dance," I said, kissing her cheek.

"Absolutely." She drew a cross over her chest. "Now go shake hands and convince everyone that CyberSecure is worth the investment."

For the next two hours, I shook hands and discussed security with half of the casino owners in Vegas. I was peopled out and couldn't wait to get back to Aurora.

After a lengthy conversation with the CEO of Oasis, I finally had to cut him off. "See that pretty woman in the blue dress?" I asked, motioning toward Aurora.

"The gorgeous blond?" he asked.

"That's the one. She's my date and I'd really like one dance with her before the night ends. So, if you'll excuse me."

"Can't blame you there. Enjoy the rest of your evening. I'll be in contact soon," he said with a firm grip of my hand.

"I look forward to it." I blew out a breath as I escaped the long-winded CEO and made a beeline for my girl. Tapping her on the shoulder, I asked, "May I have this dance?"

She turned from her conversation with Gia, Penny, and Charli, blue eyes a bit glassy from the alcohol that flowed like water tonight. "I would be honored."

I led her to the dance floor, which was less crowded than it'd been an hour ago. Taking her hand in mine, I wrapped my other arm around her waist and pulled her close as "Champagne Kisses" played. We swayed to the music, our bodies in perfect harmony. "I'm sorry I didn't get to spend much time with you tonight."

"It's okay. I enjoyed watching you."

"You did, huh?"

She nodded. "I'd say it made my panties wet, but that would be a lie since I'm not wearing any. You're sexy when you're in business-mogul mode."

"I am?" I asked as I released her waist, spun her out under my arm, and pulled her back to my chest, now thinking about her being bare under that dress.

"Whoa! You *can* dance. I had my doubts after Charli's wedding." She giggled.

"I'll have you know, I'm an expert in all things that involve my hips." My hand pressed on the small of her back, making sure she could feel my erection. The one she caused solely by being her.

"That sounds like a theory to me. We may have to test it," she teased with a smirk.

"Oh, I think I've already proven it to be true."

"More testing is always better. To be sure."

I dipped her low, so she hung over my arm and her hair brushed the floor. Kissing the column of her neck, I growled. "Testing with you is my favorite thing. I'll let you evaluate my performance for yourself."

"I think we should say our goodbyes and start right away," she said as I lifted her back up.

"I couldn't agree more."

We said goodbye to our friends, and I thanked everyone again for their support before rushing out to the valet. Our limo pulled up and I practically pushed Aurora inside.

Between the success of the launch party and the woman at my side, I was on a high and I never wanted to come down.

Chapter 36
Aurora

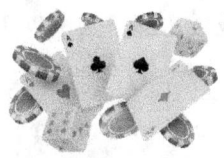

Tom fingered me in the back of the limo, and I decided not wearing panties wasn't such an awful thing. I was already one orgasm in by the time we reached my apartment.

He backed me against the door, and my purse fell to the floor with a soft thud as I wrapped my arms around his neck. "Can I have my panties back now?"

"Not a chance. They're mine." He caged me in with his arms and his eyes connected with mine. "Every part of you belongs to me."

"I see we're in bossy-mogul mode now," I teased.

"Damn right, I am. I've been waiting to get you out of that dress since I first saw you in it." With one arm behind my knees and the other supporting my back, he scooped me up and carried me to the bedroom. Once on my feet again, I bent to take my shoes off. "Those stay on," he demanded. "I want to feel those stilettos digging into my back as I fuck you."

If I'd been wearing panties, they would have been flooded. Tom was a nerdy tech guy by day, but a seriously dirty talker by night. "And the dress?"

"Oh, that's definitely coming off. Turn around."

"Bossy." I did as he asked and held my hair up. Tom kissed my exposed neck and slowly slid the zipper down. He slid the fabric off my shoulders, kissing each one, and let the dress fall to the floor.

"You are a naughty girl. No bra either?"

I looked at him over my shoulder. "I didn't want to have any unsightly lines."

"Very naughty." He kneeled and tapped the inside of my ankle. "Lift." I lifted one foot, then the other, to step out of the puddle of fabric. Tom picked up my dress and laid it gently over a chair. "Let me see you."

I turned to face him in only my black heels, feeling very vulnerable and wanting to cover all my private parts.

As if sensing my apprehension, he grabbed my wrists and held my arms out wide, preventing me from hiding. His eyes scanned me from head to toe, taking in every naked inch of my body. "You are beautiful. Pure perfection."

"Tom," I said, my voice breathy and desperate.

"Yes, angel?" His lips met my neck and glided across my bare shoulder. He licked a trail between my breasts, stopping to suck each nipple, his teeth grazing the sensitive skin and pulling them into hard peaks. "So fucking beautiful." He held my waist and fell to his knees.

My hands tangled in his thick, dark hair as he looked up at me. This man, who bowed before me, made me feel like a goddess. Never had I been so cherished and cared for. "I love you."

"I love you too." He peppered kisses along my stomach, his breath hot against my skin. Then pressed a kiss to each hip and down between them to the bare skin below, nibbling on my clit. His finger ran through my seam to the heat of my desire. "So wet for me."

"How could I not be?"

"You're my greedy girl, aren't you?" He lifted my leg and set it on his shoulder, then devoured my pussy.

My eyes fluttered and I held on to him for dear life as my insides turned to Jello. He lapped up my arousal like it was his last meal. Then, two fingers slid inside me while his tongue circled my clit. He added a third finger, and when his lips suctioned on the tiny bud, I barely had time to breathe before the orgasm seized me, sending me spiraling. I chanted his name like a prayer as my body writhed with pleasure. My unsteady body wobbled, my supporting leg ready to give out.

Tom caught me and set me on the edge of the bed. "That's my good girl."

I leaned back on my hands, still hazy as endorphins flowed through my veins. "I have one complaint."

"Funny. I didn't hear you complaining when you were calling out my name. You were so loud, I think you woke the neighbors and scared the cat."

"No complaints about that, but you're wearing too many clothes."

"You want a show?"

"I don't need a show. What I need is you naked and inside me."

He pulled on the end of his bow tie and let it unravel. The buttons of his shirt were next, revealing one inch of smooth, hard muscle at a time. "This is what you want?"

I practically panted. "Yes."

The shirt fell off his shoulders to the floor. His pants were next. I watched with rapt attention as his fingers slowly worked the button and zipper. Like a man trained in the art of seduction, his boxers, pants, socks, and shoes all disappeared in one fluid movement, leaving him standing gloriously naked before me.

"Better?"

"So much better." I licked my lips as I took in the man who'd stolen my heart.

His eyes focused on the action and his hand wrapped around his hard length, giving it a few rough tugs. "You want my cock? Then get on your knees, angel. Take it like a good girl and I'll give you everything you want."

Although I'd already come twice, my pussy flooded. This man, who was so proper by day and anything but in the bedroom, had me scrambling to my knees. I took him in my hands, pumping him up and down, then licked him from base to tip, circling the head and lapping up the salty precum leaking from it.

His hand wrapped in my hair and pulled, stinging my scalp in the most erotic way. "Don't tease."

My lips wrapped around him, and I hummed as my head bobbed, knowing it would drive him crazy. His hand tightened in my hair, and his hips jerked forward, making me gag as he hit the back of my throat. Drool dripped down my chin and onto my thighs.

Tom continued fucking my mouth with shallow thrusts. I looked up at him, his cock still down my throat. His eyes closed and his head fell back in ecstasy. His jaw clenched and air hissed through his teeth as he fought for control.

Wanting to bring him even closer to the edge, I played with his balls and gave them a gentle tug. My fingers roamed farther south, and my thumb pressed on the soft skin behind them.

He quickly pulled out. "Naughty girl, trying to get me to come in your mouth. Not happening, angel. When I come, it's going to be in that sweet pussy of yours. I'm going to fuck you slowly and thoroughly."

"Yes, please." I couldn't wait to have him inside me.

He helped me to my feet. The straps of my shoes dug into my ankles, but for Tom I'd gladly endure the pain. Leading me to the bed, he pulled back the covers and laid me down. The mattress dipped and he kneeled between my legs. His hands ran down the length of my thighs, and I wrapped them around his waist. With one hand next to my head supporting his weight, he hovered over me, his lips a whisper away from mine. "I'm never letting you go."

A tear fell from my eye and ran down my cheek. We had a long road ahead of us, a battle with my father he didn't even know he was in. I wanted to keep him forever and tell the rest of the world to go to hell. It could burn around us for all I cared. Our nights were numbered. "Make love to me," I said as I dug my heels into his back the way he demanded.

Tom lined himself up to my entrance and slowly pushed inside me, inch by inch, filling me and stretching me to mold to his body.

242

My eyes closed and a quiet gasp fell from my lips as I adjusted to his size. I'd never get used to how completely he filled me.

"Eyes on me, pretty girl."

I opened them to find him staring down at me with hooded eyes. He kissed my temple, my cheek, my lips. Each one a testament to his promise of never letting me go.

His hips began to rock at a leisurely pace. There was no hurry, no rush, no race to the end. Just love and adoration.

I wrapped my arms around his neck and ran my fingers through his hair. Our bodies moved in perfect sync, my hips meeting his with every slow thrust.

I didn't know what would happen tomorrow or the next day, but tonight we were connected as one and I'd fight anyone who tried to separate us.

Even my father.

Chapter 37
Tom

I sat in my office at Mystique on Monday, going over the spreadsheet that populated from the CyberSecure consultation interest form. It was only ten in the morning, and I already had requests from a dozen major casinos on the Strip.

The launch party had done its job. There was enough work here to keep me busy for months. Everything was falling into place as I'd hoped. At this rate, I'd have Brett's investment loan paid off in no time. And if things went as well as I expected, maybe he'd budge on the year timeline. The sooner I could be with Aurora, the better.

We hadn't gotten a chance to debrief on Saturday night, so it didn't surprise me when Brett knocked on my door a short while later. "Hey. Come on in."

He stuck his hands in his pockets and leaned against the doorjamb. "You're chipper this morning."

"Why wouldn't I be? The party was a success, and the consultation requests are already rolling in."

He stepped inside the small room and sat across from my desk. "Well, you're definitely the talk of the town."

"I am?" That was good, wasn't it? Yet, he didn't sound happy about it.

"Yep. Don't you set alerts for when you're mentioned online?"

Of course, Brett would have alerts set. He was a billionaire. His name showed up on the internet regularly. "Why would I set alerts? No one even knows who I am. No one's talking about me."

He tapped his fingertips together. "They are now."

Something was not right here, and a sick feeling filled my stomach. "I don't understand. Are people talking shit about my software? Or about me?"

Brett sighed and took out his phone. "Nah. The software got rave reviews and you're being pronounced as the next big tech genius. Nothing but praise for you. Even made it into the *Las Vegas Not So Confidential*."

It was a notorious gossip column that tore Penny to shreds when she and Brett started dating. "What the hell was Karla Blitzer doing at the launch party?"

"I invited her," he said with a shrug. "We have an arrangement. I make sure she gets into the city's biggest events, and in return, she doesn't badmouth Penny or me. It's been very mutually beneficial."

"What did she say about me?"

"It was all good." He held up his phone to read. "She said, *Thomas Bently is soon to be Vegas' newest millionaire and he's coming in hot! This swoonworthy Clark Kent look-alike is swooping in with his superpowers to protect us all from the cybervillains threatening our personal and financial information on the Strip. Have no fear, Super Tom is here! With his innovative technology, CyberSecure, casinos and guests in Vegas will soon breathe easier knowing they're not getting hacked by the bad guys. Booo on bad guys! We hate them and hope our new hero will give them a big KAPOW!"*

I laughed. "That doesn't sound so bad. I mean… it's a little dramatic and cheesy with all the Superman references, but it could be worse."

Brett's face stayed stoic as he pressed his lips together. "You should read the rest," he said, handing his phone over.

I took it and scanned to the next paragraph.

But let's get to the juicy stuff!

Oh no! That sick feeling in my stomach multiplied by a hundred.

What the ladies of Vegas really want to know is if our millionaire is single and ready to mingle. Is there a Lois Lane to his Clark Kent?
It appears there may be.
Mr. Bently showed up at his launch party with the stunning Miss Aurora LeFleur. Now, if that name sounds familiar, it should. Miss LeFleur is the sole heiress to the LeFleur Media empire. That's right, folks. She's worth millions, if not billions. It makes one wonder if Mr. Bently's superpowers aren't limited to technology... if you know what I mean.
Miss LeFleur has been seen around Vegas, and sources say she's been spending her time at Helping Hands Homeless Shelter. Not only are her pockets lined with gold, but it seems her heart is too. This beauty is a real catch. Are Tom Bently and Aurora LeFleur the new dynamic duo of Vegas? From the way they were cozied up on Saturday night, I'm thinking they might be.
But there's a twist! And oh, how we love a juicy twist.
Rumor has it that our Lois Lane is engaged to Aidan Huxley, a decorated military veteran and the son of California senator Robert Huxley. We've seen no photographic evidence of a ring (yet), but the two were regulars on the Santa Monica social scene for years. Yes, years! Friends since they were children, everyone expected the two to tie the knot. Can you imagine these two families coming together? Talk about a power couple!
Suspiciously, no one seems to know the current whereabouts of Aidan Huxley. He just POOF disappeared. One can't help but wonder... where are you, Aidan? And why are you letting Tom Bently snag your girl?
It's a love triangle we'll be watching closely. We love gossip that's not so confidential.
Are you Team Aidan or Team Tom? I know who I'm rooting for.

Below the article was a picture of Aurora and me from Saturday night, my arm around her waist. Next to it was a picture of Aurora and Aidan, his arm around her waist. The similarities were uncanny. I set the phone down, too stunned to speak.

"Did you know about all this?" Brett asked.

"Some," I answered numbly. "I knew about Aidan. I didn't know he was a senator's son or that they were engaged."

He held up a finger. "*Rumored* to be engaged. It's Karla. You know she'll take the smallest thread and run with it. Look what she did to Penny when we first got together. The woman is merciless."

I dropped my head and banged it against the desk. "It doesn't matter what's true or not true. People will believe it. Fuck. My. Life!"

"I'm sorry I invited her to the party. I never thought…"

"You're sorry? You invited that woman into my private life. And Aurora's. God! She was trying to keep her identity on the down-low, now it's splashed all over the internet for the whole world to see."

"Listen, what's done is done. There's no going back. The good news is that you were framed as the golden boy, and your software is getting good press. The important thing is to talk to Aurora and find out what's true and what's not. She doesn't strike me as the kind of woman who would lie to you about being engaged."

He didn't know the half of it! She'd been keeping secrets from day one. Our whole relationship was a house of cards built on a shaky foundation of omissions and partial lies.

I wanted to believe the story in the *Las Vegas Not So Confidential* was gossip, but behind most rumors was an inkling of truth.

My phone started pinging with incoming texts.

Charli: OMG! I'm here if you need me.

Penny: Are you OK?

Hunter: You stud muffin!

The news was spreading. I grabbed my wallet and keys and headed out the door. "I need to go!"

Brett followed me into the hallway. "Don't do anything stupid!"

Normally, that wouldn't be a problem, but lately it seemed to be my go-to. I knew she was keeping something from me, but I never thought it would be this.

Calm down! You don't even know if it's true yet.

And there was only one person who could answer that question. This time, I'd insist on the whole truth.

No more lies.

No more secrets.

No more things left unspoken.

Chapter 38
Aurora

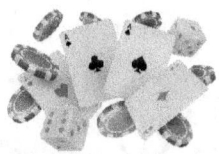

I rushed across town to Helping Hands. When Kendra called, she said it was urgent. My worst fear was that my software crashed, all the data was lost, and the shelter wouldn't get its grant. I may have started volunteering for selfish reasons, but I'd come to care about the shelter and people it helped.

Rushing in the back door, I saw Carl first. "Do you know where Kendra is?"

"Hello, to you too," he said with a smile.

"I'm sorry. Hi. Kendra asked me to come. I think there's something wrong with the computer program."

"Don't know anything about that," he said as he chopped carrots. "She's in her—"

"I'm right here."

I turned around to find Kendra clutching her clipboard. "You said it was urgent. Is something wrong with the database?"

"Nope. It's running perfectly, but there is an important matter that needs your attention. Something you should see." She walked down the hallway, motioning for me to follow.

Now I was confused. *What else could she need from me?*

When I stepped into her office, I realized we weren't alone. A man dressed in jeans and a black T-shirt, with a short beard, knelt next to a German shepherd, rubbing its back. "I don't understand."

The man raised his head and looked up at me.

Those eyes.

Green as the summer grass.

I'd know them anywhere.

My voice caught in my throat. "Aidan?"

"Hello, sunshine."

My eyes welled and tears poured down my cheeks. "Is it really you?"

"It's really me." He stood and held his arms out.

I ran.

I ran and jumped into his arms, wrapping my legs around his waist. He held me tightly and spun me around, his muscles flexing under my weight. It'd been so long, and I didn't want to let him go.

When he finally put me back on my feet, a slow clap began. Kendra and Carl stood in the doorway watching us.

Kendra put her hands to her chest. "It's moments like this that make what we do worthwhile."

"I'm glad you found your friend, Rora," Carl said.

I was still stunned. And confused. "I didn't find him. He found me. But how?"

"I'll let Aidan explain it to you. We'll give you two some time." Kendra started to walk away, but then stopped. "And don't think I don't know it's you who's been slipping those hundred-dollar bills in our donation box. Thank you," she said with a wink.

Huh?

Once Carl and Kendra were gone, the reality set in that my best friend was standing in front of me. I'd almost given up hope. Thought I'd never see him again. I rubbed my hand along his scruffy face. He looked good.

Different, but good and healthy and sober. "How? How did you know I was in Vegas?"

He chuckled.

My lips twisted to the side. "What's so funny? I looked all over the city for you, and I kept coming up empty."

"Not much has changed. You still don't check your alerts, do you?"

I waved my hand in the air. "Why would I? I don't need to read the shit people write about me."

"You probably should have read this one." He pulled out his phone and handed it to me.

I sat and read the article from the *Las Vegas Not So Confidential*. Although it sang his praise, Tom would hate the article with all the superhero references.

Is there a Lois Lane to his Clark Kent?

Oh no! The article went on to reveal my identity and the fact that I volunteered at Helping Hands. My father was going to have a fit when he saw this.

I looked up at Aidan. "So that's how you knew I was here?"

"Yep. Once I read that, I came to the shelter and asked for you." He rubbed his chin. "Did you finish the article?"

I shook my head. "Not yet."

"You should keep reading."

My eyes went back to his phone.

But there's a twist! And oh, how we love a juicy twist.

My stomach sank. Nothing that followed those words could be good. I kept reading, my heart now sinking with my stomach.

"A love triangle?"

He chuckled. "Apparently."

"Tom is gonna flip when he sees this." I worried my teeth over my bottom lip.

Aidan pulled up a chair next to me and sat. "I assume he doesn't know about me."

251

I gulped. "He knows about you. He knows why I'm in Vegas. He doesn't know your dad is a senator, or that we were supposed to get married."

He brushed my hair behind my ear. "It's a gossip rag, sunshine. It's a rumor."

I looked up at him. "But is it? Our parents started the rumor. They've been pushing us for years to tie the knot."

"Do you love this guy?"

"I do. You're going to love him too. He's sweet and thoughtful and wicked smart."

Aidan's mouth hitched up on one side in one of his classic smirks, the usual dimple in his cheek hidden behind his beard. "Good in bed?"

I rolled my eyes. "You have no idea."

He kissed my temple. "I'm happy for you, sunshine. You deserve a man who treats you right."

"When he reads this," I tapped on the phone screen, "He's going to think I've been lying to him the whole time."

"So we explain it to him. That it's what our parents want, but not what we want."

"Your dad is hiring a private investigator to find you. I convinced them to let me try first, but time is running out. What if they drag us back to California?"

"Rora, we're not children anymore. They don't control us. If we don't want to get married, that's the end of it."

That wasn't really true. Our parents had their hooks in us deeper than he knew.

Aidan rubbed his fingers over the lines in my forehead. "Quit worrying. I've got my shit together now."

With the excitement of seeing him and the article, I hadn't even asked Aidan about where he'd been or what he'd been doing. "You look good. Healthy. Happy."

"I feel good. Better than I have in a long time. I'm not sure I would have healed if I hadn't left. I needed the separation."

252

"From me? I said some awful shit to you and I didn't even get a chance to apologize. I was so worried when you left rehab."

He blew out a ragged breath and rested his arms on his knees. "From everyone. You. Our parents. My grandfather. Everyone thought I should magically snap out of it. No one understood what was going on in my brain. The weed and alcohol drowned out the noise."

"I'm sorry. I should have been a better friend. I should have been there for you."

"I don't blame you. I was a miserable son of a bitch. Barking at people all the time. Getting high and drunk. I wouldn't have wanted to be friends with me either."

My eyes welled again. "I was mad at you, but I never stopped loving you."

"I know that now, but I wasn't in a place to receive it then. I figured everyone would be better off if I disappeared."

A tear slipped from the corner of my eye. "I wasn't better off. I was missing my other half."

He smiled at me. "Sounds to me like I've been replaced."

"Never." I wrapped my arms around his neck, still not fully believing he was here. "What happened? Where did you go?"

"I hopped on a bus. Vegas seemed like a good place to get off, so I did. I wandered from homeless camp to homeless camp, sleeping under bridges. Met some people. Drank a lot of booze. Did some drugs."

My heart broke thinking of him in a camp. I'd seen the conditions, and they weren't pretty.

"Then one day, I met this guy named Dave. He was a veteran like me, and we talked a lot. He understood me. He convinced me to go to an AA meeting with him, and I did. Turns out there's a lot of ex-military guys, like me, struggling. I didn't feel so alone anymore. I started going to the veterans center and talked to a therapist. He got me on the straight and narrow and even gave me Iris."

"Iris? Who's Iris?"

Aidan patted his knee. "Come on, girl." The German shepherd, who'd been so quiet I forgot she was there, walked over to Aidan and sat at his feet. He scratched the dog's head between her ears. "Iris is a therapy dog. She's trained in PTSD."

I reached out a hand. "May I?"

"Yeah. She's friendly. This girl saved my life."

I rubbed her fluffy head. "It's nice to meet you, Iris. Thank you for taking care of Aidan." Her tail wagged as she leaned into my hand. "Where are you living now?"

"In an apartment building reserved for veterans. It isn't fancy, but it's clean."

"Do you have a job?" I knew I was asking a million questions, but I needed to know he was okay.

Aidan nodded. "I do. I work at the veterans center as a counselor. Help other guys who are struggling. It makes me happy to pay it forward. I feel like this is my calling."

"That's great. I never did think you were suited for politics."

He scoffed. "Try telling that to my family. The idea was practically beaten into me from the time I was a kid that I would follow in the family's footsteps."

I waved a hand, dismissing the idea. "Aww... fuck 'em."

Aidan bumped my shoulder with his and laughed. "I still think it's funny when you swear. If your father could hear you now."

"Fuck him too. I'm pissed at him."

"Now what?"

"Come back to my apartment and I'll tell you the whole story. You're going to be pissed too."

Though I was ecstatic that I'd found Aidan, I dreaded my next conversation with Tom. Hopefully he didn't believe the gossip.

I'd lied to him once.

I'd lied to him twice.

I wouldn't blame him if the third time he called it quits.

Chapter 39
Tom

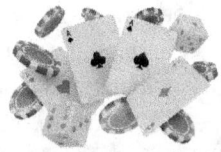

My mind ran crazy with a dozen different scenarios. She said she loved Aidan but wasn't in love with him. What if that was another lie? What if I was a way to bide her time while she looked for the man she really loved? What if she packed her bags and left, too afraid to face me after the story came out?

Each thought was a valid possibility.

But there was also another possibility.

What if the story Karla Blitzer wrote wasn't true at all?

I looked at my watch again. My ass hurt from sitting outside her door for the last hour. Normally, Aurora was home during the day, yet when I knocked on her door, all I got was silence. She didn't answer her phone or my texts.

And if I was being honest, it was the silence that was killing me.

The not knowing.

The uncertainty.

I based my life on facts and figures. Data was my friend. And I had none.

The elevator doors at the end of the hall opened and Aurora stepped out. But she wasn't alone.

A man with a dog that could chew off my left leg followed her.

I stood, ready to get the answers I needed. Regardless of whether I liked the truth or not, I needed it.

"Tom!" She ran to me and wrapped her arms around my neck.

I couldn't hug her back. Not yet.

She let go and slumped. "You read the article."

"I did." I looked at the guy with her and recognized him from her social media pages. Good-looking... no third eye, no horn, and no gnarly teeth. Instead, he wore clean, well-fitted clothes, with a fresh haircut and beard trim. Not at all what I was expecting for someone who'd supposedly been living on the streets for months.

He held out his hand to me. "I'm Aidan. Aurora's been telling me about you."

I reluctantly took his hand, and his shake was that of someone who spent hours in the gym, firm and manly. "She told me about you too, though she may have left out some important details." I should have done a background check on him as well.

Aurora bit the side of her thumb and chewed on the skin. "You're mad."

"I'm not mad. I'm confused. I want the truth. I don't want to dance around it like a campfire. If I'm going to get burned, I want to jump right into the flames."

"That's fair. Come inside and I'll tell you everything. Both of you."

The two of us followed Aurora into her apartment. Aidan sat on the couch, right where I'd made her come, and the dog obediently lay at his feet. I took the farthest chair away from him.

"Shall I get Iris a bowl of water?" Aurora asked him.

"She'd like that. Thank you, sunshine."

Sunshine. He had a cute little nickname for her? That really grated on my nerves.

I stared at the dog. "Is Iris yours?" It was a dumb question. Of course, the dog was his. Why else would it be following him around?

"Yes, she's a therapy dog trained in PTSD."

I nodded. The question about the dog was at the bottom of a long list of other questions, but it was the easiest to address.

Aurora brought a plastic bowl filled with water and placed it on the floor. Then she sat next to Aidan, which really annoyed me, but I was the dumb fuck who sat in the chair, so I really had no one to blame but myself. "Where should I start?" she asked, rubbing her hands on her thighs.

"How about the beginning?" That sounded like a fantastic place to start.

She turned to me. "Aidan and I met when we were very young. Our grandpas used to take us places together and we became fast friends. As we got older, our parents pushed us together even more. We were sixteen when the first talk of marriage between us started. It was right after my grandpa died."

My teeth ground together. "So the engagement rumor is true."

Aurora shook her head. "It's not true. I'll admit Aidan and I tried dating, but we were better off as friends. Our parents didn't care about what we wanted. After high school graduation, the pushing began. We convinced them we were too young and to wait until after college. We both went to UCLA, where we stayed friends but dated other people. We figured our parents would give up the idea of a wedding."

"But they didn't," I guessed.

"Not at all," Aidan said. "The day we walked across the stage with our diplomas, our parents set a date. They were insistent and kept pushing, making us both crazy. Aurora and I knew we didn't want to get married, so I made a rash decision and enlisted in the military. I did it to set Aurora free from me."

God, why did this guy have to be so selfless? He was making it hard not to like him.

"So you can see why I felt guilty when he came home with… issues. If not for me, he would have never enlisted."

"Rora, don't shoulder that guilt," Aidan said, grabbing her hand. "It was my choice, and I'd do it again—for you. As for my issues"—he looked

257

directly at me—"I came home damaged. Or at least that's how I felt. PTSD kicked my ass. But now I have Iris and I'm in regular therapy, so I'm doing much better," he said, stroking the dog's head.

Everything they'd said lined up with what Aurora told me. It was either an elaborate lie or the complete truth. I hadn't decided yet. I leaned forward, a bit of stress releasing from my shoulders. "That brings us to now. Why do people still think you're engaged?"

"Because of our parents," Aurora said, crossing her arms. "When I decided to come to Vegas to look for Aidan, it was because I was worried about my best friend. My father allowed it because he saw it as an opportunity to force the marriage. He hasn't stopped talking about it. He wants me to bring Aidan home, but that was never my plan. I thought if I could find Aidan first, the two of us could come up with our own plan."

I leaned back in the chair and let out a huff. This entire time, she knew her family expected her to marry someone else. "Is this why you're leaving Vegas? To marry him?" I asked with a wave of my hand.

Aurora had the good sense to look sheepish. "Yes. I didn't think I had a choice. My father said the future of LeFleur Media depended on it. That if we didn't, the company would be cut to shreds."

"What?" Aidan asked. "That's a lot of pressure to put on you." He gritted his teeth. "I could wring your father's neck."

At least he had the decency to be outraged too. I wasn't the only one blindsided.

There was one thing I still didn't understand. "Why don't you two want to get married? You have history. You care about each other. It pains me to say this, but you seem perfect together."

"We do love each other. I told you that," Aurora said. "But we'll never be more than friends. There's no chemistry. No romantic feelings."

Marriages had been made on less. Like the article said, it would be two powerful families coming together. No wonder their parents wanted it so badly.

"I can see you're skeptical," Aidan said.

"Can you blame me?"

"Not really. You don't have all the information." He grabbed the back of his neck and pulled. "I'm gay."

Whoa! Didn't see that coming.

"Aidan…" Aurora grabbed his hand.

"It's okay, sunshine. You don't have to keep my secret. I've kept it quiet since we were teenagers. It's time to tell our families. I don't want to live a lie anymore."

She nodded her head as her eyes welled. "Okay. I'll support you, but I'm not sure it's going to make a difference."

"What do you mean it won't make a difference? Surely they can't expect us to get married if I'm gay."

Yes, I wanted to know the answer to that too.

"Here's what you both don't know," Aurora said, looking between Aidan and me. "My father kept referencing my grandfather's will and trust as the reason for the marriage, but I'd never seen them. I had my mother email me a copy of both and I took them to a lawyer."

"You didn't think to tell me about this?" I asked. It was important information.

"With the launch party, it didn't seem like the right time. I needed to know what I was dealing with first. I'm in love with you, Tom, and I wanted to know what our chances were."

"What did you learn?"

"Well, there's a lot, so bear with me. Apparently, before I was born, my father made some bad decisions for the company and it almost bankrupted LeFleur Media. Your grandfather"—she pointed at Aidan—"bailed the company out. Our grandfathers made a gentleman's agreement that if the two families ever had an opportunity to join through marriage, then the debt would be settled, with both families getting fifty percent of the controlling interest. We were being manipulated from the time we were little. They were pushing us together."

"What the fuck!" Aidan held his fist to his mouth and reeled in his temper. Iris put her front paws on his legs and dropped her head in his lap. "That pisses me off. I mean… I'm not mad we became friends, but their intentions… those sneaky bastards."

259

"A gentleman's agreement isn't legally binding." Law wasn't my expertise, but I knew enough.

"You're right," Aurora said. "The agreement isn't binding, though the board will take it into consideration, but the trust is. Technically, my father didn't inherit the company. I did. My father is only temporarily in power until I meet the conditions set forth in the trust."

"Wow! What are the conditions?" Aidan asked.

"There are two," she said, holding up her fingers. "One, I have to be at least twenty-five. And two, I have to marry a man of sound moral character and reputation. Here's the kicker… the trustees must approve my marriage. The trustees include my father and the board. If I don't fulfill the conditions, I get nothing. And neither does my father. The company goes to the trust to manage as they see fit."

I dropped my head in my hands and rubbed my temples. Why couldn't I have fallen in love with the checkout girl at the supermarket? Why did it have to be the woman with the most complicated life in the country?

"Forget about the debt for a minute," Aidan said. "You don't think your dad would approve of anyone but me? Why?"

She nodded her head. "Here's where it gets interesting."

There was more? It was already beyond *interesting*, if that was even the right word. Fucked up was more like it.

"There's a clause in the trust that if I marry a direct descendant of your grandfather, then my father retains some ownership. Otherwise, he gets zippo. I'm furious with him, but I don't think he deserves to be banished from the company."

I disagreed. Her father sounded like a real prick. He'd been manipulating his only daughter for years for his own benefit.

Aidan threw his head back against the couch. "We're fucked. You either marry me, or your family loses LeFleur Media."

My mind spun. This wasn't real. Arranged marriages were a thing of the past. All Aurora's choices had been stolen from her unless she wanted to be responsible for the demise of the company.

Loyalty to me or her family… I never stood a chance.

"Not necessarily," Aurora said. "The lawyer said I could contest the trust in court. It's risky though. I'm willing to fight, but it will take some time. If I win, you and I will be free to marry whoever we want, and the company will stay intact. There won't be anything binding us together," she said to Aidan.

"It's your call," he said. "I would make the sacrifice. For you, and only for you."

Seeing the two of them together, I understood why people thought they were a couple. The bond between them went beyond friendship. An invisible thread tied them together.

"What are your thoughts, Tom?" Aurora asked.

I'd spent the last few minutes listening, taking in this huge revelation. Trent's words rang in my head, *You fight for the one you love.*

This was more than a fight. It was a war.

"I think if you're going to court, you'll need ammunition. The best defense is a good offense."

"I agree, but what?"

"If you want to prove you're capable of making your own decisions, then make them. Your father doesn't know you know what's in the trust, right?"

"He's kept me in the dark on purpose. He's counting on having the upper hand."

It was a gamble, but it could work. "I have an idea how you can flip the game."

Brett knocked me with his shoulder. "I thought I said not to do anything stupid."

"Leave him alone," Charli said. "My brother finally grew a set of balls. Don't you dare try to chop them off."

Though I appreciated my sister's support, her word choice left a lot to be desired. Sweat rolled down my back as I gave Brett a gentle shove. "Go sit next to your wife."

"You sure about this?" Charli asked.

"Strangely, yes."

She gave me a nod and stood at my side.

The room was gaudy with its red drapes and faux-gold candelabras. The smell of roses hung in the air, thick and heavy. My girl deserved better.

"Truly Madly Deeply" began to play and a hush fell over The Little White Wedding Chapel. Aurora appeared at the back of the chapel in a sleek white cocktail dress, holding a bouquet of pink and white roses, with Aidan and Iris at her side. As she came down the aisle, my heart leaped.

Yes, it was impulsive.

Yes, it was crazy.

Yes, it went against every bit of my conservative nature.

But I didn't care.

If this was our chance to be together, I was grabbing it with both hands.

When Aurora made it to the end of the aisle, I took her hand and helped her up the step. "I know this isn't what you envisioned for a wedding, but we can do it again the right way. And if you change your mind right now, I'll still love you."

She smiled at me. "I'm not changing my mind. This feels right. And you're getting to wear this tux again," she said with a wink.

"Are we ready?" the officiant asked. Thankfully, not an Elvis impersonator. Even in the current circumstances, I had more class than that.

We both nodded.

"We are gathered here today in fabulous Las Vegas to join this dazzling couple in the holy bonds of matrimony. Marriage is not simply a vow, but a contract and a partnership."

He had no idea how close his words hit home.

We'd written our own vows for the ceremony, and I went first.

"I, Thomas Bently, take you, Aurora LeFleur, to be my wedded wife. To have and to hold, in scandal and success, in tech chaos and media storms, for richer or poorer, in sickness and in health, to love and to cherish for the rest of our days. I promise to stand by your side and be the man you need me to be." I slid the ring I purchased this afternoon onto her dainty finger. It wasn't as big as she deserved, but it wasn't a tiny rock either.

Her eyes welled and she mouthed *I love you.*

Then it was her turn.

"I, Aurora LeFleur, take you, Thomas Bently, to be my wedded husband. To have and to hold when the servers crash, to fight the board and the headlines together, for richer or poorer, in sickness and in health, to love and to cherish for the rest of our days. Wherever this journey takes us, I want to do it with you by my side." She slid the simple gold band on my finger.

With tears in both our eyes, we looked at the officiant. "If any person here knows of any lawful reason these two should not be joined in matrimony, speak now or forever hold your peace."

We turned toward our friends, who surely had a million reasons we shouldn't get married, but none of them said a word. Not even Hunter, whom I was positive would take the opportunity to ruin my moment.

After a brief pause, the officiant continued. "By the power vested in me by the state of Nevada, I now pronounce you—"

The chapel doors flew open, and a man dressed in a three-piece suit yelled, "I object!" He rested his hands on his knees, panting. "I object to this wedding!"

"That's my father," Aurora whispered.

I gulped. *How? How was he here?*

Aurora shook her head. "You're too late," she told him. Then she turned to the stunned officiant. "Finish it."

"Alrighty. By the power vested in me by the state of Nevada, I now pronounce you husband and wife. You may kiss your bride," he rushed out the final words.

I took Aurora's face in my hands and kissed her with all the joy in my heart. Her arms wrapped around my neck, and for a moment, there was no one else but the two of us.

Her father stomped up the aisle, steam practically pouring from his ears. "You have no idea what you've done!"

Chapter 40
Aurora

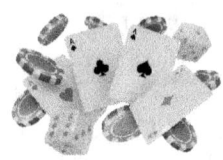

I thought I'd at least have a few days to prepare for the face-off with my father, but like everything else in my life, he had his own ideas. It turned out the private investigator he hired wasn't in Vegas to look for Aidan; he was there to watch me.

I felt violated.

Again.

My father sat across from me on his private jet, while Aidan and Tom sat in the back with Iris, quietly talking and observing from afar. I wished I was back there too, but this conversation was long past due.

"You're getting an annulment!" His fist pounded on the table between us.

I crossed my arms and leaned back in the soft leather. "I'll do no such thing."

"You think this is about me trying to control your life, but it isn't. It's structural. It's survival for LeFleur Media. Let me paint the picture for you, Aurora. When this company gets torn to shreds, they'll cancel our investigative desk. They'll replace your mother's name on the journalism fellowship. They'll cut our regional affiliates who can't meet click quotas. Everything your grandfather and I built will be destroyed because you fell in love. Well, isn't that cute? Get your head out of your ass!"

I pulled the stack of papers from my bag and slammed them on the table.

When my father saw what they were, he paled. "How did you get those?"

"It doesn't matter how. You've been manipulating me and Aidan for years. You and Mom, his parents, and our sweet grandpas. All of you! This isn't about me. This is about you and your actions. I won't let your past mistakes determine our futures."

He jabbed the pile of paper with his index finger. "It's in the trust, Aurora. We didn't have a choice."

"There are always choices. Truth should have been one of them."

He laughed. "You're so naive."

"I'm not naive. I know what's at stake. I'm willing to fight for this family and this company. Are you?"

He jabbed the papers again. "I've always fought for this company. Do you have any idea the power we'd wield if our family were to join the Huxleys? You're sitting on top of a media empire in the middle of the most volatile era of information warfare we've ever known. Facts are currency. Perception is policy. The LeFleur name alone won't shield this company when the wolves come knocking. But you know what will? A seat in Washington. A husband whose last name opens doors in the Capital. A father-in-law who doesn't just read the laws but writes them. We'll have unprecedented political power that will thrust us ahead of any other network."

I sighed. *His* head was so far up the company's ass he couldn't see anything else. "Do you hear yourself, Dad? You're not asking me to make a business decision. You're asking me to give up love for leverage. This company has been your identity for so long, you can't tell where it ends and you begin. You're willing to sacrifice your daughter's happiness for influence and control, to get back some of the power Grandfather took from you. I'm sorry you messed up, but that has nothing to do with me. All you have to do is approve this marriage, and we keep the company. It will be mine."

"Not only me, Aurora. The board has to approve too."

"I'm not afraid of the board. I'll meet the wolves at the door."

"And then what? You get your revenge by removing me from the company?"

"I have no desire to run LeFleur Media any time in the near future. Technically, I have until I'm thirty-five to fulfill the terms of the trust. You can continue as the CEO. Stand with me, and we'll contest the trust in court. I can do it alone, but we'd be stronger together."

My father sagged in his chair and pulled his tie off. "You've given this a lot of thought."

"Had you been honest with me from the beginning, we could have been on the offensive from the start."

"I suppose." He leaned on the table. "Did you marry this guy to piss me off, or do you really love him?"

"I love him. He's not some loser like you think. He's smart and sweet and treats me with respect. But most of all, he's willing to walk through fire with me. Isn't that what you want for your daughter?"

"I don't think he's a loser. He's media gold. The press can't stop raving about him."

"He's not an asset, Dad. And neither am I."

"I know, I know, I know," he said, waving a hand in the air. "If you're really sure this is what you want, I'll fight the wolves with you."

"Thank you. Now would you like to meet my husband?"

Chapter 41
Tom

"Your father hates me," I said to Aurora from my seat in the back of the jet. I'd rarely been on an airplane, let alone a private jet.

"He hates everyone," Aidan said with a chuckle. "Why should you be any different?"

"Oh, stop," Aurora scolded Aidan. "I just flipped my dad's whole world upside down; give him a chance to come to terms with that."

"How'd he take it?" I asked.

"He wants to meet you."

I took a deep breath and let it out slowly. "I figured he would."

"He's up front waiting. Do you want me to come with you?" she asked.

"Nope," I said, shaking my head. "If I'm going to earn your father's respect, I need to do it alone."

Walking to the front of the jet, I slipped into the buttery-soft leather chair across from Mr. LeFleur. He poured two glasses of scotch and offered me one. "Mr. Bently."

"Mr. LeFleur," I said, taking the glass.

He sat back and crossed one leg over his knee. "So, you're the man who stole my daughter away from a United States senator's son."

"In all fairness, I didn't know Aidan was a senator's son until this morning. I didn't know who Aurora's family was until last week. I simply fell in love with a girl. She captured my heart the first time I met her." I took a slow sip of the scotch, letting it burn my throat.

"You'll excuse me if I'm skeptical. This feels a bit like you circling the castle."

"All due respect, but I would have circled a cabin in the woods if your daughter was inside it. I'm not interested in your castle. LeFleur Media has nothing to do with me. If and when Aurora decides to take ownership is up to her. I have my own projects to keep me busy."

"Yes, I've heard. The up-and-coming tech security guy," her father said, lifting his glass. "I read the articles. *Super Tom*, I think they called you."

I chuckled. "Karla Blitzer has a way with words."

"Let's hope she's correct. Being married to my daughter is not going to be a cakewalk. Even if I give her my approval, she still has to get it from the board. She's contesting the trust. It could take years. If you're not up for the challenge, then walk away now."

"I'm not going anywhere unless my wife tells me to. Otherwise, I'll stand at her side." I set my glass on the table. "You should know she didn't marry me to spite you, though you would have deserved it. Despite your manipulation, Aurora is taking this to court for you too. She doesn't want to see you removed from LeFleur Media. She's loyal to a fault."

"I know she is."

"You should also know that *my* only loyalty lies with her. You may be the media mogul, but I have a very particular skill set. If you betray Aurora or turn your back on her, I'll dox your ass so hard you'll be feeling it for decades. Every parking ticket, every unpaid tax, and every secret rendezvous with a certain twenty-seven-year-old redheaded secretary will become public information." I may have failed to do a background check on Aidan, but I hadn't on Gerard LeFleur II. I was quite thorough and dug deep.

His forehead crinkled as he pierced me with his eyes. "Understood. Seems Aurora married a politician after all."

"Nah. I'm just a nerd in love with your daughter."

Chapter 42
Aurora

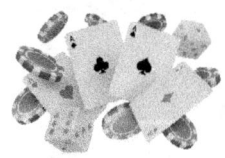

If I was going to war with the board, I wasn't going alone. They may have been a pack of wolves, but I had my own pack... my father, my husband, and my best friend. All the important men in my life were there to support me. The four of us, dressed in power suits, entered the conference room armed with facts, figures, and determination.

A dozen board members sat around a long, gleaming table. Some of them I'd known my whole life, others I'd never met. One I was very familiar with, sat with his back rigid and a scowl on his face. His eyes lit up when he saw Aidan, yet he said nothing.

All their eyes were on me.

Thanks to Brett, a new article in the *Las Vegas Not So Confidential* dropped first thing this morning. Karla was more than willing to attend our wedding and get the jump on every other media outlet. As predicted, yesterday's event was today's gossip.

The room buzzed like a hornet's nest that'd been kicked.

I walked to the end of the table and leaned on its edge. "Thank you for meeting with me on such short notice. As you may have read, I have decided not to marry into the Huxley political dynasty. I have chosen my own path, for which I need your approval."

"Request denied," former Senator George Huxley snapped. "She was supposed to marry my grandson, Aidan. It was agreed upon."

I gritted my teeth. "That is half true. Unbeknownst to us, our future and happiness were used as a bargaining chip between two old men with a debt to settle. Before Aidan and I were born, our destinies were determined."

"Is that true?" a woman in a sharp, black suit asked. She sat at the head of the table as the leader of the board.

Aidan's grandfather shrugged.

"As you know, the trustees are required to approve my marriage. Per the trust, I am to marry a man of sound moral character and reputation. I have fulfilled the requirement with my marriage to Mr. Thomas Bently, a software developer taking the Vegas Strip by storm with his cybersecurity system."

"That may be what the trust says, but I made an agreement with your grandfather. It too is in the trust and must be adhered to. The joining of the Huxley political dynasty and LeFleur Media will push this company into the future, giving us an edge no other media company can match," Aidan's grandpa proclaimed.

"Again, a half-truth. The gentleman's agreement is not legally binding; however, it is sexist and completely antiquated. Though the joining of our families would give us a political edge, what I'm offering is better than influence through marriage. I'm offering protection, innovation, and leverage through partnership with a man who built a multimillion-dollar digital security company from the ground up. This is not a consolation prize; it's a competitive edge."

The older gentleman sitting across from the senator chuckled. "What's he gonna do? Install better security cameras?"

We knew this sell wasn't going to be easy, so Tom and I developed a list of how we could help the company together, even if we decided to stay in Vegas. "I'm talking about blocking federal surveillance attempts, preventing internal data breaches, and developing software that makes our newsroom the safest source in digital journalism. Both my husband and I are technology experts. Together, we can protect this company far better than any politician."

Aidan's grandpa huffed. "All of that sounds nice, but it's irrelevant." He pounded his fist on the table. "The agreement is clear!"

I squinted at him. "The trust is clear as well. And it doesn't require me to marry a Huxley to inherit the company." Turning to the rest of the board, I made my final plea. "The real reason the senator wanted me to marry his grandson is self-serving. If I did, he would receive fifty percent of the controlling interest of LeFleur Media. He's not looking out for this company. He's looking to line his own pockets."

Gasps sounded around the table.

"Is that true, George?" the woman in the black suit asked.

"I bailed this company out when it was going down the toilet. I demand repayment!"

I passed out financial ledgers to the board members. "The debt has been paid in full, with interest. Senator Huxley also has five percent of the stock in LeFleur Media. Not only has he been paid, but he's been collecting dividends for years. Should he get an additional fifty percent of the controlling interest, he will be the top shareholder in the company. Your voices will be silenced, and you'll be beholden to him."

The woman stood from her seat. "I don't know about anyone else, but I feel betrayed and lied to. George Huxley has not been working in the best interest of this company. I'd like to file a motion to remove him from the board."

"I second the motion," another member announced.

"You can't do that!" he shouted. "Aidan, tell them I'm looking out for you. For our family!"

Aidan, who'd been quietly watching, stepped forward. "I love you, Grandpa, but I can't condone your behavior or that of Aurora's grandfather. The two of you lied to us for years. You tried to push us together, knowing we had no interest in marriage."

"You love her! You can't deny it."

"That's true," Aidan said. "But we were never getting married. I'm gay, Grandpa."

"Bullshit!" George yelled. "You're lying. No grandson of mine is gay."

More chatter erupted around the table.

Aidan shook his head. "And that reaction is exactly why I didn't tell you. You may not like it, but I'm not hiding anymore."

The senator huffed out his disapproval. "Unbelievable!"

"Thank you, Aidan," the woman said. "I know that must have been difficult, but we appreciate your candor." She turned to the rest of the board. "All in favor of removing Senator George Huxley from the board of LeFleur Media."

Several hands popped up immediately, others a bit slower, but every single member approved the motion.

"I'm sorry it's come to this, George, but the board has spoken. Please remove yourself from the room."

Aidan's grandpa pushed away from the table. "Fuck you all! You're all a bunch of spineless jellyfish kowtowing to the ridiculousness of a stupid girl!" He stomped to the door. "I hope this company goes down in flames and all of you burn with it!"

Once he was gone, I addressed the board again. "I would like to introduce you all to my husband, Mr. Thomas Bently. He'll tell you a bit about himself and answer all your questions."

Tom came and stood next to me. "Thank you for allowing me to speak with you. I'm Thomas Bently and I'm madly in love with Aurora. I'm originally from Colorado and went to school at MIT for computer science..."

Tom charmed the board with his intellect and willingness to answer all their questions. He had them eating out of the palm of his hand.

When the inquisition was over, I stepped back to the table. "I stand before you, not as someone's wife, but as the sole heiress of LeFleur Media who has challenged the antiquated agreement of two old men with a grudge and forged her own path as an independent woman. I humbly request that you approve my marriage to Mr. Bently and deem the terms of the trust fulfilled for my succession."

This was the moment of truth. We'd made a solid case, but it was out of our hands now. My future and that of the company was up to the board.

The woman in the suit stood again. "Thank you, Aurora. You've made a compelling argument. Please give us a few minutes for discussion."

I gave her a nod. Tom put his hand on the small of my back and led me from the room. Aidan and my father followed. Once in the hallway, I began to shake.

My father rubbed his hands up and down my arms. "I've never been prouder of you, Aurora. You have more strength than I ever had at your age. Whatever they decide, we'll deal with it. If it means we lose LeFleur Media, then so be it. We'll figure it out."

"Thanks, Dad." All these years, I'd been seeking his approval, trying to be a good girl. How could I have known that defying him would be the thing that truly garnered his respect?

Aidan kissed me on the temple. "You did good, sunshine."

"I'm sorry about your grandpa."

"I'm not," Aidan said with a shake of his head. "He's not the man I thought he was."

Tom squeezed my hand. "I'm proud of you, angel. And also a little terrified. The way you stood up to the board was impressive. Your grandfather was right to leave the company to you and that's why if they don't approve of our marriage, I'll step aside. We'll get an annulment so you can take your rightful place."

I grabbed him by the lapels of his coat. "You will do no such thing, Thomas Bently. I am your wife for better or worse. I won't let them determine our future. We will do that. Together."

He laughed. "Okay, boss lady." He leaned in and whispered in my ear, "As long as you know, when we're in the bedroom, I'm the boss."

I winked at him. "I'd have it no other way."

The door opened and we were ushered back into the conference room. My skin prickled with anticipation. The next five minutes would determine the rest of my life.

The woman stood. "After deep consideration, the board has agreed to approve your marriage to Mr. Bently. We pronounce Aurora Bently as the rightful heir of LeFleur Media and the new owner." Applause erupted around the table as they welcomed me into the fold.

Relief flooded me. One hurdle down, one more to go.

"Thank you. You've made a lot of difficult decisions today, and as the new owner, I'm asking you to make one more. According to the trust, once I have taken my rightful role, my father is to step down immediately. That was my grandfather's punishment for a mistake my father made over thirty years ago when he was barely twenty-five himself. Over the last ten years, since my grandfather's death, Gerard LeFleur II has run this company with integrity and in good faith. Under his leadership, LeFleur Media's profits have soared, our reach has been extended, and our approval ratings have peaked. My father has more than proved himself. I do not agree that he should be removed from the company, and I intend to challenge the trust in court."

Once again, the room buzzed with chatter.

Then I dropped the next bomb.

"As a newly married woman, I plan to spend the next year in Vegas with my husband, helping him build his company and continuing my volunteer work with the homeless. We will also be developing new security measures for LeFleur Media. I do not plan to be here for day-to-day operations, but would like to quietly observe and learn from my father over time. I ask that until we get a ruling from the court, you allow him to continue leading this company into the future. I have complete confidence in Gerard LeFleur II and I believe he's proven you should too."

The woman who'd been the spokesperson for the group turned her lips up. "I think I speak for everyone when I say we were all nervous about you immediately taking control of the company. You may be capable, but you are young. There is a lot to learn."

"I agree," I said.

"I put it to an immediate vote to allow Gerard LeFleur II to act as CEO, per Aurora Bently's request, until a ruling from the court is handed down. All in favor."

Every hand in the room shot toward the ceiling.

I laughed. "I'll try not to take that personally. You've made the right decision."

"We've all been impressed with your maturity and professionalism. We have no doubt that in time you'll make an excellent leader for LeFleur Media. Good luck to you, Aurora, and congratulations on your marriage. We'll be expecting big things from you."

"And I…" I reached for Tom's hand and joined our fingers together. "*We* plan to deliver. Thank you for your support. It means everything to us."

The board filed out of the room with handshakes and congratulations, leaving the four of us and Iris behind. "I can't believe it worked." To be honest, I was shocked. Everything happened so fast, yet we couldn't have planned it better.

"You made a very compelling case," my father said. "I'm indebted to you. I thought there was only one way forward, but you opened my eyes. I promise to keep the company safe until you're ready." He hugged me and kissed my cheek.

"I'm not in any hurry, Dad. I want to enjoy married life for a while."

My dad shook his head. "I still can't believe you're married. I didn't even get to walk you down the aisle."

"We're going to do it again. The right way. I promised Aurora she could have the wedding of her dreams. You'll get your chance."

My father shook my husband's hand. "Welcome to the family, Tom. I'm trusting you to take good care of my little girl."

"Always."

With a clap on Aidan's shoulder, my father said, "Why don't you kids come by the house. I think a celebration dinner is in order."

Aidan grabbed the back of his neck. "I think I'm going to head to my parents' house. There's a long-overdue conversation we need to have. I'm sure my grandpa has given them an earful already."

"Are you coming back to Vegas?" I asked.

Aidan nodded. "Yeah. I met someone."

I hugged him tightly. "I'm so happy for you."

"Thanks. Let's hope my parents are too."

My father and Aidan walked out together, leaving Tom and me alone.

"You know," Tom said, "I thought I had to prove that I was worthy of your love by making something of myself and being able to take care of you. But you never needed me. You were always capable of taking care of yourself."

I wrapped my arms around his neck. "I'll always need you. Without you, none of this would have been possible. You're my real-life superhero, Tom Bently. You've saved me in all the ways that matter."

"Maybe Karla was right… we are the new dynamic duo."

"Damn right, we are," I agreed. "Together we are unstoppable, now and forever."

Epilogue
Tom

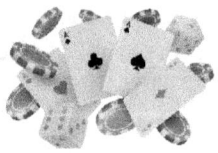

I stood and looked out the window of my new office at the Vegas skyline, jagged peaks jutting high above the glitz and glam of the Strip, where almost every casino now used CyberSecure. It was unbelievable how much my life changed in the past six months. Growing up as a nerdy kid in Colorado, I never imagined I'd have a beautiful wife, a thriving company, and more money than I knew what to do with. I questioned every day whether it was real or a dream I hadn't woken from yet.

Aurora's grandfather's trust was settled. With her father and the board on her side, the judge declared the clause in the trust removing her father from the company as overly punitive and granted Aurora discretionary authority, as the trust's primary beneficiary, to structure the company as she saw fit until she was ready to assume leadership. Gerard LeFleur II would remain CEO for the foreseeable future. Aurora and I had a lot of plans that didn't include her running a multibillion-dollar media empire anytime soon.

Her father insisted on a postnuptial agreement, which I gladly signed on the dotted line. I had no interest in LeFleur Media and was never with her for the money. I was with her for her gorgeous heart and beautiful mind. When she was ready to lead, I'd stand by her side like she'd done for me.

Warm arms wrapped around my waist from behind. "Whatcha thinking about?"

I turned in my wife's arms. "I'm thinking about how thankful I am for this life with you."

"It's kinda crazy, isn't it?" She chuckled. "How your life can be going along in one direction and in the blink of an eye you're traveling down a totally different path? I have you to thank for that."

I kissed her on the forehead. "Think your father will ever forgive me for whisking you away to a wedding chapel without his blessing?"

"He's forgiven you," she said with a hand on my chest. "Our relationship is finally becoming what it should have been all along. He and my mom are busy planning the wedding we never had for our one-year vow renewal. I've let her have carte blanche to be as over the top as she wants. My one request was for a beach ceremony. Be prepared. If you thought Hunter and Charli's wedding was snazzy, you haven't seen anything yet. It's going to be the social event of the year."

"Oh boy! That's a bit terrifying."

"You'll survive." She pulled me by the hand. "Come now, or we'll be late for the ribbon-cutting ceremony."

Aurora continued volunteering at Helping Hands, although not so anonymous anymore. She used her wealth and influence to bring more attention to the shelter. She pitched an idea to her father to do a docuseries focusing on the people society pretended didn't exist, telling their stories and bringing awareness to the epidemic. My wife was a force of nature when she put her mind to it, and she never quit amazing me.

She and Aidan teamed up to create a program specifically for veterans navigating life after the military. Today, they were announcing the new services at Helping Hands and opening the doors to the press. I would proudly stand in the crowd to watch Aurora and Aidan cut the big red ribbon together.

I doubted anything could break their unshakable bond. For as much as I hated the guy before I met him, I now counted Aidan as a good friend, perfectly straight teeth and all. He'd sacrificed so much for Aurora, and for that, I was eternally grateful. Had it not been for him, I would never have met her.

"Wait!" I stopped at my desk and opened the top drawer. Nestled inside was a collection of bow ties in various colors and patterns. "Which one?" I asked her.

She shook her head. "You're never going to give those up, are you?"

"Never. They're my trademark."

Aurora selected a turquoise-blue tie with a paisley pattern. "It'll match your eyes."

I plucked it from the drawer and fastened it around my neck. "How do I look? Is it crooked?"

She tugged on the ends and twisted them in place. "Very handsome. You're my very own Clark Kent."

I rolled my eyes. "That guy's a hack. He'll never be able to compete with Super Tom."

"You've become incorrigible." She laughed. "I'm gonna have to tell Karla to tone it down."

"Don't you dare." Not gonna lie, with Aurora at my side, I kind of felt like Super Tom. I had a flourishing business, a fancy car, a penthouse apartment, and most importantly… I got the girl.

Another Epilogue
Aurora

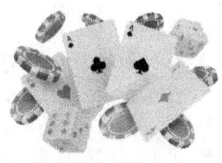

"Uh-oh. I know that look," Penny said as she bounced baby Max on her hip.

"What?" I asked innocently as I watched Tom spin around the dance floor with his sister.

"You're glowing."

"It's probably the champagne. Would you look at this place? It's practically flooded with it." That wasn't a lie. There was a champagne fountain right next to the six-tier wedding cake. My parents spared no expense for their only daughter's wedding. Though it was beautiful, all the over-the-top opulence was a bit much. I didn't have the heart to tell them I preferred the small chapel wedding in Vegas.

"Yes, the champagne." Penny gave me a gentle nudge. "You should go dance with your husband."

"I think I will." With my gown swishing around me, I crossed the dance floor and tapped Charli on the shoulder. "May I cut in?"

She let go of Tom's hand. "Of course."

"FYI… you might want to check on Carina. The guys are busy chitchatting while she gets a tongue bath from Iris."

Charli's eyes searched for her daughter and found her sitting on the floor next to the big German shepherd, covering her in kisses. "Oh dear!" She lifted her dress and scurried toward them.

Tom chuckled. "I'm glad we're not dealing with that yet."

I frowned. "When we have kids, I want to have more than one. Aidan was like the brother I never had, but it would have been nice to have a sibling."

"Okaaay. Whatever you want." He took my hand and wrapped his arm around my waist. He led me around the dance floor, spinning and twirling me.

"Do you remember the first time we danced?"

He nodded. "I do. I had a hard-on the size of the Eiffel Tower. I was so afraid of poking you with it."

"You barely touched me the whole night until you got sloshed on Hunter's bourbon and got loose lips."

"That's not a problem tonight." He pressed his hips against my stomach. "Wait! What do you mean I got loose lips? Did I do or say something else inappropriate?"

He still didn't remember that night, but I remembered it perfectly. "You didn't do anything inappropriate, but I have been keeping a secret from you."

He scowled at me. "We've discussed this. No more secrets, Aurora."

"Fine. That night was the first time you told me you loved me." I jutted out my chin. "Right before I took your room key and put you to bed."

"Ugh!" he groaned. "That's terrible. I'm sorry I love-bombed you that night."

"It wasn't terrible. I wanted it to be true. I just wish you'd said it when you were sober. I had to wait weeks for you to say it again." I stared into his eyes. "What was terrible were your jokes."

"Hey now, my jokes are funny."

I pinched my fingers together. "A little bit. I've got one for you though."

"Lay it on me."

"What does a baby spreadsheet call its father?"

He looked up at the ceiling, then back at me. "I don't know."

"Data," I said, laughing at my own joke.

Tom pinned me with his gaze. "That's as terrible as mine."

"Is it... Data?" I asked, raising my eyebrow.

He stopped dancing and held me out by the arms, glancing at my tulle-covered body. "Are you...?"

I nodded.

He wrapped me in his arms. "How long have you known?"

"I've suspected for a week, but I took a test this morning. Are you upset?"

Rocking me back and forth, he couldn't wipe the giddy grin from his face. "Not at all. Do you think he'll be techy, like us?" Tom asked.

"I think *she* or he will be whatever they want to be. They can be a tech innovator, a media mogul, a lawyer, a plumber... I don't care as long as they're happy. I don't want them to feel pressured into anything. I want them to follow their own path."

"As long as they follow their mom's example, the sky is the limit," Tom agreed.

I'd gone most of my life thinking my story had already been written. I'd never do that to our child. Dreams and ambitions came from your soul, not your bloodline. Our lives were a blank page when we were born, waiting for us to tell our story.

Mine had me running into a handsome nerdy prince who flipped my world upside down with his crazy ideas... a quickie marriage, a boardroom showdown, and a court battle. The plot twists came fast and furious and there was no lack of conflict. I was a media princess who made headlines by challenging old men and writing my own story.

With a pink plus sign, my next chapter was about to begin. Who knew how many would follow? All I knew was when I got to the end of my own fairy tale, there would be six little words... and she lived happily ever after.

Want to read the article from the *Las Vegas Not So Confidential* announcing Tom and Aurora's marriage?
Don't miss Karla Blitzer's take on their wedding!

Get the **exclusive bonus content** for free by signing up for my newsletter. This is the only place it's available!

https://bit.ly/Technically_Yours_Bonus_Content

Want to get caught up with the rest of the Vegas millionaires?
Check out:
What Happens in Vegas (Trent & Gia)
Billionaire Bachelor in Vegas (Brett & Penny)
Behaving Badly in Vegas (Hunter & Charli)

Thank you so much for choosing to read
Technically Yours in Vegas.

If you enjoyed the story, please leave a review on Amazon, Goodreads, or BookBub. They help so much!

Don't Want to Say Goodbye?

Check Out My Other Books:

Hearts Trilogy
Hearts on Fire
Shattered Hearts
Reviving My Heart

Wild Hearts Trilogy
Wild Hearts
Secrets of the Heart
Eternal Hearts

Forever Inked Novels
Tattooed Hearts: Tattooed Duet #1
Tattooed Souls: Tattooed Duet #2
Smoke and Mirrors
Regret and Redemption
Sin and Salvation

Vegas Love Series
What Happens in Vegas
Billionaire Bachelor in Vegas
Behaving Badly in Vegas
Technically Yours in Vegas

Acknowledgments

Thank you for choosing to read *Technically Yours in Vegas*. I loved telling the story of Tom and Aurora. Tom played a quiet role in all the other books in this series, but I fell in love with his nerdy, calm demeanor. I knew there had to be someone out there behind a keyboard for him. However, his tech-genius brain caused me a lot of research. I learned more about blockchain technology than I ever wanted to know. And Aurora... I have her to thank for all my new knowledge abouts trusts and corporate structure. These two ran me through the gauntlet. Yay for this dynamic duo!

To my husband~ I could have never done this without your love and support. When writing a book was just a pipedream, you were my biggest cheerleader. You always wanted to be a roadie and now you are, schlepping all my stuff from show to show and giving up your weekends. Not quite the razzle-dazzle you probably expected, but I love you for it! Thank you for believing in me!

To Linda and Heather~ You ladies are the best beta readers anyone could ask for! You've supported my journey and given me pep when mine was all gone. Your suggestions, critiques, and encouragement helped me in ways you'll never understand. Your constructive criticism improved this book so much and helped make it into something I'm proud of. I could never thank you enough for your help!

To Rose~ Girl... you make my books shine! Thank you for the extra polish you put on every manuscript. This is our seventh book together and I don't know how I survived before we met.

To my readers~ Thank you for supporting me in this journey. There are thousands of books that you could have chosen to read, and I am honored you chose mine. Please spread the word and leave a quick review on Amazon, Goodreads, or BookBub if you have enjoyed this book. Without you, writing would still be a dream.

About the Author

Sabrina Wagner writes sweet, sassy, sexy romance novels featuring stubborn men and the women who bring them to their knees. Her books will make you swoon, break your heart, and tickle your funny bone. They include found family, witty banter, and second chances.

Sabrina believes true friends should be treasured, a woman's strength is forged by the fire of affliction, and everyone deserves a happy ending. It's rare to find her without a book in her hand or a story spinning through her head. She's a hopeless romantic and knows all too well that life is full of twists and turns, but the bumpy road is what leads to our true destination.

Want to be the first to learn book news, updates, and more?
Sign up for her Newsletter.
https://www.subscribepage.com/sabrinawagnernewsletter

www.SabrinaWagnerAuthor.com